HOW COULD SOMETHING THAT FEELS SO RIGHT BE SO WRONG?

"It is an extraordinary thing," Peter said very softly. "This is a moment out of time, governed by no rules. Would it be very wrong, do you think, Hannah, if we pretended we were lovers and I kissed you?"

It seemed so right, so very right, to lift her face. His hands gently cupped it, and the hood of her cloak fell back as his mouth came down onto hers. It was warm and soft and so tender, and she gave a little moan as something stirred deep inside her, something heavy and heated. She could feel the outline of his body full-length against her, feel his radiant heat flowing into her as his mouth played on hers, asking for more. And she gave it to him, opening her mouth to his as his hands moved restlessly on her back, pressing her even more closely against him so that her breasts lay full against his chest. She was lost . . .

SIGNET REGENCY ROMANCE
COMING IN MARCH 1993

Carol Proctor
The Dangerous Dandy

Elizabeth Jackson
A Brilliant Alliance

Marjorie Farrell
Lady Barbara's Dilemma

KING
OF
HEARTS

by

Katherine Kingsley

A SIGNET BOOK

SIGNET
Published by the Penguin Group
Penguin Books USA Inc., 375 Hudson Street,
New York, New York 10014, U.S.A.
Penguin Books Ltd, 27 Wrights Lane,
London W8 5TZ, England
Penguin Books Australia Ltd, Ringwood,
Victoria, Australia
Penguin Books Canada Ltd, 10 Alcorn Avenue,
Toronto, Ontario, Canada M4V 3B2
Penguin Books (N.Z.) Ltd, 182–190 Wairau Road,
Auckland 10, New Zealand

Penguin Books Ltd, Registered Offices:
Harmondsworth, Middlesex, England

First published by Signet, an imprint of New American Library,
a division of Penguin Books USA Inc.

First Printing, February, 1993
10 9 8 7 6 5 4 3 2 1

 REGISTERED TRADEMARK—MARCA REGISTRADA

Printed in the United States of America

*To David Lyle, who without fail comes to visit
in the frenzied middle of a manuscript,
gets me out of whatever jam I've managed to
get into, and does it with great good humor.
Friends for always, dear one.*

Prologue

The first blow is half the battle.
—Oliver Goldsmith,
She Stoops to Conquer

October, 1795

"Father! Oh, Father, please! Do not be so unreasonable!" Selina Delaware pressed back against the wall as her father towered over her.

"Unreasonable? Unreasonable, Selina! It is not I who has behaved as a whore, not I who has gotten myself with the footman's brat! You have always been beyond hope, running about like a gypsy child with no regard to your station, but I thought that keeping you confined would put an end to it! And what do you do? Right under my nose you let that piece of . . . of *filth* have his way with you? And now you say that you love him, that you want to marry the man? It will not be, Selina! I shall rid you of this child here and now, and you will repent the rest of your living days of your behavior!"

Lord Delaware raised his hand, intending to beat his daughter senseless, but something took hold of his wrist and caught it in a viselike grip.

"You shan't do anything of the sort," came a soft voice from behind him. "Selina and I will marry and have our child, and you, my lord, will give her your permission. And after this night you will never lay a hand on Selina again, for we are leaving this place and making our own way."

Lord Delaware struggled to free his arm, then turned to face the dark-haired youth, who had somehow managed to intrude into the room. "You impertinent scoundrel! You are nothing more than a miserable insect to be crushed be-

7

neath my heel, and you shall be sorry for this day's work!
I shall see you in hell for what you have done to her!"

"And should you not be seen into hell yourself, my lord,
for threatening not just your daughter, but her unborn
child? Leave us be, I beg you. I will take Selina away. Let
us love each other and have our child in peace."

Lord Delaware looked into the countenance of the young
man who had defiled his daughter. He saw the clear gray eyes,
the figure still slender with youth. He saw the simple clothes,
the hands coarse from work. And he made his decision.

"Go then," he said, moving to his desk. "Leave. But
leave me to have a private word with my daughter before
you take her."

"You swear not to touch her?"

"I swear," Lord Delaware said. "Take your leavings. I
want them no more."

But as the boy turned to go out the door, Lord Delaware
pulled a pistol from his desk. And before Selina had time
to sound a warning, Lord Delaware had fired at his back.

"Martin! Oh, God, Martin, what has he done to you!"
Selina ran to her lover, dropping to her knees over his still
form. Her hand came away covered in blood and she stared
at it, and then at her father.

Lord Delaware did not even stop to look at the body as
he left the room.

It was Martin's father who responded to Selina's cries,
Martin's father who gently pulled a hysterical Selina off his
murdered son's body. It was he who took his dead child
away and left him on the side of a public road, hoping the
murder would be assumed to have been committed by a
thief, as in a way it had been. As much as he despised Lord
Delaware, he had deeply loved his only son, and Martin's
coming child needed to be protected from the inevitable
scandal as much as possible. And the woman that Martin
had so foolishly chosen to love deserved his support in her
time of need, as would his grandchild when that time came.

He knew exactly what had to be done under such circumstances, and so, despite his heartbreak, he saw that it was done.
He took Selina away. He found her a respectable husband, even
though that husband was very much older. He installed himself
in service in the household, and then, when Selina gave birth to
a daughter, he set himself in anonymity to raising her, determined she would never repeat the mistakes of her parents.

1

I am told he makes a very handsome corpse,
and becomes his coffin prodigiously.
——Oliver Goldsmith,
The Good-Natured Man, I

February, 1819

Peter Frazier knocked at the door to Longthorpe with a heavy heart, wishing himself anywhere else. He had received the perfunctory summons from Lord Blakesford the week before and had procrastinated for three days before deciding that he might as well get the interview over and done with. From everything he had heard about the man, there was bound to be a great deal of shouting and gnashing of teeth. That the earl and Peter's father had not been on speaking terms for over forty years did not auger well, never mind the unfortunate situation that had caused the earl to summon Peter at all. No, Peter was not looking forward to the next hour in the least. He only hoped to come and go quickly and with as little fuss as possible.

He stepped away from the large arched door of the inner courtyard, careful not to slip on the ice, and he ran his eye over the enormous limestone structure that constituted Longthorpe. It was a magnificent building, Elizabethan in style, and had fair taken his breath away by its size alone when he'd approached through the gate house.

But oddly, the windows appeared streaked with dirt, the place uninhabited. All the draperies were drawn, and there was none of the usual movement that one might have expected about a house of such size and grandeur. He pulled his coat more closely around his neck to ward off the bitter

wind and quickly moved back to the shelter of the arch over
the front door.

After five minutes Peter banged the door knocker again,
and five minutes after that the door finally opened a crack.
A wizened little woman appeared in the gap, gray hair stick-
ing out in eccentric tufts from beneath a frilly cap, which
appeared for all the world to be secured to her head by
clothespins.

"Yes?" the woman said suspiciously, looking him up and
down. "And what do you want?"

Peter was silent for a moment, not so much because he
was taken aback, but because he was desperately trying to
suppress a choke of laughter at the sight before him, which
came complete with an enormous pocket watch dangling
from a chain about a scrawny neck. "Lord Blakesford,
please," he managed to say. "I . . . I believe I am
expected."

"Expected?" the extraordinary woman interrupted, and
then comprehension seemed to dawn. "Oh—well, then, it's
about time. Glory be, I'm sure we should be grateful that
you decided to appear at all. We were expecting you yesterday, but you probably had to come all the way up from
London."

"Oxfordshire, actually," Peter replied, bemused.

"As close as that? Fancy. Still, better late than never.
He's in his bedroom, first door on the right, top of the
landing, and mind how you go. Don't want you knocking
into anything. He's all nice and clean for you. Bathed him
myself, I did, not that it was any pleasure." She opened the
door all the way to let him in.

Peter entered, suppressing another wave of laughter as
he saw the chicken feathers that covered her shiny black
dress from the bodice down. She looked as if she'd been
doing battle with half the henhouse. "And you would be
the housekeeper?" he inquired civilly enough, wondering
whether his crusty cousin had lost his mind or actually developed a sense of humor in his dotage.

"Housekeeper? That's a laugh. I'm a woman of all work,
I am. Call me a slave if you like. The name is Mrs. Brewster," she said, "and I don't have time for idle chatter, for
I'm cooking the celebration meal. Messier Antoine won't
have a thing to do with it, the silly man. Not that I mind—
can't abide all those sauces and puffy things myself, but

that's neither here nor there. I'm grateful to be fed at all,
and tonight there's a lot who will give thanks to have food
in their bellies. But you'd best get on with your business
and I'll get back to roasting my chickens." She pointed a
bony finger across the great hall toward the ornate wooden
staircase, then marched away.

Peter shook his head, then followed in the direction she
had indicated and started up the stairs, looking about him
as he went. The usual family portraits lined the walls—not
a particularly attractive bunch, he decided, for they all
shared a stony expression as if they thought extremely
highly of themselves and very little of the rest of the world.
That would be in keeping with what he knew of the family,
he thought wryly.

He found the first door on the right as directed and
knocked, and again there was no answer. Peter gave it a
second try and then decided that he might spend the rest
of the day waiting, so he tried the knob, which turned easily
enough.

"Lord Blakesford?" he asked, easing the door open. The
room was cast in darkness, the draperies drawn against the
late morning sun. But there was a definite hump in the bed
at the far end of the room. It appeared the old man was
sound asleep.

"Oh, this is marvelous," Peter muttered, wondering if he
should shake the earl awake and introduce himself, or if he
ought to beat a retreat and have Mrs. Brewster wake the
earl first. Whichever, the situation seemed deucedly awkward. He was just about to go back out the door, having
decided on the second course of action, when he stopped
abruptly, then slowly turned around. Something odd had
just struck him.

"Lord Blakesford?" he asked again for good measure,
approaching the bed and looking down with a certain degree
of disbelief. Oh, there was no doubt that the man before
him was Lord Blakesford, for his had been one of the portraits Peter had just seen. But that was not the cause for
his incredulity.

Took your time, didn't you—we were expecting you yester-
day, hadn't Mrs. Brewster said? *He's nice and clean for you,*
she had added. *I bathed him myself.*

Well, no doubt she had, seeing as the old man couldn't

do it for himself, given that he was quite dead and had been for a good day at the very least from the look of him.

It was the first time in his life that Peter had been mistaken for an undertaker, but there was always a first time for everything.

Peter put his head in his hands, and for lack of a better reaction, he finally gave in to the emotion that had plagued him since first setting foot upon Longthorpe soil. He howled with laughter until his sides ached.

The kitchen was easy enough to find, for he only had to use his nose as a guide. Sure enough, his quarry was standing over a large wooden table, stuffing her plucked chickens. And it did look as if half the henhouse had been purged, for there were a good thirty chickens on the slab.

"Mrs. Brewster," he began, and she looked up in some surprise.

"Is there a problem?" she asked.

"In a manner of speaking," Peter replied. "You neglected to tell me Lord Blakesford was dead."

"Dead? Well, of course he's dead," Mrs. Brewster said, looking at Peter as if he was touched in the head. "Don't tell me you lads have started taking them away while they're still alive? Not that anyone would have minded in this case, but the earl might have had something to say about it." She took a handful of stuffing and pushed it into the fowl's cavity with a great deal of energy. "As I said, I'm surprised anyone came at all. No one from these parts would touch the old fool. He wasn't diseased, mind you," she hastened to add. "His heart gave out, the Lord be praised. It was one tirade too many about the upstart new heir he was saddled with after Master James drowned last month. And that's all I need, let me tell you, is a new lordship showing up and making my life difficult. He'll probably be an exact copy of the old man. They're all the same, those Fraziers. Bad-tempered and not a moral bone in their bodies. No one shed a tear when either of the sons died, and no one will shed a tear over their father's passing, I can assure you. But speaking of that, hadn't you better get on with the job? I don't want my roasting chickens competing with the smell of a rotting corpse. Oh, the village folk are going to have a feast tonight, and you'd better get the body out of here before they decide to use it for kindling."

"Mrs. Brewster, I think I should explain," Peter said, trying terribly hard to keep a straight face. "I'm afraid there's been a case of mistaken identity. . . ."

"Mistaken identity? What do you mean, mistaken identity? That's Lord Blakesford, sure enough. Never was much to look at, and three days lying up there hasn't done anything for his complexion, but—"

"No, no, Mrs. Brewster. It is my identity you have mistaken. I am not . . . I'm not the undertaker, you see. My name is Frazier, Peter Frazier. I am Lord Blakesford's cousin." He stopped to draw a deep breath before proceeding. "I am deeply afraid that I am also the new earl."

Mrs. Brewster stared at him, her mouth dropping open. And then she gave a soundless exhale, and her eyes rolled up in her little head. She slid to the floor in a faint, taking the freshly stuffed chicken with her.

Peter managed to revive Mrs. Brewster by taking one of the many chicken feathers heaped on the floor, setting it alight, and waving it under her nose. He then put her back on her feet, reassured her that she had in no way offended him, and managed to solicit directions to the vicarage.

"Now, see here, vicar," Peter said, deciding to try one last time, "surely you cannot refuse to bury someone in the churchyard just because you disapproved of his character? I don't know that a man can be denied a Christian burial just because one has a personal prejudice against him."

"This is not a question of personal prejudice, my lord," the vicar said indignantly, and Peter felt once again that strange sense of disorientation at being so addressed. "I cannot allow a man who injured so many of my parishioners to now disturb their well-deserved eternal rest. And I might add that Lord Blakesford drove some of them to that rest prematurely."

Peter sighed and stroked his forehead with one finger. "I did not know him myself, so I cannot judge, although my parents had nothing good to say about him. However, surely you will allow that the man must be buried somewhere, vicar?"

"Naturally he must be buried, and soon. But you will see that even the undertaker's refusal to have anything to do with Lord Blakesford is an indictment of his character."

"Very well," Peter said, standing. "I cannot fight the entire village. Dear heaven, but even the housekeeper informed me that the feast she was preparing was in celebration of my cousin's death."

"Mrs. Brewster might be somewhat eccentric, but she is a woman of God," the vicar returned tartly. "She came to Longthorpe with Lady Blakesford upon her marriage to the earl, and her ladyship never knew another peaceful day until she died. And that's another reason I will not allow his lordship to be buried in my church, not in the place where her ladyship lies. She'd turn over in her grave."

"Yes, quite. Well. Suppose we compromise? If you would be so kind as to consecrate a small piece of ground on Longthorpe, I will take care of everything else myself. At this rate I can see I'll be carving the tombstone as well. It is hard to credit that one man was able to alienate absolutely everyone who crossed his path. Is there no one else at all who should be notified?"

"As far as I know, there were no friends to speak of, and you are the only relation to come calling in twenty years—and that includes the two sons, not that they were any better than he. They simply quarreled with each other and went their separate ways. As for consecrating some ground, I suppose I can do that, but only so that his lordship is buried in haste and we may all forget him as quickly as possible."

"Thank you, vicar. I do appreciate your help. I did not come prepared for this situation, and I confess, I am at something of a loss."

"I did not know your father," the vicar said, "but I have heard it said that he was not like the others in his family, that he didn't deserve what Lord Blakesford did to him. Perhaps we shall find ourselves fortunate at last and have an earl who will not abuse his tenants nor rob the people. But we shall see. It will not be an easy task for you to gain the confidence of the people, Lord Blakesford. There have been two long generations of maltreatment. It is a poor village, and the people are hardened not only by poverty, but also by mistrust of your family. That's not to say it can't be changed, but it is going to take some stellar behavior on your part. It wouldn't do to go putting your foot wrong in any direction."

"Thank you for alerting me, vicar. I will do my best to see to the well-being of your parish. Now if you will excuse me, I think I had better get on with the job immediately at

hand. Would six o'clock this evening be acceptable for the
burial? And what would you suggest I do about a-ah . . . a
container of some sort?"

"I suppose," the vicar said reluctantly, "that I could bring
a coffin when I come. Unfortunately more people die in
Kirby than I christen, and there is always a spare coffin on
hand. Might I suggest you dig the grave out in the wood
near the river? The ground would be softer there, I believe,
and there is a track that my carriage can follow. More
important, it will be well out of sight and not serve as an
unwelcome reminder."

"As you suggest. I will take my leave then, vicar, and see
you this evening." Peter collected his hat and cloak, and
went out feeling as if he'd just walked into someone else's
nightmare.

The noise and warmth of the Red Lion Inn washed over
Peter like a welcome blanket of comfort. Here was something that was familiar. He knew he would find his clothes
upstairs in the room he had slept in the night before, hanging in the wardrobe just as he had left them. He knew that
the dinner he had ordered earlier that day would be ready
for him at eight o'clock. This was an ordered, uncompli-
cated world. He could almost pretend that the events of the
last few hours hadn't happened at all, that he had not just
finished burying his cousin in the woods, like some sort of
criminal hiding a body, with a reluctant vicar in attendance
as an accomplice. He could pretend that he had not just
been handed down an unwelcome and unwanted earldom
and an enormous estate that was going to require a great
deal of time, energy, and money. For this one last night he
could simply be Mr. Peter Frazier of Kingston, Jamaica,
gentleman and man of business as he was signed in the
book.

The hot bath water he'd asked for arrived shortly, the
chambermaid giving him a long look as she poured it, and
there was no mistaking the invitation in it. She was comely
enough and would no doubt be a welcome addition to his
bed later, and for one brief moment Peter considered adding her to his list of normal, comforting things for his last
evening as a normal human being. But he quickly banished
the idea, for he needed his sleep if he was to have a clear
head on the morrow.

He dismissed the tempting maid, stripped, and sank into the water, slipping down and leaning his head against the back of the tub. It was his intention to think of nothing at all, but he quickly realized that his brain had other ideas. The events of the day simply refused to leave him, and with a sigh he resigned himself and began to analyze them. That he had a hell of a job ahead of him was extremely clear. There was the village to be thought of, the situation to be assessed. Whatever things his cousin had done must have been dreadful indeed, and it would take some time to turn that particular situation around. There was Longthorpe to be put to rights, staff to be hired, money to be found to do it all with. That was another situation that needed addressing: he would have to write to the solicitor immediately, tell him of the old earl's death and find out exactly what his financial position was, for although his pockets were well-enough lined, they weren't so flush as to be able to afford the upkeep of Longthorpe. He very much doubted that there was a steward anywhere in sight, and his own area of expertise was in shipping, which would do him no good at all on a landlocked estate. It was altogether a depressing situation and only made worse by the family history. But if there truly was poetic justice in the world, he supposed it was that Longthorpe now belonged to him, after two generations of injustice and vicious fighting. His father would probably have been happy.

"Enough!" he said and sat up with determination, applying himself to thorough scrubbing. And then, clean, dressed, and somewhat recovered, Peter wandered downstairs to have his dinner and a bottle of claret, which he hoped would restore his nerves.

"No, no—this way, Galsworthy. That's the door to the kitchen. The parlor is over here."

Peter grinned as he saw the young woman taking the elderly gentleman and turning him firmly in the opposite direction.

"I know perfectly well where the parlor is," the elderly gentleman replied. "I merely wanted to see if the kitchen is in order."

"I am sure you did, Galsworthy, but it is time for our dinner. Now where has Wesley gone to? I cannot take my eyes off either of you for a moment. . . ."

She looked frantically around, and Peter watched her face from a convenient position half hidden in the shadows. Peter found himself quite taken. She was attractive enough, but there was something more about her than merely a pleasant arrangement of features, something that he found extremely appealing although he couldn't quite put his finger on what it was. Her eyes were wide and a clear shade of gray, the lashes darkly fringed, the same sable color as her hair, her eyebrows very slightly arched. She did have the most temptingly rosy mouth, shaped like Cupid's bow in a perfectly oval face.

Other than that, she was small and slim—too slim, he thought, and he could not help but notice that her dress was not of the latest fashion. There was a definite air of impoverishment about her. But she was neat enough in appearance and well-spoken. She also seemed to have her hands full.

He stepped out into the walled garden to take a quick breath of air before his dinner and was admiring what little he could see of the view when a small boy streaked by him, and Peter made a quick guess. He stepped after him and caught him around the waist. "And might you be Wesley?" he asked the child, who twisted around and looked up at him in great surprise.

"Yes, sir," the boy answered, "I am Wesley Janes. And who might you be?"

Peter grinned. He liked spunk in a child. "I am Mr. Frazier, and I think your mother would like you returned to her."

"That's not my *mother*," Wesley said, rolling his eyes. "That's my sister." He pointed through the bow window. "And that's our butler, Galsworthy. He's looking straight at me, but I'm quite safe, as he can't see very well."

"Which I am sure you consider very much to your advantage," Peter said with a laugh.

"Well, sometimes," Wesley admitted. "But Hannah becomes very annoyed with me if I tease, like the time I switched the bottle of gin with the bottle of cleaning fluid. They were more or less the same shape, you see."

"Oh, really?" Peter asked with great interest. "And what happened?"

"Well, other than I got a great smack on my backside,

Galsworthy very nearly fed cleaning fluid to Mr. Liddle, who is fond of his gin. But I was very sorry afterward."

"I can imagine. One generally is."

"Did you often get into scrapes when you were young, sir?"

"All of the time, I am delighted to say."

"How very jolly. Did you have a sister who blistered your backside?"

"No, I'm afraid I didn't. My father was quite adept, however."

"Oh," Wesley said. "I've never had a father. I feel sure it would be quite nice. But as Hannah is always saying, it is no good to wish for things you cannot have, and one must make do with what is." He wrinkled his nose. "Hannah is a stickler for that sort of thing. I don't think she knows how to have fun."

"Oh? Why is that?"

"She insists on all that is correct. I think she caught it from Galsworthy. How is one to enjoy oneself if one is being correct all of the time?"

"I quite agree with you," Peter said sympathetically. "And what are you doing here in Leicestershire?"

"We've come to live with a relative, sir. It's what Hannah calls a difficult situation. We're down to our very last penny, and he is to take us in, as we are poor relations. Rich relatives are supposed to take in their poor relations, did you know?"

"I'd heard of the practice," Peter said, highly amused. "It seems a sensible idea."

"Hannah says it is not charity as she is to be the housekeeper, and her wages will help to pay for my school. Galsworthy is to live nearby so that I shall not feel so alone. I've never stayed at an inn before. It is quite exciting, do you not think?"

"Oh, most stimulating indeed. One has all sorts of unexpected experiences at inns. And how do you feel about going to live with your relative?" Peter asked, his curiosity aroused.

"Well, the truth of the matter is that I don't really think it is such a good idea, sir. Hannah doesn't like to speak of it, and Galsworthy won't speak of it at all, and no matter how hard I've listened against the door I haven't been able to discover why. Hannah says it is supposed to be an adventure, but she cries all the time when she thinks I can't hear. I'm not a baby who needs protecting," he added. "I'm nearly eight years old—well, I will be in seven months," he amended quickly, "and I am perfectly able to look after myself, and Hannah too."

"Indeed, I am sure you are, but you need to consider Hannah's feelings, don't you think? She is worried about you, Wesley, so I think you might go and let her know you have come to no harm. She might not like your speaking so freely to strangers."

"Oh, I know she does not, sir, but then Hannah does not hold with speaking to strangers. I think it is because she has not been about much, you know. I mean, she has been so busy looking after me, and worrying about money, and all of that, that she has not really had time. But she's very nice," he added loyally, "at least as far as sisters go. And so is Galsworthy, even though he thinks I am more of a baby than Hannah does. But I truly am not. Really, sir. I am most capable."

"I can see that quite clearly. Well, Wesley, I have enjoyed speaking with you very much. I hope to see you again."

"What a very agreeable idea. Good-bye, Mr. Frazier." Wesley went scampering off, and Peter looked after him, observing through the window as Wesley's sister bent down to scold him, then took his hand and led him through into the parlor. He was intrigued by this odd collection of people and wondered what was behind their story, but he reckoned he would probably never find out. In that he was very wrong.

2

I was never much displeased with those harmless
delusions that tend to make us all happy.
——Oliver Goldsmith,
The Vicar of Wakefield, Chapter 3

Hannah tossed and turned in bed that night, dreading the
next day. She rubbed her tired eyes, knowing there was no
other solution to their problem. They had scrimped and
saved for nearly a year while she had tried to sort out her
mother's affairs, but in the end it had made no difference.

The only alternative was hiring herself out somewhere
else as a governess or a housekeeper, but who would accept
a governess with a small boy? No one, unless Wesley was
put to work as a boot-boy in the household, and she would
not see that happen to him. He deserved far better. And
what about Galsworthy? He had given loyal service to her
family for all these years and had even stayed on after her
mother's death, putting up with no wages at all since then.
He would find no work, not with his eyesight as bad as it
was. The dear man could scarcely distinguish between a coat
and a tablecloth, save by their logical positions on appropriate objects. That she had discovered when Galsworthy
had attempted to cloak Mrs. Peterson in the finest of Irish
table linen, which Hannah happened to have hung in the
cloakroom to air, prior to ironing.

She rubbed her eyes again. No, there was no other solution, despite how abhorrent this one was. And the ramifica-
tions—well, she would simply not allow herself to think of
those. She could not think of those or she should never
have the courage to take the next step. Desperation allowed
no room for cowardice.

She turned onto her back and closed her eyes, willing

herself to sleep. But as she lay there the room seemed to grow smaller and the dark became oppressive. She found herself breathing in quick, shallow breaths and an unreasoning panic took hold.

Hannah sat bolt upright, and before she could help herself, she had jumped out of bed and started to dress. Despite the lateness of the hour and the severe dangers of going out alone, she knew she had to be outside or she would suffocate. There was a walled garden below that should be safe enough.

She quickly threw on her cloak, taking a careful look at Wesley, who was sound asleep on the trundle bed, one hand curled beside his ear, the other arm flung with abandon across the mattress. Wesley would like school, she knew he would, and being with boys his own age. He would not have to work at school as she had; she would see that all of his expenses were paid and that would make all the difference, she was quite sure. He would adjust, and soon enough he would forget. . . .

She couldn't bear to look at him another minute, for fear her heart would break in two.

It was cold outside, but the wind felt good, stinging at her cheeks, bringing tears to her eyes and making her nose go numb. She'd always found solace in the outdoors, no matter the time of year. The outdoors gave her a sense of freedom, the little she knew of it. And tomorrow even that little bit would be taken from her. Everything she held most dear would be taken from her.

She pulled her cloak more closely about her and sank onto a bench. As a young girl she'd always had such dreams—dreams for a fine future, to marry a man she loved, to have his children, to have a real family. She had learned long since that there was no place in her life for foolish illusions. But why did God have to be quite so cruel? She bowed her head, not in prayer, for she felt quite unable to address Him yet again on the subject, but because she couldn't help the tears that came, nor the sobs that accompanied them. She finally just buried her face in her hands and cried her heart out.

And then she jumped half out of her skin as she heard a masculine voice come from above her and a hand lightly touch her shoulder.

"Madam? Forgive the intrusion, but I was smoking a cheroot under the lime tree and could not help but notice your distress. Is there anything I might do to help?"

Hannah, embarrassed and badly frightened as well, looked up. "No—I beg your pardon. I thought I was alone. . . ."

She trailed off, suddenly taking in the gentleman before her. He was tall and his hair was fair, the color of dark gold, but it was his eyes that struck her. They were blue, the color she imagined the sea would be at twilight just off the coast of Sicily. They were quite the most beautiful eyes she had ever seen. And from the expression in them she could see that he was genuinely concerned. Her fear melted away as if it had been no more than an errant thought.

"Not a wise choice for a young woman to be sitting outside alone in the dead of night," he said, "but as it transpires, you are not alone, nor have you anything to fear from me. You are Miss Janes, Wesley's sister, if I am not mistaken? I am Peter Frazier. I met Wesley earlier when he was hiding from you out here."

"Oh . . . yes, he mentioned he had met someone," Hannah said, pulling her handkerchief out and wiping her eyes. "Wesley is forever getting into mischief. I suppose it is what comes of being seven and having no father to keep him in line."

"Ah, a lack of a father does make a difference. However, I found him most engaging and intelligent, although my heart did go out to your butler—Galsworthy, I believe his name is?"

"Yes, poor Galsworthy. He has been part father-figure, part unwilling playmate, and the butt of many of Wesley's practical jokes." Hannah managed a halfhearted smile. "Galsworthy has always tried to be brave about it. He is very dignified, but that dignity is sorely tested. He does not see very well, which does not help."

"Your brother was quick to point out Galsworthy's infirmity with a certain amount of glee."

Hannah nodded. "He has great spirit. But he shall be going away to school, and I am sure the masters will keep him in line." She tried to keep the pain from her voice.

"That would be a pity," Peter said quietly. "May I?" He indicated the bench.

"Yes, please do," she said, completely forgetting her usual insistence on absolutely propriety. "Why would that be a pity? Surely it is better than running wild or being tutored by one's sister?"

"I cannot say, as I do not know your circumstances, but in my experience schoolmasters can be an unpleasant bunch. But it is not my place to speak. I suppose I simply took a liking to Wesley. It would be a shame to see the spirit beaten out of him at such a young age. Are you familiar with horses?"

"I have never ridden one, although I believe I see the point you are about to make. But do they really beat the boys, Mr. Frazier?" she asked anxiously. "We were never beaten at my school, although we were disciplined in other ways."

"Boys are different," he said with a slight smile. "Hadn't you noticed?"

"Yes, of course I had. My upbringing was not that sheltered. And having a young brother has certainly driven home the lesson."

He laughed, and those beautiful eyes lit up with his laughter, creasing slightly at the corners. She could not help but laugh in response, for his humor was contagious, as if he were inviting one to join in a private joke. And then she realized with surprise how easily she had been speaking to him, quite unlike her usual self, who guarded against gentlemen at all cost. Furthermore, he had managed to distract her from her misery.

As if he had read her thoughts, he said, "Good. You are feeling better, I think. Crying is often cleansing, but then there are times that tears need to be shared. Or dried. Or laughed away, depending on the circumstances. Which do you think it is in this instance?"

"To tell you the truth, I do not know. It felt good to laugh, though. I haven't done much of that for some time. But I do not mean to complain," she added quickly. "It is merely that we are having an extreme change of situation, and I have not yet adjusted to the idea."

Peter threw back his head and laughed again, and his hair caught the light of the moon and streamed with silver amidst the gold. "You have no idea how completely I sympathize with your plight. I find myself in exactly the same predicament. If I even attempted to describe to you the day I have just experienced, you would never believe me. I can scarce believe it myself. I keep trying to convince myself that I hallucinated the entire thing and that when I wake tomorrow it will all have gone away. I do not mean to make light of your situation, indeed I do not, only to tell you that I empathize. I too was having a sleepless night because of circumstances beyond my control."

"It is that exactly," she said, feeling a sense of true affinity with him. It was as if on this last night fate had sent her a friend to give her a touch of happiness, of laughter, a small spate of relief before tumbling her headfirst into the chasm. "Circumstances are beyond my control also, and I don't mind admitting that I am afraid." Under normal circumstances Hannah would never have admitted fear to anyone, let alone to a strange man, but the circumstances were not normal and she could not have felt less like her usual self.

"Fear is an interesting thing," he remarked. "Like any other powerful emotion it can be harnessed, or it can be left unleashed to destroy. Love, hate, anger, they are all the same."

"But people cannot control their feelings so easily! I can no more help being afraid than I can help breathing. I might be able to pretend to the world that I am brave, but I cannot fool myself."

"Ah, but that is not what I am saying. It is not that one should hide from oneself—not at all. It is how one chooses to act on one's emotions that makes the difference. Here, let me offer you an example." He thought for a moment, then smiled. "I have the perfect situation, but you'll have to forgive me if I take liberties with you."

"What sort of liberties?" Hannah asked suspiciously.

"Purely imaginary. Let us suppose that for reasons beyond my control I have fallen violently in love with you."

"Really, Mr. Frazier, I do not think you should imagine any such thing," Hannah said indignantly, but she was actually quite pleased with the idea of this exceedingly handsome man being violently in love with her, no matter how ridiculous the notion.

"Oh, but I think it is a fine idea. And let us assume that you are a married woman, perhaps with children. Yes, there we are. We'll give you some children, and two sets of parents—your own and those of your husband. And for the sake of argument, we shall give me a living set of parents as well. One could safely assume there would also be extended families on both sides. Now. Here I am violently in love with you. Here you are violently in love with me."

"I am?"

"Yes, naturally you are. Why are you looking at me so? Do you find the idea repulsive?"

"Not in the least. How many children have I?"

Peter considered. "Three, I think, for you are not old enough to have any more than that. Let us make them a boy and two girls."

"Do I love them very much?"

"Oh, yes. You are a most devoted mother. However, your feelings for your husband are lukewarm at best. He is a bore."

"Oh, dear," Hannah said, her eyes sparkling. She had not enjoyed herself so much in a very long time. "How unfortunate for me."

"Exactly so. And it only stands to reason that when I happened across your path, you could not resist the strength of your emotions. Did I mention that your husband was an aged bore inclined to obesity?"

"You did not have to. I am married to him, after all. So here we are. What may I ask are we doing sitting out here in the cold?"

"We are deciding what to do with all of this violent emotion."

"Well, I suppose you could always challenge my husband to a duel," Hannah said mischievously.

"Oh, shoot him dead and be forced to leave the country, presuming I am not the one killed? No thank you. I might be violently in love, but I am not stupid. Perhaps we could sneak away, considerately leaving your husband alive and in one piece, although presumably emotionally bereft. He can always divorce you."

"But then my children would have a disgraced mother, never mind the feelings of the rest of the family."

"Yes, I can well imagine the shock and outrage," Peter said. "Well, I suppose there could always be an illicit but clandestine liaison, and no one else would be affected."

"Possible, but highly questionable. I do not know if I can hold with such deceitful behavior."

"Not to mention the frustration involved," he added. "One cannot spend one's life forever sneaking about, not that it isn't done. And forgive me, but let us not forget the complications of a child that might result."

"Well, then," Hannah said, by now completely wrapped up in the story, "might I suggest that you take yourself either to Europe or a monastery, sir, for it sounds as if you are creating the most terrible problems for me, not to mention my children and my poor bore of a husband. I am sure I will recover from all this emotional violence once your physical presence is removed."

"Ah, Miss Janes, you have proved yourself not only cold-blooded, but fickle as well. My poor heart fair breaks."

"It does not look very broken," she observed. "In fact, you look extremely pleased with yourself."

"That is because you have proved my point, for you have come up with the only practical solution to the matter. You see, despite how strongly one might feel about something or someone, in the end it makes very little difference. One must take into account all the extenuating circumstances and determine what the end result will be. In this instance, had we acted upon our feelings a great many innocent people would have been hurt."

"It was a pity about my husband, although I rather enjoyed my children," Hannah said, smiling over at him. "Why did I marry such an aged bore to begin with, Mr. Frazier? It seems most unfeeling of you to have made him so dull."

"You married him because your father insisted upon the match. He had deep pockets that your family was in need of."

"Oh, in that case I can quite understand," Hannah said, the smile fading from her face. "One's obligations to one's family are paramount. Personal sacrifice is nothing in the face of that."

"Then we are in agreement. It is not necessarily a pretty thing, but there we are. Dear heaven, but obligation is weighty. Still, life is not all gloom. There is laughter, is there not, and surely that is better than tears? One can always find something to laugh at, even if it is most often oneself."

Hannah nodded, wishing she could find something to laugh about in her situation, but nothing at all came to mind. And yet something he had said struck a chord in her. "Perhaps you are right," she said, looking down at her hands. "Perhaps my sense of humor has gone missing these last few months. Actually, to be honest, it has probably gone missing these last few years. I think I must have become as dull as the husband you assigned to me."

"I don't think that is the case, but it has been my experience that one needs a strong sense of the ridiculous to survive in this life. My mother was fond of saying that when things seemed at their very worst to look for the good in the situation, for there is a reason for everything. I have a severe case of eyestrain this evening, and I am no more enlightened than I was before, but I have had a good laugh or two."

Hannah smiled. "Maybe it will all come clear to you with time."

"Time," he said, nodding. "Yes. There will no doubt be plenty of that, providing I do not go about challenging people to duels or sit outside too long in a February night battling morality and a broken heart."

"It is cold," Hannah said, realizing how impolite and selfish she had been in keeping him from the warmth of his bed, and all because she had been enjoying his conversation so very much. She quickly stood, although she would have been quite content to sit there talking to him all night. "Thank you, Mr. Frazier. You have no idea how welcome your company has been and how appropriate your advice. I cannot explain further, but I will always be grateful that you happened to be standing under the lime tree just when you were. Our paths will probably never cross again, but I want you to know that I will not ever forget you. I wish you luck with your situation. I am sure it will work itself out."

He also stood. "I shan't walk you to your door," he said, smiling down at her, "for I wouldn't want all that honor you possess to appear compromised should we be seen together. But I too have enjoyed these few moments out of time—or so they have seemed. They have given me some comfort as well, which I did not look for, nor expect. Good night and good luck to you, Miss Janes. And I thank you. I shall not forget you either."

He took her hand and lifted it to his mouth, and even through her glove she felt the warmth of his lips as he pressed them against her fingers. Her breath caught in her throat and her eyes flew to his. She was transfixed by something she had never felt and she was quite sure she would never feel again, and she found herself quite powerless to move.

He seemed to be caught in the same place, in the same emotion, for he looked down at her with an almost perplexed expression on his face. "It is an extraordinary thing," he said very softly. "Perhaps this really is a moment out of time, governed by no rules. It might be the last time in my life that it is so. And from the sound of it, in yours as well. Would it be very wrong, do you think, Hannah, if we pretended we were those parting lovers and I kissed you farewell?"

Hannah shook her head, tears filling her eyes and catching on her eyelashes. Oh, she could pretend. She could pretend anything in this moment, for she knew she'd never have another chance. She would pretend with everything she had, and she would make the memory last for the rest of her life. It seemed so right, so very right to lift her face. His hands gently cupped it, and the hood of her cloak fell back as his mouth came down onto hers. It was warm and soft and so tender, and she gave a little moan as something stirred deep inside of her, something heavy and heated.

He seemed to feel it also, for he deepened his kiss as his hands left her face and his arms drew her more closely to him, one hand returning to tangle in her hair. She could feel the hard outline of his body full-length against her, feel his radiant heat burning into her as his mouth played on hers, teased her, asking for more. And she gave it to him, God help her, she gave it to him freely, opening her mouth to his, letting his tongue taste and explore as his hands moved restlessly on her back, pressing her even more closely against him so that her breasts lay full against his chest. And yet she had no remorse. She reveled in every last touch, every last taste, every breath that mingled with his, memorizing it all, offering herself in equal measure. She was lost, lost in the moment, lost in the pretense, but it made more sense than anything had in a very long time.

And then he suddenly pulled away and released her. "I . . . I apologize," he said shakily. He was breathing hard. "I became carried away. Please forgive me."

Hannah stared at him for a moment, disoriented, her heart pounding ferociously. She raised a trembling hand to her mouth, only now becoming aware of what had just happened.

"I . . . I must go," she said, her voice unsteady. She wanted to stay, she wanted him to kiss her again, she wanted things she knew she shouldn't, and it didn't seem to matter. But somehow she managed to bring herself under control. "Good . . . good-bye," she said. And then she turned and quickly walked away. But as she went she felt his eyes on her, and it was as if he were still touching her.

His whisper floated to her on the wind just before she went in. "Good-bye, sweet Hannah. Fare thee well. . ."

She closed the door behind her and nearly ran up the stairs.

When she had finally changed into her nightdress, the process slowed by badly shaking fingers, she went to her bedroom window and picked up the edge of the curtain, looking out over the garden. She sighed and rested her head against the cold glass for a moment, feeling turned quite inside out.

What she had done was very wrong, she knew that of course. She had behaved like a complete wanton. She had committed the unforgivable sin and allowed herself to become carried away.

But for some awful reason there was a part of her that did not care. He had called it a moment out of time, and it had been, a moment in which she had been someone else, someone lovely, desirable, and unfettered. The past had been swept away, the future had ceased to exist, and she had lived simply in the moment. It hadn't hurt to pretend to be those two people, had it? Not really—it wasn't as if she would ever see him again. It wasn't even as if it had really been her. It had been a heartbroken women putting duty over love. And he, her heartbroken lover, had gallantly and bravely accepted her decision.

Hannah sighed, for she secretly had an incurably romantic nature that she spent a great deal of time trying to conceal from herself and the rest of the world. She couldn't help herself: her hand slipped to her mouth again, as if to feel the touch of his lips there.

A shadow shifted and her heart gave a sharp, almost painful tug as she saw that he had not gone in after all, despite the cold. He had been standing quite still, very much as she had left him, but now he stepped out into a pool of moonlight, and she saw him stoop and pick something up. It was the handkerchief she had used to dry her eyes. She hadn't realized she'd dropped it.

He looked at it for a long moment, then carefully folded it and tucked it inside the breast of his coat.

Hannah's heart wrenched and a tear slid from the corner of her eye. *If only,* she thought. *Oh, if only life could have been different. . . .*

Then practicality took over, and she dropped the corner of the curtain and climbed into bed, knowing reality was only a few hours away. Tomorrow would bring all sorts of shocks and she needed to sleep if she was to have the strength to bear them.

3

The best-humored man
with the worst-humored muse.
—Oliver Goldsmith,
Whitefoord

Peter returned to Longthorpe early the following morning.
The first thing he did was to inspect the vast house. He
could not quite accustom himself to the idea that this was
now his home. The only real measure of comfort was that
it was the place his father and grandfather had spent their
boyhoods, and so he supposed he was not as complete an
intruder as he felt. It was immediately clear to him that the
place had been shut up for a long time, for with the exception of the library and the dining room, everything was
under Holland covers, the draperies closed. He went from
room to room, letting in the gray sunlight, for he had always
abhorred darkness, to the extent of having to have a candle
burning in his bedroom when he was a child. Fortunately
he had outgrown that need, but he still had a great liking
for sunshine and never slept with the draperies in his bedroom drawn.

Each room was a surprise: from beneath the covers
emerged treasures of all sorts. The pale light revealed fine
tapestries and superb paintings. Peter found himself quite
astonished. His father had not done justice to Longthorpe,
or perhaps his cousin had collected many of these pieces on
his own. But if so, then why hide them away in such a
fashion? It was a puzzle, to be sure, as was the lack of staff.

When he had finished his inspection he went back to the
library, which in contrast to the rest of the house was a
jumble of odds and ends and looked as if it hadn't been
cleaned in years. He rummaged in the overstuffed desk for

paper, quill, and ink and settled down to writing a few necessary letters. There was quite a bit of explaining to be done.

He finished the first letter to his good friend and business partner, and his hand automatically reached for the sealing wax. He paused, realizing that from now on he would be using the Blakesford seal rather than the Frazier coat of arms impressed on his signet ring. And with an ironic smile, for the first time he franked his own letters, scrawling "Blakesford" across the top. He knew that the moment Edward, who had been accustomed for fifteen years to scrawling "Seaton" across his own correspondence, saw the frank in Peter's handwriting, he would understand what had happened without having to read the lines inside. Edward would then no doubt laugh himself silly.

"Good morning, Mrs. Brewster," Peter said when she appeared midmorning dragging a broom across the hall in a halfhearted fashion, which explained why the rooms in use appeared so dirty. "Do you think you might change the bedclothes in the late earl's bedroom and give the room a thorough cleaning and airing? I shall be moving into it today. Thank you. I hope your roast chickens were a success."

Mrs. Brewster nodded her little head. "They were. And speaking of food, what do you want to do about Messier Antoine? You'll be needing someone to cook the meals—if you can put up with his Frenchie airs and graces, that is. Couldn't keep a single footman between his lordship and the messier, never mind a butler. As for the kitchen maids, neither of them could keep their hands off, so the girls never stayed long. The last year it's been just the messier and me, and the messier I could do without."

"Hmm. Why don't you ask Monsieur Antoine to come and speak to me? I am sure we can work something out. Am I to understand you and he are the only staff? There are no parlor maids, not even a gardener?"

"You have it exactly, my lord. The old man was too tight in the purse to pay for more than the bare necessities, although he wasn't about to give up his Frenchie cook, not on your life. Liked his food, he did, if nothing else ever suited him. Spoiled the messier rotten if you ask me, giving him anything he wanted just so as to have his sauces and suffles. I don't know which had the worst temper, I really don't, but the messier always got his way in the end, threatening to leave every time his lordship made a noise. I hope you don't mind my speaking plain, my lord, but it's God's truth and I don't believe in mincing words."

"I have found that it is always better to be well informed than to be caught by surprise, Mrs. Brewster. I take no offense at all in plain speaking. Are you planning on staying on here yourself?"

"You have no obligation to inherit his lordship's leavings, mind you, nor his poor wife's old auntie, but if you're so inclined, I'll stay. I have nowhere else to go. Anything has to be an improvement on the last earl, may he burn in hell. I reckon you'll do."

"Thank you, Mrs. Brewster," Peter said dryly. "You are most kind. I shall do my best to oblige you."

"Then I am sure we will get along famously."

"If you do your best to oblige me as well, I am sure we will," Peter said with a slight smile. "Now, if you would be so kind, there are letters by the front door which need posting. And if you'll give this room a good dusting I would also be very appreciative."

"Very good, my lord." Mrs. Brewster bustled around for a few minutes, very effectively redistributing the dust around the room and over Peter as well, and Peter decided that she might do better consigned to the laundry room. He really had to do something about hiring a housekeeper and a butler and let them get on with seeing to a proper staff. Mrs. Brewster had obviously been taken in as a poor relation and had no idea of how to run a house. And this Monsieur Antoine sounded as if he was going to be a handful. Peter rubbed his temples and indulged himself in one wistful thought of ocean breezes and flower-scented air.

"So. And you are the new lordship?" Antoine marched into the library with nary a knock and looked Peter up and down as if it were a military inspection and he were the general. In his mind Peter was clearly the new recruit.

Peter gave him the same dispassionate inspection and decided that Antoine put him in mind of a weasel, complete with sharp nose and small button-shaped eyes. He already had the headache from trying to work out his cousin's bookkeeping system, which seemed nonexistent, and his patience was in short supply.

"I am indeed," he said, taking Antoine's measure and

deciding instantly on a course of action. "And I take it you are the chef. I understand that you prepared very creditable meals for my cousin, monsieur, and I understand that he much appreciated you. However, I do have requirements other than good food."

"Other requirements, my lord?" the man said, looking thunderstruck. "What requirements could there be other than the brilliance of my food?"

"The first is good manners. That applies not only to me, but to anyone else in this house, including the staff."

"I am not accustomed to being ordered about in such a fashion," Antoine said with an indignant sniff. "I am an artiste, not a servant."

"What you are, monsieur, is a man in my employ. Should you wish to remain at Longthorpe you will respect my wishes. I require very little: timely meals, no extravagant spending, and a willingness to work. That does not seem like very much to ask. If you think it is going to task you overmuch, then you are quite free to go."

"But my lord, you have no understanding! The earl, he was a gourmet, he had appreciation for my art! It cannot be created like that, pouf! It must be contemplated, there must be the suffering, the process. How am I to create in an atmosphere of this distrust? My soufflés, they will fall, my sauces, they will curdle! This is not possible for me!"

"Very well," Peter said calmly, but ready to throw the paperweight at the silly man's head. His nerves were already stretched to their limit, and he really did not think he could take much more. "If it is not possible for you, then find another position."

"You do not appreciate Antoine," the man said, looking close to tears. "I knew it would be so. No one appreciates my greatness. The earl, he was the only one who appreciated my art. For him I created, day after day, night after night. We wept together over the brilliance of my meals. We tasted, we discussed, he understood true genius, the earl. What am I to do now? Who is to understand me?" He drew a very large handkerchief from his apron and wiped at his eyes.

"Monsieur, you must do as you please. I would be happy to give you a chance if you can work under the conditions I have set out. If not, leave. Now. For your wages."

"Three hundred guineas a year," Antoine stated, his eyes miraculously clearing. "It is what the earl has paid me."

"I sincerely doubt it. One hundred would be outrageous, but we shall settle at one hundred ten. You won't do better."

"If my expenses are included as well, it is done," Antoine said with alacrity.

"Those expenses are limited to your room and board," Peter countered, wondering why he was bothering at all. He enjoyed a decent meal, but he didn't have to have it shoved down his throat with pretentiousness and pay for the pleasure with an absurd salary. Still, it would have been unfair of him to dismiss the man out of hand, no matter how strong his inclination.

"The earl saw to my journeys back to France, so that I should be inspired by new ideas," Antoine said, waving the handkerchief in the air between thumb and finger.

"I am not in need of your inspiration, monsieur. Should you find yourself in need of it, then you can amply afford to take yourself back when I have no need of you here. Are we quite finished? I have a great deal to do."

Antoine was clearly considering a tantrum but must have seen it would have been pointless, for he bowed. "As his lordship wishes. I shall apply myself to dinner. It will be ready for you at eight o'clock."

"Six o'clock would suit far better. And I do not require very much this evening. I do not have an appetite. A boiled egg and toast will do very well."

"My lord! I do not cook nursery food!"

"Monsieur Antoine, if you cannot prepare a boiled egg and toast, then you are no chef. One must be able to stretch from the most complicated to the most simple. Do you think you can manage that?"

Antoine thought this over for a moment and then wisely conceded the point, for he could see which way the wind blew should he not conform. "Very well, my lord. It shall be as you command."

"Thank you, Antoine," Peter said. "And Antoine, in the future when I ask to speak with you, you will please knock and wait for an invitation to enter before doing so. You may leave now."

Antoine pulled himself up, considered a parting shot, reconsidered, and took himself off.

When the door had shut behind the obsequious man, Peter buried his face in his hands. It obviously was not enough having inherited Longthorpe, he had to take on Antoine and Mrs. Brewster in the bargain? The old earl was probably laughing from beyond his grave. Still, it was no more than he had expected. Life was going to be brutal for a time.

He leaned back in the chair for a moment, his mind drifting back to the interlude in the posting-house garden the night before, and he smiled. It had been an extraordinary meeting and that had been no snatched kiss. It had been given and taken freely, in a way that would never have been possible under any other circumstances. It really had been as if they had been suspended between two worlds, or at least he knew that was how he had felt, as if everything had been slightly unreal. He strongly suspected that Hannah had felt very much the same way, given her heated and unexpected response. He hadn't expected his own very heated response, come to that.

He wondered what it was about her that had affected him so strongly: she was certainly attractive enough, but her face would not have launched a thousand ships. Perhaps it was her vulnerability that he had found so endearing. He knew he'd had an unfair advantage, for he had known much more about her than she about him: young Wesley had been most informative on the subject of his sister, and he had used that knowledge to cut deep below the surface.

It had not been hard to put a few of the pieces together and come up with the conclusion that Hannah had led a life of hardship, heavy responsibility, and little frivolity. It seemed a damned shame that she was now to be locked away as someone's housekeeper and her poor brother sent to some miserable school or another.

It really was too bad. Had there been no consequences to consider, it would have been easy enough to have concluded the evening on a more intimate note. Two lonely souls sharing a bit of human comfort on a cold winter night; oh, that would have been a cheerful occasion.

Peter sighed. Never mind. He'd have to find his bit of human comfort elsewhere. He couldn't go about ruining innocent young women, no matter how attractive and sympathetic he found them. It was a damned shame that his mother had raised him to be a gentleman. It played havoc with one's loins.

And thinking of his loins, he would have to turn his attention to his obligation in that direction as well, now that his situation had so drastically changed. But that was a matter that at least he could put off for a time, for Longthorpe and the welfare of the village had to take precedence over everything else, including producing an heir.

Peter went back to attempting to sort out the earl's papers, but he couldn't help feeling depressed.

Hannah left Galsworthy and Wesley at the Red Lion. Only Galsworthy knew it had been a final good-bye, and he had borne it well. She would not think of his white face, nor his shaking hands as he had clasped her own between them. She would certainly not think of how he had held a sobbing Wesley back as she had walked out of the door. At least Wesley had believed he would see her again. It would take a number of months and a few very careful letters before he understood the truth of the matter.

It was a bleak day, the sun obscured by clouds, and the wind blew sharply from the north, cutting straight through her cloak. She spent the entire walk refusing to think about anything at all. For the first two hours she concentrated only on putting one foot in front of the other, but by the time the third hour had passed she not only felt frozen nearly solid, but also quite sick, for with every footstep she was walking farther away from the people she loved and coming closer to her unavoidable fate and the man who was solely responsible for all their misery.

The house finally appeared, huge, forbidding, a brownish gray mass of stone and windows surrounded by white snow and the bare, dark outline of branches. She had seen drawings of it, for it was one of the older and better known houses in England. To see it with her own eyes only drove home its grandeur.

Hannah swallowed. Under any other circumstances she would have considered it an honor to be housekeeper to such a place, could have immersed herself in her work, felt proud to be a part of such magnificence. But instead she felt nothing but resentment and dread, and she had to force herself through the courtyard to the front door. It took every last shred of determination to make her hand lift to the door knocker and let it drop. It fell, pounding against the heavy wood with what sounded to her ears like a death knell.

After a period, the door opened and an odd-looking little woman appeared. "Yes?" she said. "And what do you want?"

"I'm here to see Lord Blakesford," Hannah replied, thinking that what she'd really like to do was to turn tail and run. She concentrated on trying not to shake.

"What for?" the woman asked, and Hannah blinked, for she found this a very strange way to answer an earl's door. Hannah might be destitute, but she had her standards.

"I believe he is expecting me," she said with as much dignity as she could muster.

"Well, why didn't you say so? People never say what they mean," the woman grumbled. "Right this way." She led Hannah across the massive hall and opened a door off to the left. She stuck her head in. "There's a lady here to see you, your lordship. Not bad-looking, either, and seems proper enough, although a bit raggeldy-taggeldy. Do you want to see her?"

Hannah couldn't quite believe her ears. Galsworthy would have had an apoplectic fit had he been there, despite what he thought of the earl. "Manners are manners," he was fond of saying, "no matter what the circumstances." She heard a murmured response from inside, and she steeled herself as the little woman nodded at her.

"He says to go in," she announced, then vanished around a corner. Hannah swallowed through a dry mouth, asked God's forgiveness, and walked through the door. And stopped dead in her tracks as she saw the gentleman who was sitting behind the marquetry desk and looking up at her expectantly.

"Good God," he murmured, slowly putting down his pen. "Hannah." He looked as dumbfounded as she felt.

"Mr. Frazier?" she managed to say, going first white and then beet red and hoping the man had an identical twin, but knowing in her heart it wasn't so. "Mr. Frazier, is that you?"

"The last time I looked," he answered, looking down at himself as if he wasn't quite sure. He looked up again. "What in the name of heaven are you doing here?"

"I came to see his lordship. I have an . . . an appointment."

"No . . . oh, no," Peter said in disbelief. "An appointment. You have an appointment."

"Yes. With the earl."

"Dear Lord in heaven. How extraordinary."

She did not know how to respond to that exactly, and she went an even deeper red, for she realized that he must be the earl's private secretary. She hoped fervently that her mortification did not show, for her pride was the one thing she had left to her, and she had no intention of losing it. She summoned what was left of her wits about her and tried to look sensible.

"He is definitely expecting me today, if you will check his book, please, or announce me, or do whatever it is you usually do when the earl has an appointment."

"This is not possible," Peter said. "I do not believe it."

"I cannot think why you find it quite so extraordinary. People do make appointments, you know, and I am no exception. But I suppose that you are surprised that I have an appointment with the Earl of Blakesford at all."

"Oh, yes. Very."

Hannah, not sure what to make of that response, cleared her throat. "Well I have. And as I am equally surprised to find that you work here, that makes us even, although I confess that I find this very awkward."

"Awkward? Oh, you have no idea," he said, and he leaned his forehead against the palm of his hand. His shoulders started to shake, and she saw with some surprise that he was quite beside himself with amusement.

"What do you find so diverting?" she asked, stung to the quick. "I do not see anything the least bit humorous about the situation. In fact if you had any sensitivity at all you would remember that I was deeply upset last night at the prospect of coming here. And had I known you worked for the earl I most certainly would never have . . . never have—"

"Let me kiss you?" he asked nonchalantly enough.

"Yes," Hannah replied. "I thought you were someone quite different."

"How curious. Who did you think I was?" he asked mildly.

"A stranger. Well, you were a stranger." She bit her lip

in an agony of embarrassment. "And I would have you
know that I am not in the habit of . . . I don't usually—"

"Kiss perfect strangers?" he finished for her.

"Yes. I mean, no," she said, close to tears. Instant death
seemed a particularly attractive notion in that moment. "I
most certainly do not."

"I should hope you do not. And I would have you know
that I don't usually go about kissing perfect strangers either.
But by the time I got around to kissing you I didn't consider
you a stranger in the least. I felt as if I knew you quite well
in an odd sort of way. Did you not feel the same way?"

"Yes, but . . . see here, Mr. Frazier, we ought not even
to be having this conversation now or referring to what
happened between us. It was most improper. We should
not have spoken to each other at all last night."

"Perhaps not, but we did, and I thought we managed to
converse perfectly well, didn't you?"

"Yes, but I thought . . . I thought I would never see you
again! I spoke freely and without thought. And anyway, it
was different. You said so yourself."

"Yes, and I meant every word. It was different. But tell
me, Hannah," he said more gently. "Why have you come?"

She lowered her eyes. "I told you, I came to see the earl.
Please do not make this any more difficult for me than it is
already."

"But I do not try to do so. You have seen the earl," he
said. "You are seeing the earl."

Her head jerked up, and she looked around the room in
alarm but there was no one else, only the two of them. "Do
you jest with me, Mr. Frazier? I find nothing amusing in
it."

"I do not jest in the least. You see, Hannah, I forgot to
introduce myself properly last night, not yet being in the
habit. I am indeed Peter Frazier and hope I always will be.
But the good news, or the bad, depending on how you look
at it, is that I am not employed by Lord Blakesford. I *am*
Lord Blakesford."

He might as well have announced he had just been released from Bedlam.

4

"Did I say so?" replied he coolly; "to be sure,
if I said so, it was so."

—Oliver Goldsmith,
Citizen of the World

Hannah blinked. Then she blinked again, as if to clear her
vision. But there he sat, looking at her quite calmly. She
could see that he was not teasing her.

"You're mad," she said. "That's what it is."

"Wouldn't *that* be convenient," he replied. "But I am
afraid I am quite sane."

"But I know Lord Blakesford," she said, "or at least I
did, a few years ago. And you are not he."

"No, I am not. Nothing like. But I am Lord Blakesford."

"Oh, dear God," she said, sinking into the large chair
opposite the desk, for her body had gone weak with shock.
"But how? Are you sure?"

The laughter she had so loved the night before was back
in his eyes, but this time she did not find it amusing in the
least.

"Naturally I am sure," he said. "If you think, you will
remember that I told you I too had found myself caught in
circumstances beyond my control. These are those circumstances. You cannot honestly believe I am mistaken in my
own identity?"

"But I thought you were the secretary! What happened?
I do not understand! There cannot be two Lord Blakes-
fords, can there?" she asked, searching her memory for
precedent. "No, I am quite certain there cannot be," she
said decisively.

"No, there cannot," he agreed. "It is really quite simple.

41

The ninth Earl of Blakesford died suddenly four days ago.
I am now the tenth earl.''

"Died? He's dead? Oh, dear heaven. Dear, dear
heaven.''

"I rather wonder about heaven myself, given what I know
of his moral character," Peter said, observing her curiously.

Hannah just nodded, her head spinning with shock as she
tried to take the implications in. He was dead, God be
thanked. But one hand slipped to cover her mouth as she
realized that with the earl's death any hope of a decent
future for Wesley had also died. Yet at the same time a
tiny selfish feeling of thankfulness crept in, for it meant that
at least she would see Wesley again.

Her gaze wandered to the window as she frantically tried
to think what to do next. She had spent her last pound that
morning. Now there was nothing—except for her mother's
pearls, the one thing she had resisted selling. Perhaps she
could pawn them until she could think of something else.

"Hannah? Are you still with me? Just at this moment you
look as if I had told you your dearest friend had died, which
surprises me, given the person we are discussing.''

She dragged her eyes away from the window and back to
his face. "It is not that," she said, sitting up straighter. "I
cannot regret his passing. It is only that the news comes as
a shock.''

"Yes," Peter said with a grin. "I found I had the same
reaction. However, I do believe the shock I received was
slightly more overwhelming than your own.''

"I can imagine, discovering you were suddenly an earl.
But then you must have expected it at some point? Heirs
are usually brought up to assume their responsibilities.''

"Not this one. I learned I had come into direct line only
last week. I was a lowly second cousin, you see, and until
recently Henry had two perfectly sound sons of his own.
I was brought up on an island in the Caribbean with no
expectations and nothing to do with this branch of the
family.''

"Oh, how very difficult for you," Hannah said, suddenly
feeling very sorry for him.

"It is not easy, no. But I have no choice in the matter,
have I?''

"No, you haven't, and how much more awkward for you
without any training. It must be terrifying to have no idea

of how to go on. It is no wonder that you were distressed last night."

Peter looked at her for a long moment, then dropped his eyes to his folded hands. "How good of you to understand," he said. "Of course, I have only been at it a day. I am sure I will somehow muddle through the rest of my life. I am quite accustomed to making a fool of myself. At home one thinks nothing of it."

Hannah nodded. "English society is very different and must seem very rigid in comparison. Here there are rules for absolutely everything. Galsworthy has devoted his life to teaching them to me in the most minute detail."

"Oh, yes. Galsworthy," Peter said thoughtfully. "Has he indeed? In that case I am sure you would make a much more correct earl than I."

"Oh, piffle," she said, forgetting herself for a minute, "that is ridiculous. I cannot help having had the rules drummed into my head all of my life, just as you cannot help having grown up as you did. You mustn't despair over your lack of knowledge. That is the sort of thing that can be corrected easily enough. It is not as if you are lacking in moral character, which is far more important. You told me yourself last night how you felt about putting duty and obligation and responsibility to others before your own desires, and those are the things that are most important in a peer, far more important than knowing which fork to use or when to bow and to whom. You have noble blood in your veins and that will show through."

"Thank you, Hannah," he said gravely. "I find your faith in me most heartening."

"It is faith in yourself that you must cultivate. If you behave as an earl, with full confidence in your rank, then people will treat you as an earl."

"Will they? How interesting. And if I behave as I always have, how will they treat me then? As a savage?"

"I never said you were a *savage*," Hannah said indignantly. "I would never be so rude. You may have been raised around such people, but I am sure that you behave as a man of gentle birth should. Usually." She stood and pulled on her gloves. "I must be on my way," she said, thinking that if she were to pawn her pearls, she needed to collect them from the inn and find a pawnbroker. "May I

wish you luck in all your endeavors? I am quite sure you
will catch on to your new position very quickly."

"Hannah, please sit down."

Hannah looked at him with surprise. "I beg your
pardon?"

"I asked you to sit down. We have not finished."

"But I must go. I have things I must attend to."

"And I have questions to ask you. Please, Hannah, do
not be stubborn."

"Very well. It would be churlish of me to refuse." She
removed her gloves again and sat, folding her hands in her
lap. "I really do not know how I can further help you, but
I will try to answer your questions. However, I truly do not
have much time. What do you wish to know? I assume this
regards the rules of etiquette?"

Peter's lips twitched with amusement. "No, it regards
you. Why did you come to see my cousin?"

Hannah, taken by surprise, colored. "I . . . I came to be
his housekeeper," she said.

"Because you are, or were, a relation of his, is this not
true?"

"But why would you think . . . Oh. Did Wesley say something to you?"

"Only that you had come to Leicestershire to take shelter
with a wealthy relation. He did not say that the aforemen-
tioned relation was the Earl of Blakesford or naturally I
should have said something to you at the time."

"Yes, I'm sure you would have," she said weakly.

"Now, if you please, Hannah, will you enlighten me as
to how you and I are related? I find it is a rather compelling
point. I am sure you would agree."

"But we are not related," she blurted, then blushed even
more hotly. "That is, I am not related to you. Not in the
least. It is Wesley who is your relation."

"How very interesting," Peter murmured. "It is a most
reassuring thought that I have not been going about kissing
a maiden aunt. In what way am I related to Wesley and not
to you, if I may ask?"

"I . . . if you please, I would rather not say."

"Wouldn't you? Why is that? Hannah, there is really no
need for you to look as if I am about to draw all of your
teeth. It is a simple enough question, and one that I consider important."

"But why?"

"Because I like knowing who my relations are," he said with exasperation. "Now, applying logic to the situation, it occurs to me that you and Wesley must have a father in common. Therefore Wesley and I must be related through his mother."

"It is exactly the other way around," Hannah snapped, for she found his acuity extremely irritating. The man had no regard for privacy, but then she ought to have learned that the night before.

"And yet you have the same surname? An unusual situation. The laws of consanguinity come to mind."

"The law had nothing to do with it. If it had done, we should not have found ourselves in this mortifying situation."

"Ah," Peter said, grasping the point surprisingly quickly. "Wesley is base-born, then?"

Hannah dropped her eyes, belatedly regretting her outburst and feeling excruciatingly embarrassed.

"I see I am correct. I also assume your mother is no longer living?"

"She died a year ago."

"I am so sorry. And Wesley's father?"

"Please, my lord, may we not discuss this any further? I find this conversation most uncomfortable. You have guessed the truth of the matter, and there is nothing more to be said. I really should like to leave."

"Hannah, Wesley is not the first illegitimate child to have been born into the world, nor will he be the last. It is not an uncommon situation."

Hannah stared at the floor, wishing to drop directly through it. "There is no need to point out the fact to me, my lord," she said in a low voice. "And this is not a proper subject for discussion."

"The devil with the propriety. It is a necessary subject and there is no need to look so distressed. I am most certainly not about to pass judgment. Does Wesley know the truth of the matter?"

Hannah looked up. "Yes . . . but he does not know the identity of his father, and I would prefer to keep it that way, at least until he is older."

"That is your right. But you will please tell me, for I would like to know our connection. It must be close if my cousin Henry agreed to take you in. Henry had two sons. Would Wesley's father happen to be one of them? James drowned last month, which might be why you have been forced to come here.'

"I know nothing of James."

"No? Then it would have to be his older brother Rupert. No, that's impossible. Rupert died in the Peninsula nine years ago, and Wesley is not yet eight. Hmm. I am the only other living Frazier male that I know of, and I am not Wesley's father. Or I don't really see how I could be, but I suppose anything is possible. I have not led a completely pure life."

Hannah stared at him in astonishment, not quite able to believe that he would say such a thing to her. But then again, there was something about Peter's complete disregard for correctness that was a blessing: he was nearly impossible to shock. She had never imagined that anyone could be so casual about the stigma of illegitimacy.

"I hope to heaven your silence does not imply that Wesley is mine, Hannah," Peter said, breaking into her thoughts, but she noticed that he didn't look particularly concerned. No doubt he wasn't. No doubt people in the Caribbean went about casually conceiving children on whomever they could interest and no one raised an eyebrow. What a delightfully tolerant society, she decided. It was no wonder he had thought nothing of being alone with her in the dead of night and kissing her as he had. People must behave like that all the time in the Caribbean. Perhaps it had something to do with the climate.

"Hannah?" he repeated. "You have the most peculiar expression on your face. He could not possibly be my child, could he?"

"No, of course he is not. And you really must learn not to make such comments, my lord, or you shall have all those very proper people you wish to make an impression on falling to the ground in a faint."

Peter laughed. "Ah, well. Perhaps it would do them good, but I suppose I ought at least to attempt to behave. Decorum is a very awkward thing, to be sure. But to return to the matter at hand, who is Wesley's father? If he is a relation of mine, perhaps I can intercede on the boy's behalf."

"I cannot see how, my lord, unless in inheriting the earldom you also became divine. Wesley's father is dead. It seems you have stepped into his shoes."

Peter sat back in his chair with an audible exhalation of air. "Good God," he said for the second time that day. "You do have the gift of surprise, haven't you, Miss Hannah Janes?"

"I beg your pardon. I do not intend to surprise in the least. I have always been told that it is a most unladylike thing to do."

That made Peter smile. "That is the first I have heard of that particular stricture. It sounds very dull, but then most strictures are. So," he said, rubbing his cheek with his index finger. "Wesley is Henry's natural son. That really is a most interesting development."

"I am not sure why I even told you," Hannah said, fidgeting with her gloves. "It is not as if there is anything that you can do about it."

"You have a strong point, Miss Janes, and a way with an understatement. Indeed, the deed has been done and cannot be taken back. That is the drawback to biology."

"Biology cannot be held to blame," Hannah said bitterly. "It is the weakness of the human spirit to resist it that creates the problem." She rose, thoroughly sick of the subject. "I really must be leaving. Thank you for your time. I will not take any more of it."

"Sit down." Peter's voice was unexpectedly sharp, and for the first time he sounded every inch an earl. Hannah immediately complied without thinking, but something inside of her registered deep surprise.

"Now," he continued, and his voice had assumed its usual calm tone, "you will please recover your reason, Hannah. You cannot honestly think that you can drop a piece of information like that in my lap and then walk away, assuming I am going to do nothing? You may think me a barbarian, but you also know I am not without a certain sense of duty. Wesley is my cousin, base-born or no. Wesley, had he not been base-born, would now be the tenth earl. However, there is no way to remedy that situation. The laws of succession must stand. That is not to say that Wesley should be cast out into the street with nothing but a stale crust of bread cast after him. After all, Henry was willing to acknowledge him, although I must say that does surprise me."

"He was *not* willing to acknowledge him," Hannah said, determined to have the truth between them if Peter insisted on pursuing the subject. "He was willing to pay the minimal amount for his schooling. The condition was that he never lay eyes on my brother. Ever."

Peter absorbed that. "What about school holidays? This is an extremely large house; surely they would have inadvertently stumbled upon one another at some point?"

"Wesley was never to set foot upon Longthorpe soil," Hannah said as evenly as she could manage. "Not under any circumstances."

Peter's mouth tightened. "All right. That much is in character. But what does not make sense is why you were to come to Longthorpe as a housekeeper, of all positions Henry might have chosen. In the first place, it is more than apparent that my cousin had no interest in keeping a house. It appears he spent a lifetime creating a mausoleum. Furthermore, why would he want any reminder of a child he adamantly refused to see? Bringing the child's sister here would have been a constant reminder, or so it would seem to me."

Hannah bit her lip. "I imagine he thought to humiliate me," she said, thinking that in that moment, even from beyond the grave, the old earl had managed to achieve his goal.

"Forgive me, but in what way would you have been humiliated?" Peter leaned slightly forward over one arm, his posture casual, but that unsettling, keen look was back in his eyes.

"He knew how very much I had always . . . always disliked him," Hannah answered tonelessly. "It annoyed him in the extreme, although he disliked me in equal measure. I imagine he considered it a personal victory when the bothersome daughter of his discarded mistress was finally forced to write to him and beg him to support Wesley. I had to sell my mother's house and all her possessions to pay her debts, and there was no other choice but to throw ourselves on his mercy. He obviously did not feel that was humiliation enough. He wished to see me completely miserable, and he knew that to be forced to live as a servant under his roof, separated from my brother, would accomplish that, as well as making Wesley miserable. So he wrote back and laid out his conditions. The tone of his letter made his intentions very clear. Does that answer your question?"

"Hannah, I do not mean to add to your humiliation by having you speak of it. It is only that I must know the full story," Peter said, his voice now gentle, so gentle that it made her want to cry. "What, exactly, did my cousin's letter say?"

"I was to be here today to take up my position. Galsworthy was to look after my brother in the future. I was to communicate with Wesley only through Galsworthy. I was not ever to see Wesley or Galsworthy again." She forced back tears. "I do not know what else to tell you."

"You are sure there is nothing you wish to add?"

She shook her head. "Nothing."

"Good."

"Good?" she asked incredulously. "I cannot see what you can possibly think is good about any of this!"

"Can't you? I consider that singularly unimaginative of you, Hannah. It seems to me it is all quite clear." He touched the tips of his fingers together and looked over them at her.

"What do you mean?" she said, her eyes flying to his in confusion.

"What I mean is that Wesley shall have a home here for as long as it suits him. There is no question of that."

"Wesley . . . here? With you? But why? Why would you offer such a thing?"

"I am not my cousin, Hannah. I have no ulterior motives. I only want to do what is right. I cannot give Wesley Longthorpe, but I can give him a home and financial security. Does that not seem fair?"

"F-fair? Oh, my lord—it is more than fair! It is unbelievably generous!"

"And so why do you look so crestfallen?"

"Do I? I do not mean to—it is only that I shall miss him most dreadfully. But that is of no significance, none at all in the face of his future."

"Hannah, for a woman who strikes me as being possessed of a fine intelligence, you are being very obtuse. I have no intention of separating you from your brother. You will naturally come here to live as well."

"To live . . . my lord, forgive me, but as kind and as attractive as the offer is, it is quite impossible."

"Impossible? Why? It makes perfect sense."

"But it is impossible. I am an unmarried woman. You are an unmarried man. It cannot be. Society will not countenance such a thing, and your position would be compromised. Please believe me."

"Let me worry about my position, if you please. There is nothing at all inappropriate in my offer. In fact I will countenance nothing else. What good is having money and position and a huge house if one doesn't use them to sensible purposes? I certainly do not want to rattle about here on my own with only Mrs. Brewster and Monsieur Antoine to keep me company. What a dreary thought. And speaking of that, I find that I am in desperate need of a shortsighted butler. I don't suppose Galsworthy might be available?"

"Galsworthy?" she said, distracted. "You want to employ Galsworthy? Oh, I am sure he would be extremely pleased. I have not been able to pay him for over a year, and no doubt he would be grateful for the wages."

"That would be marvelous, for as you must have seen, Mrs. Brewster isn't quite the thing as far as butlers go. She is lacking a certain delicacy of approach, do you not agree? I believe Galsworthy would improve my image tremendously."

"You are quite correct," Hannah agreed, relieved to have her beloved Galsworthy taken care of, although she would miss him dreadfully as well. But at least Wesley would have someone who loved him at his side. She swallowed hard against the lump in her throat and tried to look cheerful. "Galsworthy would be a definite improvement over Mrs. Brewster, even if he is old and can't see very well. But he tries very hard to make up for it. You are very kind to consider him."

"Not at all. As I explained to you, I am in need of any and all help that I can acquire, and the sooner the better. Galsworthy will do very well, for he seems a very loyal sort, and I am sure he will keep a watchful eye on me."

"Oh, yes, he is very good about that sort of thing. He knows a great deal about all kinds of matters, and he is very good at being flexible in his work."

"Excellent. Perhaps he would be good enough to double as a valet, then. As for Mrs. Brewster, I do feel that in all good conscience I must keep her on. She deserves a citation for having put up with my cousin. It is no wonder she is peculiar; actually, if truth be told, I rather enjoy her. If my instincts are sound, the woman has a good heart. What she does not have is a way with the broom, never mind the door."

"What will you do with her? I cannot imagine what she would be suited for."

"It occurs to me that she would be better off returning to something approximating her original position, which I gather was that of companion to her niece, the late Lady Blakesford. She would have to be of respectable family, although it is hard to tell now."

"It does take a stretch of the imagination," Hannah agreed.

"Indeed, but my cousin was a stickler for family credentials, and his wife came from an impeccable background. Perhaps Mrs. Brewster came from one of the lesser branches of the Abingers. In any case, she would make an adequate chaperone, would she not?"

"Most unlikely, and in any case, whom would she chaperone?"

"Why you, naturally. It would be a nominal position, of course, but it might do to lend some sort of respectability to the arrangement. What do you think?"

"I think you are the most unconventional, not to mention the most stubborn, hardheaded gentleman I have ever come across! I have told you that your proposal to have me live here is an impossible one, and you refuse to listen to me!"

"Naturally, for you are so caught up in your conventions that your common sense has gone missing. Hannah, for the love of God give it up, for I cannot continue to argue with you. Wesley is my relative and should be living here. You and Galsworthy and Wesley are a family. It would be stupid if not unconscionable to separate you. Will you make everyone miserable just because you feel the urge to stand on a misplaced sense of propriety?"

"It is not misplaced, my lord," Hannah said indignantly.

"Oh, yes it is. It is mightily misplaced. In fact it is absurd."

"Oh, and this is coming from the man who kissed me last night in the middle of a garden, a common *public* garden at that, without a single chaperone in sight or even a proper introduction? Who do you think you are to be talking of proprieties?"

"You were there too, Hannah," he pointed out.

She colored. "And I shouldn't have been. I know I behaved disgracefully last night, and you must think me a
fallen woman, especially after what you now know about my
mother. But despite what you might think of my behavior, I
assure you that I am not that sort of—"

She was cut off by an incredulous sputter and then Peter's
hands came down hard on the desk and he leaned forward,
staring at her. "Are you out of your mind?" he said. "Sweet
Christ, but what can you be thinking? Do you believe me
to be so totally depraved—or perhaps so totally devoid of
any sort of understanding—that I would take advantage of
you, never mind under my own roof? Even a moron such
as myself knows better than that. Let us not even bother to
bring honor into it!"

Peter looked thoroughly dangerous in that moment and
Hannah felt like an utter fool. "But I didn't mean to imply
. . . that is, I wasn't entirely sure," she stammered. "After
last night, you might have thought anything of me."

"My dear girl," Peter finally said, having regained his
control, "I may have my flaws, but I am not completely
corrupt. I kissed you last night, yes, and I enjoyed every
moment of it. It is true that I ought not to have been kissing
you at all, and for that I apologize. But one kiss does not
make you a fallen woman in my eyes, nor myself a degenerate wretch. I shan't be kissing you again, so you needn't
worry that I am going to be lurking in dark corners, waiting
to leap out at you."

Hannah looked down, unable to meet his eyes. "Very
well. We shan't speak of it again," she said in a small voice.

"All right, then. When I told you that I will look after
Wesley, I meant exactly that. I think he would be happiest
having his sister and his old friend here with him, and I am
sure you would agree. I intend nothing more than that,
Hannah. I most certainly do not intend the seduction of a
young woman I have offered to take into my protection.
However, lest you now jump to the conclusion that instead
of offering you a carte blanche I am offering you charity,
let me put your mind at further ease and add that I was
also hoping that you might oversee Longthorpe's domestic
arrangements. I do not wish you to be housekeeper, but
more to act as a . . . let me see, perhaps as my assistant.
Would that be acceptable?"

"If the situation were any different I would be happy to act as your assistant. But despite all of your persuasive arguments, it still would not be correct for me to live here with you," she said, looking up at him. "I apologize for having implied that you would behave less than honorably, for I can see now that you would not, but it would still be taken very wrong in the eyes of the world, no matter how innocent the arrangement."

"And you called me stubborn? Dear heaven, Hannah, you could wear down the pope with your moral stances. But please listen to one more piece of reason. We do have a relative in common, have we not? I do not think anything more needs to be said to the world at large than that. You are my cousin by association, and as such you have come to help in setting up my household. Is that not eminently sensible? Such things must occur all the time, sisters coming to help out their brothers, cousins to help cousins? I am in desperate need of help, surely you can see that? Will you not take pity on my predicament?"

"It is true that you will need help . . ." she said uncertainly, teetering on the edge of surrender. "After all, you will have to go up to London at some point."

Peter rubbed his eyebrow with one finger, then looked up at her. "I am not entirely unused to London, Hannah. I have been before."

"I did not mean to offend you, my lord. What I mean is that you have never been there as anything other than plain Mr. Frazier. Expectations were not high. Now you will find they have changed, and the circles you move in will be different."

"And how is that?" he said, regarding her with extreme curiosity. "Do you think my friends will suddenly decide I have become too grand for them?"

"No, my lord," she said, trying to be patient with him, "it is only that you will be expected to associate with people of your own kind—other peers, the cream of the *ton*. Eventually you will be expected to take your seat in the House of Lords. I suppose I could help you attain some of the necessary polish. . . ."

Peter passed a hand over his face, then looked back at her with a neutral expression. "Oh, that is very kind of you, Hannah. Really, you are most considerate, offering so selflessly to correct my behavior."

"Not at all. It is nothing after what you have offered to us. And I enjoy being useful, rather than feeling like a burden. And what I don't know about gentlemen, or peers, I am sure Galsworthy will be able to tell you. He was with a . . . a most elevated household, before he came to us."

"Was he?" Peter said. "How very estimable. But given that, maybe you had best consult with Galsworthy first. He might not want to take on such a weighty responsibility as myself."

"I am sure that he will. He has a very good heart. I am completely devoted to him, and despite our family difficulties, he never once hesitated in his devotion to us. I am quite sure that he will show you the same allegiance."

"I am overwhelmed by all this devotion," Peter said dryly. "Then it is arranged. You will all three of you move to Longthorpe this afternoon."

Hannah wavered for a final moment. She felt as if her entire life was hanging in the balance. And then Peter smiled at her, and all resistance melted away. "Very well, although I am sure you are only asking us to stay out of the kindness of your heart."

"Nonsense," Peter said firmly. "Although it is true that I have never believed in breaking up families—and Wesley will not be sent away to school, by the by—it is also true that I am in need of your services, and Galsworthy's also. And speaking of Galsworthy, where are he and Wesley? Have they already left for the school?"

"No. I left them at the Red Lion. Galsworthy is awaiting the money the earl was to send once I appeared at Longthorpe. He wasn't prepared to give me a farthing for Wesley in advance."

"Ah. Of course he wouldn't. Well, I imagine Galsworthy will be very happy to see you again and hear the good news. Shall I drive you in my carriage, or did you have the carriage you came in wait?"

"I didn't come in a carriage. I . . . I walked."

"You walked. I see. You walked the ten odd miles from the Red Lion in this weather. No doubt you were in need of the exercise?"

"I spent the last of my money on Wesley's breakfast," she said quietly. "And I did not mind walking. It took my mind off my troubles."

"I see," Peter said, and Hannah could not help noticing that his eyes had suddenly and inexplicably darkened. "However, you shall not walk back. If you will give me a few minutes, I will harness the horses and bring the carriage around. There is not yet any stable help."

She heard him call loudly for Mrs. Brewster as he left, and his voice sounded curt, almost angry. "Tell Monsieur Antoine to prepare a decent dinner for two, Mrs. Brewster, and also to have an early dinner sent up to the nursery. Tell him he can consider the exercise a test of his abilities."

There was a burst of protest from Mrs. Brewster, and then Peter's reply. "I don't care in the least if he has a tantrum, Mrs. Brewster. Deal with it. If there is no dinner, then there will also be no Monsieur Antoine, and you may tell him I said as much. And you will please prepare three bedchambers for immediate use. One is for Mr. Galsworthy, the new butler. He is not a young man, so something near the warmth of the kitchen would do well. One is for Miss Janes—a suite with an attractive view if you please, near the nursery. And the third is to be made up in the nursery for Master Janes, who is seven. Thank you. My relatives shall be living here permanently."

She heard Mrs. Brewster's surprised squeak in reply, and then he said something else more softly that she could not make out at all. And then the front door closed behind him and the crunch of his boots on the snow came faintly through the closed window.

Hannah squeezed her hands tightly together in her lap, closed her eyes, and whispered a fervent prayer of gratitude. She considered God not a distant deity, but more like a close personal friend who lived in another, kinder place. She gave thanks to have a roof over all their heads and for the blessed stroke of fortune that had felled the earl and given them Peter instead. She gave thanks that she would not be demeaned and humiliated every waking hour, nor live in fear of having to fend off unwelcome advances from the old reprobate. But most especially she gave thanks that she would not be separated from her beloved Wesley and her dear friend Galsworthy. She would have her family after all.

But oh, dear Lord, she added at the end, *why, after all*

these years, did you hand me such a heaping platter of good fortune, and then oversalt it with impossible irony?

There was no answer to that question, not that she'd really expected one, so she opened her eyes, sighed, and decided that common sense and correct behavior were the only things that were going to get her through this new and entirely unexpected situation. God certainly did have an odd sense of humor.

5

A book may be amusing with numerous errors,
or it may be very dull without a single absurdity.
> —Oliver Goldsmith,
> *The Vicar of Wakefield*

"Do you mean *my* Mr. Frazier, Hannah?" Wesley said, his brow knotting as his eyes searched his sister's face. "He is the rich relative who is to look after us? But why didn't he say something yesterday when I met him? I told him my name and why we were here. Are you quite sure it is the same man? I think you must be mistaken, Hannah, for I do not really see how it can be. *My* Mr. Frazier has fair hair and blue eyes and a nice smile. And he is very, very tall and smartly dressed."

"Yes, I am quite sure it is the same person. He didn't say anything to you because he had no idea who we were. He didn't know we were related."

"But how can he be an earl, Hannah? You really must be mistaken, for surely you of all people know that earls are not gentlemen, they are lords. He said most distinctly that his name was Mister Frazier."

"Yes, I know," Hannah said patiently. "But he's only just become the earl, you see. The old earl died a few days ago, and so he is not yet accustomed to using his title."

"And would the new earl be married?" Galsworthy asked, looking inscrutable. He had been listening in complete silence until now, showing no emotion at all after his initial start of surprise when Hannah had walked through the door.

"No . . ." Hannah said, knowing just what Galsworthy was thinking. "But he is a most generous and morally upstanding man, nothing at all like the last earl."

"And exactly what is your position to be?" Galsworthy asked.

Hannah frowned. "Well . . . I am not exactly sure what it means, but his lordship says I am to be his assistant. I assume that means in domestic matters."

"His assistant. I see. Well, we shall see what we shall see, Miss Hannah," and then he firmly compressed his lips as if not to let another word slip out on the subject.

"Well, I think it is very fine, Hannah," Wesley said, "and you look much more cheerful than when you left this morning. Will you still be allowed to visit me at school?"

"Oh, Wesley, I nearly forgot! That's the best news of all. You shan't be going away to school. Lord Blakesford is quite insistent that you stay at Longthorpe."

"That is very fine news," Wesley said with a sigh of contentment. "Very fine. I had not really wanted to go away, Hannah, at least not all that much, for I should have missed you most awfully. I do like Mr. Frazier so, and it will be very nice all of us living together, I think. Don't you think so, Hannah?"

"Yes, I do. And Lord Blakesford likes you too, very much indeed."

She suddenly noticed that Galsworthy's expression had turned cloudy and she realized what he must be thinking. "I am sure you will find no real fault with him, Galsworthy," she said with a little smile. "He considers himself quite a business to take on, but he would be very appreciative if you would take him on nevertheless and be his butler—and also his valet. If you are willing, of course."

"Naturally I am willing, Miss Hannah. I am always pleased to be of service." Galsworthy's dignity had returned with alacrity, but Hannah could see the tears suddenly shimmering in his eyes, and she knew the relief he too must be feeling.

"Where is he?" Wesley asked, jumping up and down on one foot. "I should like to thank him! I think it is all terribly exciting!"

"He is outside waiting with the carriage. He thought this might be news I would want to deliver privately."

"Then I shall go outside directly. May I, Hannah? You gave me such a telling off yesterday for going out without asking."

"Yes, of course. We will join you shortly. I just need to arrange for the baggage to be brought down."

Wesley streaked away, and Galsworthy cleared his throat. "And does his lordship know the truth of the matter, Miss Hannah?" he asked more severely.

"More or less," she said, wondering which particular part of the exact truth Galsworthy might be referring to. Galsworthy had an uncanny ability to divine truth out of the most obscure situations.

"Begging your pardon, Miss Hannah," Galsworthy said, and Hannah prepared herself, for Galsworthy only ever begged her pardon when he was about to say something unnerving. "I feel I ought to be informed as to his lordship's exact understanding." He fixed her with a foggy but firm eye.

Hannah reached out a hand and gently touched Galsworthy's shoulder. "I told him the most important details. He is aware of Wesley's paternity and how the situation came about."

"Very good. And as for your own situation, Miss Hannah?"

"If you are asking whether I told him the truth of my own paternity," Hannah said, facing the matter square on, "no, I did not. I didn't really see how he would have benefited from the knowledge that my father was some footman or other."

"That is none of his lordship's business that I can see, Miss Hannah, and that is certainly not what I was referring to. I refer to his lordship's intentions toward you. It is not an issue to be sidestepped."

"His intentions are nothing but proper, Galsworthy. I made very sure of that. He only wants to see to Wesley's well-being."

"As you think correct, Miss Hannah," Galsworthy said darkly. "However, one never knows. Assurances have been made before with dire consequences. There is a good reason for observing the proprieties, and I do not see them in place in this matter."

"Galsworthy, you and Wesley and I are to have a proper home again. That is all that matters. His lordship has accepted Wesley as his cousin, and I do not think he will go back on his word to Wesley or to me. But speaking of proprieties, there is something I should forewarn you about. It concerns his lordship."

"Yes?" Galsworthy said, one thick white eyebrow inching up like a caterpillar toward his balding scalp.

Hannah wanted to laugh. She had never known anyone as suspicious as Galsworthy, although in her twenty-three years, she had seen enough to understand why he might be suspicious of his own sex. "It is nothing like that, Galsworthy. It is just that his lordship is a bit backward."

"Backward, Miss Hannah?" Distrust had been replaced by carefully controlled astonishment.

"Yes. Not in his brain, but rather in his manners. He has not had a normal upbringing. It is our duty to assist him in the correct behavior, for he was not groomed for the earldom. He is something of a . . . a *country* sort of person."

"Do you mean a country bumpkin, Miss Hannah? I may tell you I am up to nearly anything, but if you expect me to make an earl out of an onion—"

"It's not quite as bad as that," she said soothingly. "All that will be required is subtle instruction here and there. You shall see soon enough. But come, Galsworthy, his lordship awaits. Let us attend to the baggage. And try not to worry. All will be well."

"It does seem a far superior situation to the one we were all heading for, Miss Hannah, but I cannot be comfortable until I see the circumstances for myself. I simply cannot." He moved away, grumbling under his breath, and Hannah was relieved, for it meant Galsworthy was back to normal.

Hannah finally persuaded Wesley to eat his supper and be tucked up in bed. He had been racing about the house and grounds ever since alighting—or more accurately, she amended, leaping from the carriage. Peter had not objected in the least, quite amiably taking Wesley down to the stables to help him feed and stable the horses and put the carriage away.

"Are you going to be able to sleep, my darling?" Hannah asked, smoothing the dark, slightly damp hair off Wesley's brow as he burrowed under the covers. "I know it has been an exciting day for you."

"I shall lie awake for a little while, for I need to think over everything. It is a splendid house, is it not, Hannah? There are more rooms than I can count, and they all have wonderful surprises in them. I found one whole room, like a big hall, that has suits of armor and spears and all sorts of other things under the covers. And—"

"I know. There is much to be discovered, and you may start first thing in the morning after your breakfast, as long as you don't get under Mrs. Brewster's feet. She is not accustomed to having people about."

"What a funny little woman. But do you know, Hannah, I think I rather like her. She puts me in mind of a sparrow."

"A sparrow? Yes, I can see what you mean, although I hope you don't share your impression with Mrs. Brewster."

"I wouldn't do that, Hannah. But what do you suppose Galsworthy must think? He gave her a most interesting look as he went marching off to the kitchen, although it is hard to tell what he actually saw of her. Why do you suppose she wears clothes pegs in her cap? And what did Galsworthy and Mr. Frazier—that is, Lord Blakesford—have to talk about behind closed doors for so long, Hannah?"

"I imagine they were discussing Galsworthy's new duties, Wesley. It is usual for an employer to interview his servants before hiring them. No doubt he was instructing Galsworthy as to how he would like things done."

"Will he be instructing me as to how he'd like things done, Hannah? Suppose I don't get it right? Will he send me away do you think?"

"I don't think you need worry about that, Wesley," Peter said from the doorway, and they both turned to look at him in surprise. "Had I been sent away for all of the things I didn't get right at your age, I should have traveled three times around the world by the time I reached fifteen."

Peter advanced into the room carrying two candles. Hannah immediately stood, slightly nonplussed at his unexpected appearance in the nursery. She was under the impression that gentlemen took no interest in such things as bedtime, or in any children's activities, for that matter. But then, Peter did not do much of anything like an ordinary gentleman.

"I came to bid you good night, Wesley," he said, "for if you feel in any way as I do, it must seem mightily peculiar to be going to sleep in a new house, especially one as large as this. I brought you some extra candles, just in case you wake in the night and need to find your way. I often become disoriented when I wake in strange surroundings, and I am forever barking my shins on the furniture and cracking my head on errant beams, although you have nothing yet to fear from the latter. These candles seemed sufficiently tall to burn until dawn."

"Oh, thank you, sir," Wesley breathed, and Hannah felt a lump rising in her throat. She would never have expected such thoughtfulness nor understanding of a small child's fears, not from a man with no children of his own.

"Not at all," Peter replied with a smile. "Now, where I come from, the nights are far shorter, and a great deal warmer. One can have the window open year-round and listen to the music of the sea."

"Oh," Wesley said wistfully, pushing himself back up. "Will you tell me, sir—I mean, my lord? Where is this place, and how can the nights be shorter? I had always thought that the night was the same length everywhere in the world."

"It is an island called Jamaica, and I shall explain it all to you tomorrow when we go to feed the horses their breakfast. I'll expect you at eight o'clock promptly. And Wesley, you must call me Cousin Peter, for we are family, and family must be at ease with each other. But now I think you should sleep, for we have all had a big day. I am looking forward to your help tomorrow."

Wesley grinned at him, and the gap where his front tooth had not yet come in showed lopsided. "Good night, Cousin Peter. I am very happy that we are to be living with you in your fine house."

"And I am very gratified that you should feel so," Peter said, bowing. "I shall leave you with your sister. Hannah, do join me downstairs in the library when you are finished. Galsworthy has somehow located sherry, for which I am indebted to him for life."

He softly closed the door behind him, and Wesley nodded with satisfaction. "Don't you think I was right, Hannah? Isn't he splendid?"

"Very splendid, Wesley," she said. "Now say your prayers and go to sleep. I mustn't keep the earl waiting."

Wesley slipped back down under the covers with a contented sigh. "Do you know," he said with a yawn, "I have just decided that life might be rather nice after all."

Hannah looked down at him, and then she pulled him to her in a tight hug. "Do you know, my darling," she whis-

pered, "I believe you might be right. I think you are going
to be very happy here." She rested her chin on top of his
sweet-smelling hair and she felt his sigh against her
shoulder.

Hannah began to wonder just how much Wesley had been
pretending happy anticipation of school for her sake and
how much he might actually have divined of her misery and
shared in it.

"Hannah?" he murmured sleepily, and his next words
confirmed her suspicion. "Are you going to be happy now?"

"I think so, Wesley," she said, her heart feeling as if it
might break with tenderness for him. "I think we are all
going to be very happy."

She couldn't help but hope that at last it might be the
truth.

The start of dinner went smoothly enough. Peter did not
slurp his soup, Galsworthy did not miss the glasses when he
poured the wine, and not only that, he had somehow found
the time to polish the silver and lay the table with the
proper china and crystal. It all seemed a very adequate pic-
ture and an auspicious beginning for the training of an earl.

"The pattern is Limoges," Hannah said to Peter, who
seemed to be examining the bottom of his soup bowl with
some interest. "It is made in France. The crystal is Water-
ford, which is produced in England."

"Really?" Peter said. "And what nationality would you
ascribe to the beetle?"

"The beetle?" Hannah said, wrinkling her brow. "What
beetle?"

"The one who is trying very hard to avoid death by
drowning in the bottom of my bowl. Or do you think the
chef intended him as a garnish?" Peter, who did not seem
the least disturbed, lifted the insect out of the tomato bisque
with the tip of his spoon and placed him gently upon the
linen.

"My lord," Hannah said, not sure whether to be more
appalled that the beetle had been in the soup to begin with
or that Peter felt it proper to send it crawling along the
table. For the sake of practicality she decided to focus on
the latter. "I do not think, my lord," she said tentatively,
"that the ladies of the *ton* would be thrilled with sight of
an insect upon the dinner table."

"No! Surely the ladies of the *ton* cannot be such a tight-laced bunch. Why, in Jamaica such things are a natural occurrence. One comes to expect a good spider or two to drop in for a casual taste. I have heard our local ladies say that it is the mark of a good cook. Galsworthy?"

Galsworthy instantly appeared from behind the door.

"My compliments to the chef. His soup is superb, and tell him I was most impressed by the creativity of his garnish."

Galsworthy bowed. "Very good, sir."

Not a minute later, a very small, thin man appeared in the selfsame door, his eyes flashing with indignation. "What is this the Galsworthy has said to me, my lord? I have made no garnish for the soup! It is a tomato purée with only *la crème*. The Galsworthy is a fool, *une bête, n'est-ce pas*? My soup, it is superb, *oui*?"

"Your soup is indeed superb. However, Galsworthy passed on my comment most correctly." There was a distinct sniff of satisfaction from the shadows, which both Antoine and Peter ignored. "It was indeed garnished, and with what might initially have been mistaken for a mushroom had it not had three pairs of legs."

The little man went instantly purple and his even smaller eyes narrowed until they were no more than slits. *"Voilà!"* he cried, his hands flying up into the air. "It is that Brewster woman! Nevair, but nevair, does she look to see if the china is clean! She is the filthiest woman I have evair had the misfortune to come across! One look from her is enough to curdle even the simplest of my sauces!"

Peter leaned back in his chair and folded his arms across his chest. "If I am correct, Antoine, I believe I asked you earlier today to request permission before you came bounding into a room. I do not much enjoy being interrupted in the middle of a promising meal by strong emotion. If you please, you will now remove yourself and attend to the rest of dinner. If you do not feel Mrs. Brewster can be relied upon to see that unwanted substances do not appear in your culinary efforts, then you might check the state of the china yourself. And you will in the future, should you be unfortunate enough to make the same mistake of bounding where you have not been invited, acknowledge the other occupants of the room. Hannah, this is obviously the chef, who will no doubt benefit by your advice in decorum. Antoine, you will defer to my cousin in all matters, for Miss Janes will be acting in the capacity of lady of the house. Thank you, Antoine. I happily anticipate the next course."

Antoine's mouth worked spasmodically, looking very much like the rapid opening and closing of a very small purse, and Hannah wanted desperately to burst into laughter. But Peter seemed to be doing very well with deflating his new chef's airs, and levity would have been inappropriate.

Antoine turned abruptly on his heel and disappeared through the doorway again, his back very still and almost quivering with hurt indignation.

Once the door had closed Peter turned to her. "I fear Antoine has a creative temperament," he said. "No doubt it will produce miracles in the kitchen, but I worry for the state of my nerves. I am not accustomed to dealing with temperament."

"But you were very firm with him, my lord. It was exactly the right approach to quell an unacceptable attitude."

"Was it? How very reassuring to know I handled the situation correctly. It is not that I am entirely inexperienced with staff, you understand. I have a shipping business, did I tell you? But dictating to sailors and merchants is very different from attempting to reason with a French culinary artist."

"I have confidence that you will soon grow accustomed, my lord."

"Peter."

"I beg your pardon?" she said, wondering if he was in the unfortunate habit of talking to himself.

"Peter. My name is Peter."

"Oh. Yes, I know. But I cannot possibly call you by your Christian name."

"You cannot? Why not? Is there some prohibition of which I am not aware?" He regarded her innocently, and Hannah realized what a truly enormous job lay ahead.

"No, I cannot. In the first place, it would be incorrect for us to be on such familiar terms. In the second, it is my job to train you to the earldom, and you must become accustomed to being addressed as 'my lord,' or 'your lordship' or 'Lord Blakesford.' Only your intimates may address you more familiarly. From this day on, you are 'Lord Blakesford,' and 'Peter' only to a very select few. In Wesley's case, to address you as 'Cousin Peter' is correct, which is why I did not offer an objection. You are, after all, related by blood, even if the relationship itself is not entirely correct. In my case, there is no true relationship, save through my brother, which makes our situation quite tentative."

"Tentative?" Peter asked with interest. "How is that? I do not feel the least tentative. Ought I to?"

Hannah gave him a look of exasperation. "It is as I explained. I am in a situation which constitutes that of a poor relation. One exists somewhere in limbo, above the servants but below the salt, if you see what I mean. You do understand the latter expression?" she added, for clarity of instruction was everything.

"I believe so," he said mildly. "Having spent much of my life below the salt I find it a most comfortable place."

"Yes, but it is time for that to change."

"Whatever for? I have always prided myself on how long I can hold my breath."

"Hold your breath? What has that to do with placement at a dinner table?"

"I have no idea," he said. "I was referring to diving in the ocean. How did dinner tables come into the subject?"

Hannah thought for one moment that she saw a devilish gleam in his eye, but then she decided that she must have been mistaken and it had been a trick of candlelight, for he looked vaguely confused.

" 'Below the salt,' " she explained carefully, "means that one is not seated in a position of honor. It has to do with where the salt cellar is placed."

"I am sure it makes perfect sense," Peter said and turned his attention to Galsworthy, who was carefully making his way in with the platter of fish. Hannah gave up the point, and conversation mostly ceased as they applied themselves to the excellence of Antoine's cooking.

Course after course appeared from the kitchen: after the fish they were presented with fowl, game, mutton, a number of savories, cheeses, even a soufflé which had risen quite beautifully.

"Ah, the suffle," Peter murmured.

"It is pronounced soufflé," she whispered. She hoped he wouldn't mind her forwardness in correcting him in the presence of his butler, but after all, he was now an earl, and he couldn't afford such mistakes.

"Thank you," he said, his face quite without expression. "I shall keep that in mind. You must feel very free to point such things out to me. I am an enormous believer in education. I am sure I shall be most enlightened by your particular storehouse. Tell me, Hannah, for I find that I long to know. How and where were you raised?"

"In Reading, although I was sent away to school in Essex when I was nine."

"At nine? That is rather early to go off, especially for a girl."

She sensed genuine surprise beneath the words. "It was because my mother couldn't have me at home."

"And it was at this school that you learned all about being a lady, yes?"

"Yes . . ." Hannah did not find it necessary to add that she had learned more about being a lady by waiting on the other students. The old earl had not been interested in providing any extras, and so Hannah had paid for her board in work. That had not been so bad. It had been the attitude of the other girls that had been humiliating, although it was true that some had been kind, had offered her their dresses when they had outgrown them, or shared the cakes and sweets sent from home. Really, it had only been a few who had been truly dreadful and malicious. She remembered Pamela Chandler in particular.

"Hannah? Where have you gone? Back to Essex?"

She pulled herself back to the present. "I beg your pardon. I did not mean to wander."

"I often wander myself when I remember my school days, although I usually wander in the opposite direction and as far away as possible. I did not much enjoy them. It is why I do not think Wesley should be sent away. He can have a tutor here who could teach Wesley his lessons and prepare him for a higher education."

"Oh, but I can do that!" she exclaimed.

"Hannah, my dear, I am afraid I am going to need you for other things. And in any case, do you not think that it is about time that Wesley too has exposure to other people and situations?"

"I am not sure what you mean, my lord," Hannah said uncomfortably. "He has been content until now."

"Perhaps. But until now his opportunities have been limited. He needs a normal boyhood, Hannah. He can have one here, but I think that you might enjoy a little freedom from each other. I don't mean that I think you are unworthy to the task of raising him, for you have already done a wonderful job. I was only suggesting that you will both be busy with other pursuits."

"You are probably right," Hannah said reluctantly. "I suppose I am going to be busy if I am to help you to bring Longthorpe up to scratch." *And bringing you up to scratch is going to be extremely time-consuming,* she added to herself, watching as Galsworthy placed the finger glass in front of him. Peter glanced down at it, then looked up at her. He opened his mouth as if to ask a question.

"It is a finger glass, my lord," she said quickly. "The finger glass is always presented before the dessert."

Peter closed his mouth again and gazed at her with fascination, his fingers toying with his wineglass.

"It is not for drinking, it is for washing. Look, like so." She dipped the corner of her napkin into the tepid, rose-scented water, then delicately touched the napkin to the corner of her mouth and the tips of her fingers.

"Very pretty," he said, watching her lazily. He took a sip of his wine.

"It is not meant to be pretty, my lord," Hannah said with exasperation, "it is meant to be practical. One is not obligated to wash, naturally, but if you have inadvertently soiled yourself, this is your opportunity to correct the situation."

"I see," Peter said with a relatively straight face. "Cleanliness is everything."

"Exactly," Hannah said, beaming approval at her pupil. "Would you like to try, my lord?"

Peter picked up his napkin, inserted it into the glass, then gave himself a good wash.

"My lord! You are not meant to be taking a bath! A little delicacy of manner would be appropriate. I realize that this is all very new to you, but try to remember that a peer must be a model of refinement."

Peter choked, then quickly covered his mouth with his napkin, loudly sneezing into it in a most ungentlemanly fashion.

"Oh, have you something caught in your throat?" she asked with alarm, for his eyes had begun to stream.

"I . . . I must have sw-swallowed the wrong way," he

managed to say, recovering. "I beg your pardon." He wiped his eyes with the back of his hand. "I begin to think you are going to make all the difference to life at Longthorpe, Hannah. In fact, I do believe you might very well be a true blessing in disguise. And speaking of Longthorpe, we ought to discuss what needs doing. The entire place will need a thorough going-over, as it's been shut up for so long, but one of the first things to attend to will be staffing the house. I imagine most of the servants can be drawn locally, or at least I hope so. I gather the villagers are not well off, and it would be nice to give them some support. The only trouble is that I have absolutely no experience in training servants."

Hannah noticed Galsworthy pulling himself up a little straighter as he removed the finger glasses and placed the dessert in front of them. Dear Galsworthy took great pride in knowing exactly what the right thing was and how to make it happen as it ought. "I quite understand. But do not worry. Between Galsworthy and myself, I am sure we can manage," she said.

"I was counting on it. I am going to be overrun with other things for some time, between a business to run and this estate to pull into order."

"And will you be returning to the Caribbean when you have accomplished that task?"

Peter looked at her speculatively, but his eyes held laughter. "I wonder why you ask. Are my manners so appalling that you have decided there is no hope?"

"No, of course not. It is just that you have a home, a business there. I thought you would eventually want to return to what is comfortable for you."

"That would be a strong temptation, but I do not think it would be an effective solution to this particular problem. I have made up my mind to reside here permanently, and I shall simply have to hope that my bones eventually adjust to the cold and damp and that I do not expire from an advanced case of consumption before producing the obligatory heir."

"Oh. Yes, of course . . . an heir. I hadn't thought of that. You will be requiring a wife."

"It is one of those expected things that goes along with the business of producing heirs, yes."

Hannah dropped her eyes, for she hadn't thought of this

particular aspect of his situation. "I am sorry. You must hate what has happened to you after the freedom you have had."

"I cannot say I hate it, Hannah, although I am far from overwhelmed by joy. I did not wish for it, I would never have asked for it, but it is now mine. I have always believed very strongly in family, perhaps because of what was done to mine. In any case, this is my family legacy. I have a responsibility to it, to everything and everyone it entails. There are many people less fortunate than myself who are dependent on this legacy. That may sound feudal, but it is true. And I believe that responsibility has been badly neglected for a good half century. It is up to me to correct whatever wrongs have been done."

"I understand," she said very quietly, seeing the hard irony in his eyes where laughter had been only moments before. "I do understand what you mean, although my responsibilities have been nothing next to what you are taking on. I want you to know that I will happily help you in any way I can. It is the very least I can do."

"Why, Hannah, that is very good of you. To be truthful, I do not know yet what help I might need, but I deeply appreciate your offer. I truly do."

"It is nothing, nothing at all next to what you have done for us. If in any small way my knowledge of social proprieties can help you to succeed in your mission and take your rightful place, I shall feel most content."

Peter scratched his cheek with one finger. "Ah, yes," he finally said. "The social proprieties. Well, in that case, as I wish you to feel content here, then I shall have to set myself to being most attentive to your instruction. I shall try very hard to improve. Tell me what is next, Miss Hannah Janes, for I find myself most anxious to hear."

"Well, my lord, if we were dining in company, the ladies would excuse themselves and leave the men to their port. It is always passed from right to left, by the by. But as we are alone, it would not be incorrect for us to retire to the library for conversation."

"Would a game of cards be in order? Or do you consider that vulgar, playing cards with the opposite sex?"

"Not at all, as long as one does not play for stakes. Although it is my understanding that ladies in the fast set will do so."

Peter sighed. "No stakes. Very well, we shall play for simple pleasure. I imagine that is proper enough. So, shall we retire to the library?" He rose. "Galsworthy, you may tell Monsieur Antoine that in future we will require only what two people can comfortably consume when we are dining by ourselves. I do not hold with waste. However, you might diplomatically add that as a test of his talents he created a superb meal and may stay on. Thank you."

"Thank you, my lord," Galsworthy said, bowing.

Peter led Hannah from the room, but she noticed as she followed him out that a small smile played about the corners of his mouth, and she wondered what had put it back on his face.

Mrs. Brewster finished washing up the dishes while Galsworthy dried and Antoine banged pots and pans about in the corner, muttering under his breath.

"A cup of tea, Mr. Galsworthy?" Mrs. Brewster asked, ignoring Antoine.

"Thank you, Mrs. Brewster," Galsworthy said, settling down at the long table in the middle of the room. "It has been a long day."

In truth, it had been a day filled with surprises, and he still did not know what he made of the situation. He did, however, feel enormous relief that Hannah was not running straight into a situation bound for disaster. Or at least he did not think she was. He had not yet sized up this new earl. He only knew what he had made of the last one.

"I can just imagine what a day you have had. Goodness, a man of your respectable years coming to a place like this under these peculiar circumstances. It would knock the stuffing out of anyone. But I must say I am happy for the help and the company. There's some who are worse than no company at all. There's some who don't know about keeping to their place. There's some who are just too big for their britches."

Antoine turned and glared at her. "If you are referring to me, madame, I suggest you hold your wagging tongue. One of these fine days it will fall out of your head."

"I'll speak as I see fit, messier. And I was speaking to Mr. Galsworthy, not to you, so you can just keep yourself to yourself."

"*Mon Dieu*! It is not enough that I have to live with you

day in, day out? Now I have to listen to two of you in my kitchen? And I should like the key to the wine cellar returned, monsieur. It was most impertinent, taking it off my hook without asking."

Galsworthy sniffed. "The wine cellar is a butler's responsibility, and that is how it will stay. The key shall reside with me."

"I shall speak to his lordship ovair this outrage!"

"His lordship has already given his instructions. The key stays in my pocket."

"Don't I just know why you want the key, messier?" Mrs. Brewster said, offering Galsworthy sugar. "Well, let me tell you something—there's going to be no more pilfering from his lordship's private stock. You may have been able to bamboozle the old man, but you're not going to bamboozle this one. Three hundred guineas a year, my foot."

"Aha! Listening at doors again! I should have known!"

"You should just count yourself lucky that I didn't tell his lordship what else I know. Getting his lordship in his cups every night, and then cheating him at cards. A disgrace is what I call it. And if I hadn't thought that he deserved what he got, I would have gone straight to him with the truth and seen you out on your ear."

Antoine, who had gone bright red, snatched up a carving knife and began waving it over his head. "For your tongue, madame. It will make fine chicken food if it doesn't poison them first!"

"Perhaps," Galsworthy suggested quickly, "it would be best if we let the past rest in the past and start out fresh, with our best foot forward. Please, put the knife down, monsieur. Violence never solved anything."

"She is a foolish, lying old woman, monsieur, and I will not be slandered so! I will not! And as for you, you do not tell Antoine what to do, or how to behave in his own kitchen. I suffair you only because I am forced to it. I do not know what this stupid new earl thinks he is doing, hiring an old butlair who can hardly see where he is going."

"That is quite enough, messier," Mrs. Brewster snapped. "You may have heaped your phlegm on me all of these years, but your reign is over. I heard his lordship perfectly well, and if you do not behave yourself, you will not last past breakfast. It would behoove you to remember that. I do not think that his lordship will take kindly to your abusing his new butler.''

"And valet," Galsworthy added. "I am to act as his lordship's personal valet. It is a most trusted position, monsieur. Valets have their employer's ear."

"Bah. I go to bed. You give me the headache, both of you." Antoine pulled off his long white apron and flung it over the back of a chair, and then stomped dramatically out of the room.

"My goodness," Galsworthy said mildly. "What a very unpleasant man."

"You don't know the half of it, Mr. Galsworthy. His fingers are stickier than his pastries. But I reckon that will stop now. Oh, life is going to change, I can see that. You don't know what it's been like all these years, watching his lordship close up the house, dismiss the staff, those that didn't walk out. He was the most miserly person I've ever had the misfortune to know. Wouldn't spend a penny on anything but his food and drink, except for buying things and more things for this place and then putting them under those sheets. Now in her ladyship's day, oh, you should have seen it then!"

"You have been here for some time, then, Mrs. Brewster?"

"Well over thirty years, I have. I came with my dear Sarah, I did, to keep her company and give her a start in a strange new place. She was just a slip of a girl, young and innocent, with no idea of the monster she was marrying, poor soul. There were parties at first, and the house was all opened up and nice. Fine ladies and gentlemen came to stay. But then his lordship became more and more peculiar. He was jealous of her, you see. He didn't want to share her with anyone. He wouldn't even let her go up to London to see her friends. She was just like one of his things that he collected, something to be shut away in the dark. It wasn't surprising that she lost her health and wasted into nothing."

"His lordship seems to have had that effect on people," Galsworthy said dryly. "Do go on, Mrs. Brewster."

"She came to him at eighteen and died before her twenty-fourth birthday, poor girl. It nearly broke my heart, it did. She was a good girl, not deserving of his ill-treatment. At least the two boys gave her some happiness, although it's a blessing she didn't live to see what spoiled wastrels they turned into. I can tell you they led me a merry dance."

"It is a shame to hear it, Mrs. Brewster. It must have distressed you to see that happen."

"I stopped wasting my time worrying over them years ago. I just did the job I was told to by his lordship, kept my mouth shut, and kept up Sarah's things, just as she wanted. 'Auntie Eunice,' she said to me on her deathbed, 'Oh, Auntie, don't let him shut up my room too. Keep the light coming in, keep it pretty for me.' So I did that, just like I promised, and I looked after her grave, too, poor angel. He never went into her room again after the day she died, so he was never the wiser. But I will tell you, my angel's death pushed him right over the edge. If he had been mean before, he became meaner and angrier and more hateful by the year."

Galsworthy nodded, thinking that Hannah's mother had had much of that anger taken out on her. But he said only, "How unfortunate."

"But here I am going on and on, and not letting you get a word in edgewise. Oh, it is going to be a joy having things back to normal, a little boy in the house, and that nice mistress of yours. She seems a kind enough soul, and well-mannered too. Manners go a long way."

"Indeed they do, and Miss Janes is a very good and conscientious woman, Mrs. Brewster. And the earl also seems to be a decent enough man."

"We shall see about that," Mrs. Brewster said tartly. "Things aren't always what they appear on the surface, and let us not be forgetting his lineage. Dreadful debauchers, those men. The only good thing I can think of is that when the solicitor came to inform his late lordship of Master James's death, his lordship went into conniptions at the very idea that this one was going to inherit. Never seen a rage like it. He was furious with Master James for being so irresponsible as to drown and let such a thing happen. Can you imagine? That poor solicitor was picked up and thrown out the door by his collar. I've never seen anyone scurry away so fast."

"You know what is said about the bearer of bad news . . . ." Galsworthy said wisely.

"Just so, Mr. Galsworthy. Just so. I knew you were a clever man the moment I laid eyes on you. Oh, yes. Life is going to be improving, I can see that. As for his lordship, I'll be consulting my tea leaves in the morning, and the cards, of course. That is bound to tell us much. But for now it is time to attend to other things."

She hopped up from the table and went over to the enormous hearth where a kettle had been heating, poured out steaming water into two copper tubs, then threw a handful of herbs into the water and stirred. "Twice a day, Mr. Galsworthy, and a nightly nip of brandy, and you'll live to be hundred whether you want to or not."

She carried one of the tubs over to him and put it on the floor. "Off with your shoes, now, and put your feet in there. It makes all the difference in the world. If we are going to bring this place up to snuff, then you need all the help you can get. I'll just get my own foot bath, and the bottle can come out, now that the messier's gone off to bed. I have my own supply, I do, and he's not coming near it."

Galsworthy wondered if it was quite correct to remove one's shoes in front of a female not one's wife, but then he decided that it was for medicinal purposes, which excused much. He dutifully took off his shoes and placed his feet in the water, leaning back and relaxing as the steam billowed comfortingly up around him. He was beginning to think that life had taken a very distinct turn for the better.

Now there was only Hannah to worry about, and with the handsome new lordship in close proximity, he was going to have his work cut out for him, most especially given his lordship's alarming bloodline. He could only pray Hannah had not inherited her mother's profligate nature. He hadn't spent the last twenty-three years looking after her and teaching her correctness and self-control to have her go astray now.

It seemed a rather inflammatory situation, he thought glumly. Galsworthy sat back to inhale the pleasant vapors of the steam. He might as well enjoy his creature comforts while he could. Sleep was clearly going to be in short supply.

6

Far other aims his heart had learned to prize,
More bent to raise the wretched than to rise.
—Oliver Goldsmith,
The Deserted Village

Peter spent much of the night lying awake, contemplating the underside of the canopy above him. To say he was overwhelmed with what he had just been handed would have been a supreme understatement. Forty-eight hours ago he had not had a relation in the world. Now he had not only one by blood, but an entire handful by association, including Hannah Janes, of all people. And therein lay his problem and the cause for his sleeplessness.

Never, if he had spent years thinking up an impossible fiction, would he have come up with something quite so extraordinary as having the woman he had come dangerously close to compromising the night before, march in through his new front door and announce herself a destitute relation by association of a bastard cousin.

He rolled onto his back and folded his hands behind his head. It was truly absurd: the good Lord had not only dropped the earldom on him; he had also dropped Hannah Janes alongside and complicated the matter by missing his aim and dropping her in the wrong location and a day too early.

Had they not met the night before, the situation might have been a great deal easier. They would have started out correctly, two strangers with only a small boy and some bad luck in common. But oh, no. He had to have gone stumbling across Hannah in the garden, had to have felt the need to insinuate himself into her affairs, to dry her tears, to have a deeply personal exchange of conversation. And then, like a complete idiot, he had finished it all off by taking her in his arms and kissing her as if there were no tomorrow. The only problem was that there had been a tomorrow, and it had brought Hannah Janes right along with it. So much for acting on impulse—one always paid for it in the end.

He didn't so much mind taking on the responsibility: that was part of the job that accompanied the earldom. But if God had had to go dropping Hannah Janes into his life, could He not at least have had the consideration to have given her a spotted face and bad teeth and a figure like Mrs. Brewster's? Life sometimes seemed altogether unfair.

Peter groaned and pulled the pillow over his head.

Pamela Chandler was reading the morning paper as she always did: she went directly to the section that dealt with births, marriages, and deaths. It was the most elucidating part of the paper, although the marriage portion always depressed her. Why she, at four-and-twenty, had not managed to catch a husband was beyond her. She was not unattractive, she had a healthy portion to offer, and a fine family lineage. She had tried and tried and tried, but nothing seemed to work. It was a miserable state of affairs, and one she was determined to correct, for she really did not think she could bear her dear mama for very much longer.

"Pamela, dearest, what news?" her mother asked, pushing toast into her mouth with one hand and brushing crumbs off her ample bosom with the other.

"Let me see, Mama. Oh, look here, Selby has had another daughter. He must be furious. That is the fifth, is it not, and no son yet. Imogene will be beside herself, for he was most firm on the matter of a son this time."

"Indeed. It probably would have been best if the girl had died in childbirth. It is clear that she is not going to do her duty by him. A pity. You would have made him a fine wife, Pamela. All that land, and such an old title . . . if only you'd tried harder."

"Yes, Mama. Oh!"

"What is it, dearest?" Lady Chandler looked up with interest, for her daughter sounded truly alarmed.

"It is Lord Blakesford, Mama. He has died. Mr. Frazier has succeeded him. Listen!" She read the obituary with great concentration.

"Fancy that! And you were up at Seaton only a week or so ago when he learned he was in direct line. Now there is an opportunity, my puss, if ever I heard of one."

"I think not, Mama," Pamela said. She really did not see how she could throw herself across Peter Frazier's matrimonial path again, not after the lecture he had given her the last time around.

"You think not? And why is that, may I ask? Pamela, darling, your papa and I have done everything we can for you, but the expense of Season after Season is becoming a burden. We cannot go on like this. This year you will find a husband, and if you cannot find one with a title and a fortune, then you will have to marry without benefit of either. There are not so many unmarried earls running around, my puss, that you can afford to pass up an opportunity such as this."

"Yes, Mama," Pamela said miserably. "I know. But Mr. Frazier made it most clear that he had no interest in me."

"That was before this happened. He will be looking for a wife now, see if he isn't. There will be the fortune, and Longthorpe—well! Do you want to let that slip from between your fingers?"

"No, naturally not, Mama. It is said to be one of the country's finest houses."

"That is exactly right. Now, let us apply ourselves to rethinking the situation. If you are to catch the Earl of Blakesford, it will require some strategy. It occurs to me that a condolence call might be just the thing. After all, you *are* well-acquainted—why, just think, you are such dear friends with the Marchioness of Seaton, and that upstart is married to Blakesford's closest friend. The entire world knows of the connection between you and Eliza, after all, and how kind you were to her when she was a nobody."

"Yes, but Mama, that does not give me the same connection to Lord Blakesford as Eliza has," Pamela said doubtfully.

"Nonsense, my pet. Naturally it does. You were all in Jamaica together, were you not, during that one Season? It would be quite rude if you did not express your sympathies."

"But, Mama, he is so well-connected, he will no doubt have half the *ton* expressing their sympathies."

"Well, naturally he is well-connected. His father was a

Frazier, after all, and a splendid emissary for his country. Your papa always had the highest regard for the man. We shall ignore his wife's unspeakable background. Imagine, a Cit's daughter. I never did understand why that didn't hold Thomas Frazier back, but never mind. He made a splendid chargé d'affaires to the Crown in spite of her. Now, Pamela, you must be a friend to the new earl in his time of need. Christian charity is everything. Let me see . . . we should put off our visit for just a short while so as not to seem too eager. Perhaps a month would be just right. If we strike early, we can make an impression just before the Season begins. You don't want to give every other mama and her daughter a chance in the crush of London, and you can be sure that Blakesford will be hotly pursued." She rang for more tea and toast and added an order for buttered scones and jam.

"Now, my pet. Let us think about your wardrobe. It must be appropriate for the country, naturally, but useful for town as well. Perhaps a little more than we had budgeted might be worth its weight in gold. Isn't that right, my pet?"

"Yes, Mama," Pamela said, knowing that there was no arguing with her mother. And she really could not afford to throw away any opportunity, no matter how slim it seemed. Maybe there was hope after all, if this time she could just manage not to make any mistakes.

Peter saddled up his horse and set out for the tenant farms. He thought it would be a fine idea to start assessing the condition of the estate, although fifteen thousand acres was going to take some time. The farms seemed the best place to start, for surely the inhabitants would be able to tell him what he needed to know.

He'd been forewarned by the vicar to expect poor conditions, but he was not prepared for the sight that met his eyes when he rode into the first and largest of the farms. Poverty was evident everywhere. The road ran with mud, there was a stench of filth, and the children who stared from the door were dressed in no better than rags.

He dismounted, feeling quite sick, and he made his way around a large puddle of murky water that stretched in front of the door. The children had vanished around the corner. He knocked.

"Good morning," he said to the woman who opened the

door to him. She was heavily pregnant and looked tired and pale, and she also looked frightened when she saw him. "Would your husband be at home?" he asked.

"He hasn't been home for eight months," she said. "He's gone to work the mines, like everyone else. It's what I told the last man, not that his lordship didn't know it perfectly well, seeing as Sam had been his foreman." She started to close the door again, and Peter put his hand out to catch it.

"Please," he said. "Your name?"

"Mary Baker, as if you didn't know it." She pushed a hand across her forehead. "And if you've come for the rent, there's none to be had. Are you going to evict us?"

"Evict you? Is that what you'd been told?"

"I was told that my family would be out in the street if I didn't have the rent by this month. Well, I don't have it, nor anything to give you in its place. The last of our savings went for last month's rent."

Peter was angry, very angry, but he tried not to let it show. "Mrs. Baker," he said gently, "you are most certainly not going to be evicted, have no fear. Things have . . . they have changed. Lord Blakesford is dead."

"I heard." Her chin trembled but she held it up defiantly. "And I heard there's a new lordship arrived already. So what has changed?"

"A very great deal. May I come in?" Peter asked.

"If a gentleman like yourself wants to come into a house that doesn't belong to me, who am I to object?" she said bitterly. "But it's not much to look at. You won't be getting much for it, nor for any of the others when you try to sell."

Peter removed his hat and entered the dark interior. There was a young child lying on a mattress by the smoldering fire and a kettle hanging on a hook in the hearth. A half-eaten loaf of bread sat on the table. The child began to cough, and his mother went to bend over him and adjust the thin blanket.

"He is ill?" Peter asked, moving across to them.

"It's the whooping cough," she said tonelessly. "Poor Johno's going down fast. We lost one last year the same way."

Peter knelt by the rough mattress, stroking the hair off the fevered child's brow. He judged the boy no more than three, if that. "How long has he been like this?"

"Two weeks now. I can't afford to have the doctor come."

"I'll send the doctor around as soon as I can. Has Johno had anything to eat?"

"Only bread soaked in milk," she said, looking bewildered by his concern. "But it's all we have, save for a chicken Eunice B—" Her hand went to her mouth as if she'd said something she ought not to have.

"It's quite all right, Mrs. Baker. I know all about the chickens that Mrs. Brewster cooked, and I am very glad she did."

"I beg your pardon, sir," she said more slowly, "but I took you for one of his lordship's men. But you cannot be. Who are you, and why are you looking for my husband?"

"If you'll sit down with me, Mrs. Baker, I think I can explain everything to your satisfaction. I also have a great many questions to ask you, if you wouldn't mind giving me some of your time. . ."

Peter left an hour later, much enlightened and even angrier than he had been before. He decided to pay another visit to the vicar.

"My lord, this is a surprise," the vicar said, showing him into the parlor. "I was in the midst of writing my Sunday sermon, but I suppose I can take some time. Not much, mind you, for my sermons take me days to write and it is already Tuesday. I am renowned throughout the county for their fine content. Fresh, every time. I am not the sort of person to use the same set of sermons over and over, not like some. Have you come for sherry, perhaps?"

"Vicar, I most certainly have not come for sherry. I have come because I want an explanation and some advice, and neither would wait. What in the love of God has been going on about here? I have just come from Mary Baker's house, and she was quite eloquent about the conditions of the local people, whose misfortune has been mostly brought about by the actions of my cousin."

The vicar scratched one very large ear, then lowered his gaunt frame into a chair and indicated another to Peter. "I informed you that he was the devil himself with morals to match."

"You did indeed. I just had not thought that even the devil would do such harm to innocent people, especially those who depended completely upon him. What can be done?"

The vicar shook his head sadly. "The heart has gone out of the people. They've been hungry for so long that they stopped fighting years before. The land has been exhausted and there are no resources left. As you probably realized from talking to Mary Baker, most of the men have been forced to leave for the mines. Disease is rampant and there is no money for medicines. Entire families have been decimated. What is needed more than anything is a large influx of money to put these good men and women back on their feet. Anything would help, but if you truly care as you say you do, then you will try to replace what has been stolen. Your cousin lined his already full pockets at the expense of his tenants."

"I will do what I can. But as you pointed out to me, there is no goodwill toward my family, and I can tell you that the few people to whom I spoke this morning were none too pleased to see me."

"They will accept you only when you have proven your good intentions, my lord. Your cousin not only cheated and stole from the men, he badly used their women, and his sons did as well—all debauchers, those men. There is a good reason that Longthorpe has not been staffed for years."

Peter only shook his head, but his gut was churning. "If you please, Vicar," he said tightly, "will you announce at Sunday services that there is work waiting for anyone who wishes it? If it comes from you they might listen. All they have to do is appear at Longthorpe. I will speak to any men who wish to apply. I am most badly in need of stable help, and my cousin will be needing a household staff."

"Your cousin, Lord Blakesford? And what cousin is this, may I ask?"

"Miss Janes and her younger brother are connected to me through their mother. They have come to Longthorpe to live."

"Oh? Might this be the young woman seen walking down the main road yesterday morning and disappearing through the gates of Longthorpe? There has already been talk."

"Vicar, let me assure you that it is all perfectly respectable. Miss Janes has been kind enough to offer to help me put Longthorpe back on its feet, for I cannot do it on my own. Believe me, Miss Janes is more full of the proprieties than you and I put together."

"I hope you are correct, my lord. As I warned you, your moral character will have to be proven."

"Yes, Vicar, you warned me," Peter said wearily, fed up with the entire issue. He also saw that the vicar was going to need some more concrete persuasion as to his good intentions, and he mentally took another large chunk from his pocketbook. "Oh, by the by, Vicar, I have noticed there is a large crack down the side of the bell tower. It seems to me that it ought to be repaired before any further damage occurs. Fourteenth century, is it not?"

"Indeed it is, my lord," the vicar said, a hopeful gleam leaping into his eye. "That crack has only grown worse over the years. One day the entire tower is going to come down and the spire with it."

"No doubt. I wonder if you could estimate what it would cost to have it fixed. I should like that to be one of the first things I do."

"Thank you, my lord! I shall be very much in your debt! We all shall, for the church has always been the pride of Kirby! Why, they say that Queen Elizabeth herself attended a christening there. It is very good of you, my lord, to think of it!"

"Not at all. I consider it my duty. Thank you for your time, Vicar. No, that's quite all right, I can show myself out. Please, return to your sermon."

Peter drew in a deep breath of fresh air as he left, then cast his eyes up at the crisp blue sky, wondering if there was any chance at all that his cousin had ascended to heaven, or if he'd be better heard by glaring down at the ground.

"You self-serving bastard," he muttered from between gritted teeth as he mounted his gelding. "I hope you can hear me, for I intend to undo every last wrong you committed. I swear on my father's grave that these people will not suffer a moment longer than necessary. Dear God, but I pray you are rotting in hell." He kicked the horse into a canter and headed back to the village to find the doctor and send him to see to Johno Baker.

Hannah heard about it when Peter returned and vented his spleen. He hadn't actually meant to vent his spleen in front of her, but she had been up on the library steps dusting books when he came storming in, spitting invective from between his teeth.

"My lord," she said hesitantly from her perch, "you seem upset. Is there anything I can do to help?"

He looked up, startled. "Hannah. I apologize. I hadn't realized you were in here. Forgive me . . ." He shoved his hands onto his lean hips and stared down at the floor.

"What happened?" she asked softly.

"Nothing. Exactly nothing. I went off to speak to the villagers. No one was interested. Oh, the vicar will take my money for the church, but no one else wanted a thing to do with me—except for one Mary Baker, down on the south farm, and she was convinced I'd come to evict her. But at least she was good enough to listen to me and answer my questions. She had a sick child to tend; maybe she just didn't have the energy to throw me out."

"Oh, I am sorry. But surely they'll come around when they've grown accustomed to you. You'll see. It will all work out."

"Will it?" He gave her an ironic smile. "Perhaps. But life does not necessarily go according to even the best-laid plans. If it did, none of us would be in this position, would we?"

Hannah looked down at the rag in her hand. "No. It is true."

"Never mind. Don't concern yourself with my troubles, Hannah. I did not mean to pull you into them."

"But I don't mind. I want to help."

"It is good of you. But I am the only one who can atone for my cousin's sins." He moved over to the desk and picked up a paperweight, balancing it in his hand. "Excuse me, Hannah. I have some letters to write."

Hannah left him alone in the library, but the very first thing that afternoon, determined to do something to help, she went marching off to find the Baker's farm. Wesley carried a basket of food, and Hannah hauled blankets and some of Wesley's clothes that he had nearly outgrown.

"Mrs. Baker?" she said when the door opened. "My name is Hannah Janes, and I've come from Longthorpe with some things for you."

"From Longthorpe, Miss?" Mary Baker said with astonishment. "Things for me? Are you sure his lordship won't mind?"

"He won't mind in the least. He was outraged by the conditions he found everywhere. These are some clothes that my brother, Wesley, is no longer in need of. Wesley, make your bow to Mrs. Baker, and then go and play with the other children while Mrs. Baker and I visit together."

Wesley, delighted to escape, disappeared around the corner of the house where the young Bakers had vanished at their approach. Mary Baker asked Hannah in, and she was appalled to see with her own eyes what Peter had described. But she did not let it show, and she made herself right at home, determined to make a beginning at building a relationship of trust between the village and Longthorpe.

She found Mary Baker surprisingly easy to talk to, and Mary's curiosity about Hannah's arrival at Longthorpe brought the story pouring out. ". . . And so just when I thought all was lost and I was at Longthorpe's threshold, about to throw myself on the mercy of the horrible old earl, there was the new Lord Blakesford, and he wouldn't hear of anything else but having us come to live with him." She handed Mary the fresh hot cloths for Johno's chest.

"Really, Miss Janes? What a stroke of luck for you then."

"Oh, please, do call me Hannah. I'm nobody grand in the least. If you knew how I was raised, you'd laugh."

Mary looked over at her and managed a weary smile. "That fine?"

"We weren't considered entirely respectable. My mother was . . . well, the truth of the matter is that after my father died, she took—protectors." Hannah didn't really know why she was confiding this to a woman she'd never met before, but she had taken an immediate liking to Mary Baker, and sensed a kindred spirit in her. And she had an instinctive feeling that if she opened herself up, she would elicit trust in return. Besides, she was badly in need of a friend, and she knew that Mary Baker wasn't going to be one to care whether she was entirely respectable or not. It would be nice not to be snubbed.

"Like that, was it?" Mary said with a wise nod. "Not easy on a young girl."

"Oh, I spent most of the time away at school, at least until Wesley came along and I was needed at home. By then I was sixteen and old enough to better understand the comings and goings. My mother had a great many friends."

Mary covered Johno's chest and placed the new, warmer

blanket over him, then put the kettle on. "And all of them gentlemen, no doubt?" She offered Hannah a chair at the table.

"Every last one. You have no idea how I longed for a normal life: a father to sit by the fire reading his paper, going off to work in the morning and coming home in the evening for dinner."

"Sounds nice," Mary said wryly. "I had a father. He more often threw his shoes at us when he came home for his dinner. But now my Sam, he's a good man, and educated, too. He's worked hard all of his life to improve his lot." She sighed and pushed a fallen strand of hair off her cheek. "It's been a terrible thing, watching what's happened to him. He worked day and night to improve conditions any way he could, all to have the profits taken away by his lordship and put into that house, and not back into the farms and fields like they ought to have been. No, all his lordship ever did was raise the rates, and the last few years he went and rented the fields to the huntsmen for their sport, so we couldn't even scratch a living out of the soil anymore. I can't tell you how many of our boys were sent to jail for poaching, when all they were trying to do was put food in their family's bellies. Ah, well. There's no point complaining now. It's said and done, isn't it, and the men have gone to the mines. We all have our tragedies to bear in this life."

"True enough," Hannah said. "But that doesn't mean that things can't change. It will take a little time, perhaps, to put things to right, but Lord Blakesford is determined to do so."

Mary just gave her a dubious look. "We'll see. The day my Sam comes back to work the land again is the day I'll believe it. Although the doctor did come for Johno . . . he said his lordship had sent him and paid him for it. I was that surprised."

"He's a good man, Mary, I'm sure of it."

"Couldn't be that you might be taken in by that handsome face of his, could it?"

Hannah blushed furiously. "No! It's not that at all!"

"Now, you see here, Miss Hannah Janes. You may think it's nothing to do with that, but you take a piece of advice from one who's been around a little longer than you and seen what's what up there on that hill. All those high and mighty Frazier men had handsome faces. You should have seen the two sons, and may God be praised that neither one of them lived to make our lives more miserable. There was many a village girl who was taken in by pretty manners and sweet words and lived to regret it. So don't you go making up your mind about his lordship after only one day, when you don't have anything more to go on than an invitation to live up there. Handsome is as handsome does, and to date that line of handsome has done nothing good. You watch yourself, that's what I say."

"I will watch myself. But his lordship has sworn that his intentions are honorable, and in any case, Mrs. Brewster has been assigned to protect me, and Galsworthy is worse than any dragon at the gate. I think you're wrong about him. I truly do."

Mary tapped her swollen belly. "This child has its father's name and so do the others playing outside. They might not have much, but they have that. You just keep that in mind when those arms are around you and that handsome face is pressed to yours, making you forget everything else."

Hannah suddenly felt very uncomfortable, for the memory of Peter kissing her in the garden came flooding back, along with her reaction. She *had* forgotten just about everything, hadn't she? What if it happened again? Peter had said it wouldn't, but he was a man, after all, and worse, he was a Frazier. They said such things ran in the blood.

"That's right, my girl," Mary said. "Now, I normally wouldn't talk so personally on such short acquaintance, but you didn't have a mother to advise you properly, so you listen to me now. It's easy enough to let your heart lead your head and let a man talk you into his arms and his bed. And the men, they can hardly help themselves—it's part of their nature to try to take advantage. It's all lust to them and doesn't mean a thing, no matter what they might say. And let me tell you, lust has led to more heartbreak than can be counted. But you just remember that a girl's virginity is worth its weight in gold. You be sure you get a ring on your finger before you go offering anything else. Now, I've spoken my piece and that's that. We won't say any more on the subject. So why don't you tell me about your brother Wesley? He has the look of mischief in him, that one. High-spirited, is he? Looks like he could use a good dose of country air. I can always spot a city child a mile away.

Never mind, he'll get plenty of fresh air and exercise out here."

Mary Baker watched as Hannah left, her brother in tow. She hoped her words had taken hold, for she had a certain feeling that Hannah was already besotted with his lordship and just didn't know it. She liked the girl: she seemed to have a kind heart and a pleasant nature, and she didn't want to see anything happen to her. But it didn't bode well, the two of them living up there alone together, Eunice Brewster or no. All sorts of things could happen in the dark of night when blood was running hot.

She sighed, wondering if the girl's optimism about the new earl had any grounding in fact, for she could surely use her Sam at home. She rubbed the small of her back, then turned and went back inside to tend to Johno and carefully put away the precious basket of food that Hannah Janes had brought.

"Dear God in heaven," Peter said with a choked laugh, coming out of the house as Hannah and Wesley were coming across the courtyard. "What have the two of you been up to? You look as if you've been playing in a swamp."

He looked them up and down, and Hannah glanced down, only to see her sodden muddy skirts and mud-caked boots.

"We went to the Bakers' farm and there were boys there—oh, and one girl," Wesley said, hopping with excitement. "I made friends with them, especially Frankie. Hannah made friends too, with Mrs. Baker. We brought them food and clothes and things. I like living in the country! I've already discovered lots of things that I never knew before, and Frankie says he'll teach me to climb a tree properly, and—"

"That's very nice, Wesley," Peter said with a smile. "But for now, if you would, please remove your boots by the door and take them back to the kitchen so that Galsworthy can clean them. And while you're back there you might consider a bath."

"Oh, not a bath," Wesley said with a look of disgust. "Must I?"

"Yes, you must. As for you, Hannah . . . Hannah? Why are you staring at me as if I had suddenly grown two heads?"

Hannah, who had been wondering if his head was truly filled with wicked and licentious thoughts, went a dull red. "I . . . no reason," she stammered.

"Really? From the look on your face anyone would think I had grown two horns and a tail in your absence. Have stories about me struck horror into your heart already, Hannah?"

"Oh no, of course not!" she said, mortified that he had practically read her mind.

"No?" he said, frowning. "Are you quite sure?"

Hannah frantically cast about for an excuse. "I was just wondering if you were about to tell me to bathe, too, given the way you were looking at me."

"Despite what you might think, I wouldn't be so presumptuous," he said curtly, his face going suddenly cold. "Although I am sure you don't have to be persuaded to change your clothes. As I remember, it was you who was lecturing me about cleanliness."

"I am sorry if my appearance offends you, my lord. We could not avoid the mud."

"Naturally not. I would like to speak to you, Hannah. Come to the library before dinner, will you?" He turned and strode away, leaving Hannah burning with humiliation.

Two hours later she marched into the library as commanded. She had bathed, then taken out her second-best dress and brushed it carefully. No one, most certainly not an uncivilized, licentious earl was going to make comments on her appearance, and she was not a child to be lectured for coming home with mud on her skirts.

"I am here, my lord," she said. "Was there something you wished to say to me? Other than telling me to wash?" Her tone was glacial.

Peter looked up from his paper, and he did not look particularly pleased to see her. "I beg your pardon? I believe I said nothing of the sort."

"You implied it, my lord. And I will tell you here and now that it is most improper to make comments of such a personal nature, implied or not. I have always made an effort to keep a neat and clean appearance, even when I had very little to work with."

"Oh, for the love of God, Hannah," Peter said, tossing his paper to one side, "I have no idea what put this particular bee in your bonnet, but I assure you that I meant no personal comment about your appearance. However, I am interested in this sudden show of indignation. Could it be that Miss Prunes and Prisms Janes actually has a temper?"

"Nobody ever said there was anything wrong with trying to behave in a proper fashion," Hannah snapped. "And I think it most ungrateful of you to cavil at a little mud that I happened to pick up on an errand made on your behalf! I'll wager you've been muddy more than once in your life!"

"Good heavens, Hannah. Naturally I have, given that I grew up with the pigs. We wallowed together on a daily basis. It's a miracle I've turned out as well as I have, don't you think?"

"Oh!" Hannah said, feeling like throwing something at his handsome head. "You are impossible!"

"Not really. Actually, I am usually very reasonable. Why don't you come down off whatever bough you've flown up onto and be reasonable yourself? I don't know why you have chosen to take such offense where none was intended."

Hannah bit her lip.

"You don't take very well to being teased, do you? Has it ever occurred to you that you are far too serious by half?"

"I am not," she said indignantly.

"Oh? Tell me, when is the last time you did something just for the fun of it?"

Hannah frowned, for in truth she could not immediately think. And then she brightened. "I took Wesley and Galsworthy to London for Wesley's seventh birthday. We went to Vauxhall Gardens and Madame Tussaud's. Wesley was thrilled."

"No doubt. And no doubt you worried the entire time about the expense, and how to pay for the extra ices, and if you could afford to buy a balloon, and how you were going to manage the cost of the coach. I am quite certain you did not stop at an inn."

"How did you know?" she asked with surprise.

"My instincts are most sound."

"I am sure they are," she snapped, uncomfortably remembering again what Mary Baker had said about men and their instincts. "But I really have no interest in what your instincts do or do not tell you. You may keep them to yourself."

Peter looked at her long and hard, and Hannah was

forced to look away, for she found it most uncomfortable to meet that penetrating gaze. But when he finally spoke, it was in a mild enough tone of voice.

"You need to exercise your sense of humor, Hannah. I happen to know that you have one lurking in there somewhere, but it seems to have gone missing."

"My lord, you may have spent your life in frivolity up until now, but I have not had the luxury."

"Perhaps not," Peter said, his eyes snapping with sudden anger. "But do keep in mind before you start passing judgment that you know very little about me. I do not take kindly to being second-guessed. I have had quite enough of it for one day."

Hannah had the grace to color. "I beg your pardon."

"Thank you. Now, to the original reason I wished to speak to you. I have decided to teach you to ride."

"To ride a *horse*?" Hannah said, nearly choking on the word.

"Naturally a horse. I don't see any camels wandering about, do you?"

"But I don't ride, not at all. Not ever. I can't."

"Don't be ridiculous. Of course you can. You must be able to get about, after all, and a horse is the best way to do so. I cannot think that you want to wallow in mud every time you decide to do a good deed, although I really couldn't give a fig about the state of your skirts."

"Oh," Hannah said, unable to respond to this sally. She was consumed by complete, mind-numbing panic. She hated horses. They terrified her. She couldn't think of anything more awful than being forced to climb on top of one.

"I thought it might be easier on you if you could get about on horseback," Peter continued. "There happens to be a mare in the stables that I brought along, a very biddable sort. You might remember her as the chestnut harnessed to the carriage yesterday."

"But I have nothing to wear," she said, that hopeful idea suddenly occurring to her. Imminent death did wonders for creative thinking.

"I noticed some trunks full of clothing upstairs," he parried. "I am sure there must be a riding habit amongst them from one time or another. I shouldn't worry about style: there will be no one but me to see, and what do I care?

Really, all you need is something practical. We shall begin tomorrow morning at ten o'clock."

"But I don't want to!"

"Nevertheless, you shall. Do not argue with me, Hannah. I am not in the mood for it."

Wesley came dashing in at that very moment, fresh from his supper and ready for bed after his strenuous day, and so it was an end to the conversation—not that there was anything left to say. Hannah could see that Peter's mind was made up on the subject, and that he was on the very brink of losing his temper. And that surprised her greatly.

She took Wesley upstairs, thinking that Peter was not at all what he had originally appeared, for the calm, easy-going facade he showed to the world concealed something far more turbulent beneath the surface, and she had just had a glimpse of it. She knew he'd had an unpleasant day, and she felt bad that she had angered him, although she wasn't really sure how or why. He had been prickly all day. But really, did he have to be quite so unreasonable? It wasn't her fault, after all, that the villagers didn't like him. It wasn't necessary to take out his spleen on her.

He did not speak to her when she came back to the library, nor did he offer her his arm when Galsworthy announced dinner. In fact, he more or less ignored her. Oddly enough, it hurt.

All in all, dinner was a very quiet affair. Hannah went to bed early.

Peter did not go to bed at all.

7

How small, of all that human hearts endure,
That part which laws or kings can cause or cure.
                                    —Oliver Goldsmith,
                                    The Traveller

Peter was waiting in the hall at exactly ten o'clock when
Hannah came down. She had not slept well and looked
slightly haggard. Furthermore, the riding habit she had dug
out of one of the trunks upon trunks of old clothing made
her feel like an impostor, for it had clearly been cut for a
very fine lady, and not someone the likes of her. If she
hadn't been so terrified she would have felt very silly. But
all she could think of was that she was to be flung onto the
back of a horse and dragged to her death.

"Why, Hannah," Peter said civilly enough, looking up as
she came down the stairs. Although she could see that he
had recovered his temper, he looked tired. "How interesting to see you dressed so. You remind me of the portrait
in the gallery, the one with a woman and two dogs. Have
you seen it? I believe it is Henry's wife, Sarah, I think her
name was. The dress looks identical."

"I have not yet been into the gallery. But I am sure you
are correct and the dress must have been hers." She twisted
her hands together, wishing the curtains would spontane-
ously combust so that Peter would be forced to abandon
the lesson in favor of saving the house. But the curtains
remained as they were, and Hannah could see she was
doomed.

Peter opened the front door and stepped back to let her
go through. "Tell me, Hannah," he said as they crossed the
courtyard and went through the gatehouse, "Wesley seems

to have a penchant for suicide. Does he attempt to kill himself on a regular basis?"

"Oh, no," Hannah said with alarm, momentarily forgetting her panic over a horse in favor of a greater terror. "What has he done now? I thought he was safely shut away in the nursery with his lessons! He's not hurt, is he?"

"Not for the moment. Catastrophe has been averted. But I begin to sympathize with your previous plight. Caring for the boy must have taken eight arms and at least four pairs of eyes in the back of your head. I happened to be coming back from the stables earlier and heard a strangled cry coming from above the front door. Wesley had somehow contrived to climb out of the clock tower window and been caught by the back of his britches when the clock chimed the hour and the metal soldier came out to sound the gong. I had a most interesting time extricating him from his predicament. I doubt that is a stunt he will attempt again."

Hannah, whose face had gone chalk white during the telling of this story, stopped dead in her tracks. The thought of what might have happened was too awful to contemplate. "Oh, thank you—and thank God that you came along at that moment! I don't know what I am going to do with him! One cannot take one's eyes off him for a moment!"

Peter shook his head with a laugh. "He is a little devil, isn't he? He has the energy of five boys his age, and that is saying something. But do not worry. He just needs to run it off, and the country is the perfect place for that. I think he is in serious need of companions his own age."

"I suppose you are right. But then the Lord only knows what trouble he will manage to find."

"All children find trouble. It's healthy. But it's usually healthier when they find it together, for then one can sound the alarm when the other is in a tight spot. This Frankie Baker sounds an ideal companion for Wesley."

"He is a little urchin, but his mother seems solid enough."

"Yes, she struck me as that also. And by the by, I didn't thank you properly yesterday. I was truly grateful for your concern toward Mrs. Baker. It meant a great deal to me that you made the effort to visit her, mud and all." He smiled down at her. "Don't worry about Wesley, Hannah. I was very like him at the same age, although I had the advantage of being allowed to run fairly wild in the country instead of being cooped up in a town. And I was fortunate enough to have had parents to guide me. It's harder on Wesley. But he'll find his way soon enough. He has character aplenty and spirit, and the boy is by no means stupid. All that will stand him in good stead once he gets his bearings."

"Oh, I hope so. I truly do. I have done nothing but worry over him. He has always seemed so determined to go in exactly the opposite direction given him!"

"It's only because he's been so busy rebelling against life that he has not yet taken breath to see that it's not all running against him. Give him some time. He'll settle down. I don't think shutting him in the nursery to study when you're not there to watch him is any solution. I don't mean to interfere, but I have a feeling that he'll be better off if he's allowed to run free for a while. Give him a taste of that, and he'll stop thinking that life is about escaping. There's plenty of time for lessons."

Hannah nodded, feeling slightly shaken. Peter had cut straight to the heart of the matter, and his acuity amazed her. The man had so many twists and turns to his character that she felt almost dizzy—it was going to take her some time to get her own bearings. One moment he was cool and removed, virtually unreadable. The next moment he was filled with amusement, and she had no idea why. And she had learned the night before that he was more than capable of treating her to a powerful blast of silent anger. And now that was gone without explanation as if it had never existed, replaced by this gentle concern. It was simply too confusing. She stole a glance over at him, wondering what went through that convoluted brain of his. Was he really the seducer she had been warned against? It made her head ache to ponder, and in any case, she had more immediate things to worry about, such as confronting a horse.

Peter ducked his head as they passed under a low-hanging branch and crossed over to the stableyard. "Here we are. Wait here just a moment and I'll bring out your mount."

He produced the mare from one of the stalls and led her over to Hannah, who was quaking in her boots.

"Hannah, allow me to introduce you to Justine. Justine, meet Miss Janes. You are to be very kind to her, Justine, for she has had no experience at all with one of your kind.

Hannah, put your hands on her mane and give me your foot."

Hannah looked at him, her heart hammering in her throat. "Are you sure this is a good idea?" she asked, trying to sound calm.

"Naturally I am sure. How else are you to get about? There is food to be taken to the sick, medicines to be given, infants to be delivered—"

"*Infants* . . . oh, you are teasing again," Hannah said, not quite sure that he was.

"Never. Don't tell me that with all of your other accomplishments you don't know how to deliver an infant? Really, Hannah, and I thought you knew everything."

Hannah blushed and then wished she did not have such a tendency in that direction, for Peter seemed to have an uncanny ability to keep her cheeks flaming. "It is not correct even to speak of such things. I should advise you to be exceedingly cautious when referring to anything to do with such matters. In fact, I should advise you not to refer to such matters at all. A woman is confined, and that is an end to the subject. Oh . . ." In her distraction she had scarcely noticed that Peter had somehow managed to jack her up onto the horse's back. She looked down at him, then at the horse's neck. "Oh, dear. How very odd this is. What do I do now?" Her heart was pounding furiously.

Peter considered. "You might want to pick up the reins?"

"Oh, yes. Of course." She gingerly gathered the reins in her hands.

"Hannah, they are only two pieces of leather, not vipers about to attack," he said, and he reached up and arranged everything correctly. Hannah felt quite sorry when he took his hands away again, for they had felt so—so efficient.

"Now, I shall lead you around the courtyard, and you shall stay firmly put on Justine's back. She is a good, solid mare, and you will come to no harm."

He started walking in front of them, and Hannah felt as if she were sitting in an extremely unsteady rowboat that might tip over at any moment, for she found herself swaying alarmingly from side to side. She was sure that the only thing holding her on was the pommel her knee was wrapped around. Her bones felt as if they might snap with tension, and after the second time around the courtyard she could take no more. She gave into her panic, doing the most sensible thing she could think of. She dropped the reins and clutched Justine around the neck with both of her arms.

"My lord . . ." she said in a choked voice. "I think perhaps we should stop now."

He looked over his shoulder and the expression in those deep blue eyes held nothing resembling sympathy or compassion. In fact, she realized with annoyance, they held unholy amusement.

"It might help if you tried to relax," he said. "Poor Justine must feel as if she is carrying about a sack of potatoes."

"A sack of potatoes? My lord, I find you most unkind. It is not at all correct to refer to a woman of your acquaintance as a sack of potatoes. You might be advised to attempt charm if you are thinking of winning a wife." Hannah felt quite ridiculous lecturing him from her undignified position.

"I beg your pardon," Peter said contritely. "It is only that it was the first image to come to mind."

"I am sure I do not look like a sack of potatoes in the least. At least I don't think I do, although I must confess that I find myself most uneasy. This is not a natural position for me."

"Nor for the horse. I imagine Justine thinks you mentally unhinged, for I can say with a fair amount of certainty that she has never been ridden with someone wrapped around her neck before. Here, why don't you sit up, and we'll try it one more time?"

"No, I think not. I do not believe that will help. I should like to get off, please." Hannah's teeth had begun to chatter.

"Very well, Hannah," he said. "Perhaps it is enough for the first day. Tomorrow we shall try again."

"Whatever you wish." She was so pleased at the prospect of being let down that she would have agreed to anything in that moment. He reached up to her and took her around the waist.

"Hannah, you will have to let go of your death clutch if you wish to dismount. Justine is not going to oblige you by lying down."

She reluctantly released her arms and Peter lifted her off. But her knees wobbled terribly when she was finally on solid ground and she nearly fell. Peter was obliging enough to hold onto her until she had steadied. "Oh," she breathed. "Oh, that is much better."

"Yes, I have to say you do not look quite so green. I'll just put Justine away and then walk you back to the house. Why don't you sit over here on the mounting block until you feel more steady? You look as if you are about to keel over."

And he looked about to split his sides with laughter, Hannah thought. She would have loved to wring his neck for his amusement over her plight, but she was not about to admit to him just how badly frightened she had been. She would show him, she would. Cowardice might have been built into her nature just as recklessness had been built into Wesley's, but she was not about to give Peter the satisfaction of proving the point.

She would learn to ride, even if it did end up killing her, and by God she would ride to hounds before she was finished, see if she didn't—if she survived that long.

As soon as they reached the house, Hannah fled up the stairs and down the shadowy corridor to her room. She was so lost in contemplating her misery that she didn't at first notice Mrs. Brewster coming to a screeching halt at the far end of the hall, her hands flying to her throat as all the color drained out of her face.

"Sarah!" she said in a strangled sob. "Oh, Sarah, you've come back to me! Oh, my angel! Ooohhhh. . . ." She tilted alarmingly to one side.

Hannah came back to earth, took in Mrs. Brewster's little white face and the peculiar angle she had assumed, and picked up her skirts, running to catch the poor woman as she was dropping to the ground.

"Mrs. Brewster, what is it?" Hannah said, waving her hand over the woman's face. "What happened?"

Mrs. Brewster opened her eyes. "You are no ghost," she said accusingly. "Why, you are not my angel at all—you are Miss Janes!"

"Yes, I know," Hannah said, pulling Mrs. Brewster back up to standing. "Oh, I am so sorry. It is the riding habit that must have alarmed you. I borrowed it for a lesson, for I don't have one of my own. I truly am sorry to have given you a shock."

Mrs. Brewster's face worked for a moment as she assimilated this information, and then she unexpectedly broke into a contented smile. "Not at all, my dear," she said, patting Hannah's arm as if Hannah were a child. "Thinking on it, it makes perfect sense, now doesn't it? You help yourself to any of those things I packed away. Anything at all. Now why didn't I notice before?"

"Notice what?" Hannah asked with confusion.

"Why, the omens, child, the omens. The cards pointed to it just this morning—and the leaves? Did they not say the same thing? I've been seeing them for days now, indeed, and I just did not understand."

"Mrs. Brewster, what omens? What are you talking about?"

"Never you mind. Don't you worry your pretty head. I'll bring up your hot water in just a moment, my lamb. Maybe you would like to lie down for a bit? It is good for the complexion to rest after exertion."

She gave Hannah's arm one more reassuring pat, and skimmed away, looking pleased as could be with herself and Hannah both.

Hannah looked after her, wondering if Mrs. Brewster was entirely altogether in her upper stories. She hadn't paid Hannah a moment's attention until this moment, and suddenly she was behaving as if Hannah were a beloved child. Hannah decided that it would be a waste of time to try to puzzle this out, and went to her room to change. She had enough to worry about without adding Mrs. Brewster's mental health to her list.

"There is a gentleman to see you, my lord," Galsworthy intoned, entering the library with a silver plate outstretched before him. "His card."

Peter put his pen down, took the card, read it, and immediately stood. "Send him in, Galsworthy."

"Lord Blakesford," the gentleman said, entering. "This is an unexpected turn of events, so soon on the heels of our last meeting." He shook Peter's hand, then sat in the chair Peter had indicated. "I would extend my sympathies, but I know that is not necessary in this case."

"My dear Nichols," Peter said, sitting opposite him, "your sympathy would be appreciated. Not for the passing of my cousin, mind you, but for the mess he has left me. Thank you for coming so promptly; I find I am in need of a great deal of information, not to mention your legal advice."

"Certainly, my lord. From the way you described the circumstances in your letter, I can imagine you have had a number of shocks."

"Yes, you could say that, and the situation has managed to further complicate itself. Did you know that my cousin left a seven-year-old son whose existence he was well aware of? Wesley Janes is his name."

"Ah," said the solicitor. "I cannot say I am altogether surprised. It would not surprise me if his lordship had left behind a number of bastard children. But how has the child come to your attention?"

"His sister brought him here. Apparently she had made some kind of arrangement with Henry. The boy was to be sent off to school."

"How very peculiar. Your cousin could not abide children, including his own. Why would he take on a small boy? He couldn't have thought to do you out of the succession, could he? It wouldn't have been legal."

"No, I don't think it had anything to do with that. So he never mentioned Wesley, or made any provision for him in his will?"

"No, my lord. It is the first time I have heard of this. There are no provisions in his lordship's will at all for anyone."

"I see. Well, that brings me to my next question. How exactly does the estate stand? Is there money?"

"Money, my lord?" Mr. Nichols said, looking astonished. "I should say so. At last accounting there were nearly two million pounds in investments and then with the other properties, the income is . . . my lord?"

"Two million pounds?" Peter choked. "Two *million*?"

"Yes, my lord. I thought you would have had some idea of the extent of the inheritance."

"No. I had no idea. None. Oh, my God. No wonder my father would never speak of it. Half of that income would have been his?"

"Yes, my lord. But for that peculiar clause that was added by the seventh earl about marriage, after the problem developed."

"Oh, the one about the earl approving the wife of the

heir before the inheritance could be handed over? The one Henry used to cheat my father?"

"Indeed, my lord. Sadly, it still stands as part of the entailment."

"What . . . what are you telling me, Nichols?"

"I am afraid you are going to need a wife, my lord, before the income is yours, free and clear."

Peter stared at him.

"And I am also afraid that your wife must be deemed suitable."

"But Nichols, for the love of God, I am the earl. Who is to deem my wife suitable if not me?"

"In a situation such as this, the executor of the will, my lord. That would be me."

Peter rested his forehead against the heel of one hand. "This is absurd."

"Indeed my lord. But it is the law. I am sure it will not be any sort of problem. Have you a wife in mind?"

"No, of course I haven't a wife in mind! I hadn't quite gotten around to that yet. You might appreciate that there really hasn't been time, Nichols."

"I do indeed, my lord. I appreciate your entire predicament. I wish I could be more helpful. I would give you the entire sum right now if I could, but I cannot."

"I've inherited a madhouse," Peter said dryly. "That's what it is. Henry cheated my father, hoarded the Blakesford fortune, and didn't use it to any good at all. In fact, from what I can see, all he did was use the money to add to the treasures of Longthorpe while the village starved. Now, here I am with the inclination to help these poor people rebuild their lives and pride, and I'm stuck with no resources."

"Until you marry, my lord. All you need do is find a suitable woman, and your problems are solved."

"Oh, perfect. I am to go up to London, randomly pick out some miss with the right family connections who would just jump at the opportunity to be countess of Longthorpe, bring her home to reign, and you will then give her the nod and give me my income. Is that correct?"

"It would be nice if you could find a wife to be fond of, my lord," Mr. Nichols said.

"*Fond?* I don't have time for fondness, Nichols. And when did fondness become a criteria for marriage?"

"I was merely suggesting, my lord—"

"Thank you, Nichols, but I don't need any suggestions, not in this matter. In fact, let us drop the subject entirely. I will do my level best to find someone suitable as quickly as possible, and we will leave it at that. Now. Let us get down to the details of the estate. . . ."

Mr. Nichols left some three hours later, and Peter breathed a sigh of relief. His head was swimming with facts and figures and the prospect of handling these new concerns. And this business of a wife—he could scarce believe it.

He had not been looking forward to the task of finding a wife to begin with, but to have his hand forced in such a way was infuriating. And to have to have his choice of wife approved by his solicitor—a man he had only ever met twice, at that—it was downright demeaning! It would have been nice if he'd at least been able to take his time, to choose with care, perhaps find someone he might eventually grow to love.

But life, Peter had discovered, was not about the accommodation of his own needs or emotional desires. In any case, love had a way of complicating matters. He had learned that lesson years ago, and thinking about it, he really wasn't sure if he wanted to put himself in the path of that kind of agony again.

Peter sighed heavily, then rose and poured himself a healthy measure of cognac, for the past didn't bear thinking about. He needed to concentrate on the future.

Maybe a loveless marriage wasn't such a bad idea after all. His life had been upset enough as it was, and he had enough to deal with without having to go through any more emotional gymnastics.

He supposed he ought to consider himself fortunate that he'd had thirty-three years of freedom, stop feeling sorry for himself, and get on with the business at hand. He'd marry the first available woman whom Nichols might consider suitable, and that would be an end to it.

Peter examined the snifter in his hand, swallowed the entire contents in one gulp, and threw the glass across the room. It didn't even give him the satisfaction of breaking.

"Oh, to hell with it." He pulled on his coat and went out for a very long walk.

*   *   *

"I am telling you, Mary, all the signs are there!" Mrs. Brewster perched on the edge of her chair and peered across the table at her younger friend. "I checked and then checked again. I don't know why I didn't see it the minute his lordship walked in and young Hannah practically on his heels the very next day."

She laid the cards out on the table in a pattern, then examined each intently as it came up. "There. There is the house, you see that, in the position of the immediate future to come. And here, and here—you see!" she cried triumphantly. "What did I tell you! The king of hearts and the queen right next to him! The king of hearts, now he symbolizes a man fair in coloring, a good man, one appearing calm on the surface, but with a fierce and sensitive nature beneath. Hmm."

"Is that his lordship, Eunice?" Mary asked, leaning her fist on her chin.

"And who else? Naturally it's his lordship. It shows that he's generous, too, and wise, but he has had some terrible disappointments."

"And the queen?"

"Now the queen, she is of good virtue, practical, and wise, and symbolizes a good wife and mother. Now, what does that tell you?"

"He'll be marrying, then," Mary Baker said, scratching her chin. "But how do we know it's Hannah he's to marry?"

"Because all the other omens are there," Mrs. Brewster said impatiently. "The tea leaves showed a young woman traveling to a great house and taking up an important position. That would be countess, of course. It was just the same for my Sarah when I read her cup before her marriage to that dreadful earl. But this time the leaves showed good fortune ahead, not like before. I tried to warn my Sarah against him, I did, but she wouldn't listen, taken in by those dashing good looks."

"Yes, but Eunice, I still don't understand how you know the woman is that nice Hannah Janes? His lordship could be bringing anyone home as his bride."

"Well, look here," said Mrs. Brewster, tapping at another card. "Here is the seven of spades. Now that means a dark-haired girl who comes to live in the countryside after finding a place for herself there. What more could you want? Do you know any other dark-haired girls who have recently arrived on his lordship's doorstep? And here, the eight of diamonds. Now that means haste or swiftness, or sometimes it means quarrels. *But* it also represents arrows—could be the arrows of jealousy, but I'll wager it's for Cupid's arrows, see if it isn't."

"Well . . . you've never been wrong before, Eunice. Wouldn't that be something, Hannah Janes and his lordship? Maybe some peace will come to the village after all, if he's like that king of hearts you turned up."

"Well, he has to be, doesn't he? The cards never lie. Now all we have to do is help them along. Haste it says, and I reckon haste is what it means, if nothing is to come between them and their good fortune. For like I said, it also means that there's something that could get in the way, something to do with jealousy and quarreling, and this one, the three of spades, that's division and heartbreak. We'll have to guard against that, now won't we?"

"Indeed we will, Eunice, and I'll do my bit, whatever I can. It's a shame. I just finished warning her away from him, worrying over her virtue I was, although she swears that she's not fluttery over him in the least. Not that I believe her, mind you."

"Well, if she isn't fluttering over him now, she will be in no time. You just leave that part to me."

"Right, Eunice. I don't suppose there's anything in there about my Sam?" Mary asked anxiously. "Or about Johno, although he's doing much better, thanks be to God."

"Let me do a new reading, one just about that, then. Now let me see . . ." She shuffled the cards and started setting out a new pattern.

8

Sweet as the primrose peeps beneath the thorn.
—Oliver Goldsmith,
The Deserted Village

Antoine sat brooding in his room, thinking that his life had taken a distinct turn for the worse. It had been nearly a week since his lordship had arrived, a week of pure, unadulterated hell. His kitchen had been turned upside down, with Galsworthy, the horrible old man, issuing orders and behaving like God himself. *He* was supposed to be God, was he not? Had not his old lordship called his cooking as close to heaven as one could come on earth?

But oh, no. The new lorship did not want the greatness of his meals. He wanted simplicity. "Simplicity, bah!" Antoine muttered to himself. His lordship kept a sharp eye on the bills, insisting that they be brought to him every day, so that Antoine could not add his usual surcharge, which was *comme il faut* in the great houses.

His lordship had no appreciation for art. He was a silly boy, that one, playing at being an earl, but that wouldn't last long, for the man had no true authority. Antoine knew. A peer should behave like a peer; he should look down his nose at the world, despising it. His old lordship, now *he* had known how to behave. But this one, this one went around on his horse, talking to the commoners as if he were one of them. Oh, yes, Antoine had seen him at it in the village. This one dirtied his hands in the stables. This one, and Antoine shuddered, did not know how to dress. He wore not the finest fashions, nor any rings but one gold signet, no ornate fobs on his waistcoat, only one silly watch. And his waistcoats—they were not embroidered with fine colored silks. Half the time he went without his jacket altogether! It was a disgrace. And that hair. Had no one taught him to dress it properly? It was short and merely brushed, and he had no side-whiskers to speak of. He probably could not even grow a proper beard, Antoine decided with a sniff. He probably knew nothing about women, either, not like Antoine.

Now that Mademoiselle Janes—well, he knew all about that kind. All prim and proper on the surface, but just waiting to be taken to bed. He was not fooled in the least. He saw the way she looked at him, when she thought he was not looking. But he watched her always out of the corner of his eye when she came into his kitchen. And he knew why she came, oh, yes. It was not to give the orders; it was to look at him, to admire him. One day he would give her exactly what she wanted, when the Galsworthy was not around to watch over her with those nasty little eyes.

Antoine shuddered. He could not stand the Galsworthy. He despised him. He suffered intestinal complaints over him.

Antoine would need to take a vacation soon, go to France to take a cure for his nerves. No one understood him in this house. No one appreciated him. No one even spoke to him, except to be rude and unfeeling. The Galsworthy and that Madame Brewster—they had teamed up against him, and it was horribly unfair. Tears came to Antoine's eyes. They were detestable, those two. They needed to be put in their place. Order needed to be restored, that was all. Imagine the impudence of the Galsworthy, taking Antoine's precious cellar key! Oh, the insult had left him weak for days!

A little gleam came into Antoine's eyes as an idea struck him. Oh, yes, it was perfect. He would teach the Galsworthy a lesson, and that would be the end of that.

Hannah dressed for dinner, aided by the patting and cooing on Mrs. Brewster's part that had been going on for days now. She couldn't make it out in the least, nor Mrs. Brewster's sudden effusive goodwill toward her, not to mention toward Peter, whom she never ceased to praise to the skies. Peter was well enough in his own way, Hannah supposed, although she could have done without having him heave her on a horse every morning whether she liked it or not. Oh, well. He was clearly not going to give up in his efforts, so there was nothing else to do on that front but endure and hope that her heart wouldn't stop. At least Wesley was happy, for he had been off playing with Frankie Baker every day and ignoring his lessons entirely, and he did seem happier for it. And he also loved his time with Peter, who devoted an hour to him every night.

She went downstairs, hearing their voices drifting up from the library. A burst of high laughter rolled out of the library, followed by a deeper laugh that she knew to be Peter's.

When she entered, the two of them were stretched out on the floor in their customary positions, an array of soldiers between them, arranged into two armies. They were preoccupied and so did not notice her, and she watched with interest as Peter engaged his army with great ferociousness, only to be sent into retreat by Wesley's riposte.

"Good charge!" Peter said with relish. "You'll make a fine general, my boy. Tomorrow night I shall reclaim my advantage, though, but for now it is time to put the brave men away. Oh, hello, Hannah," he said, looking up, and pushed himself to his feet. "Sherry?"

"Hannah, look! I outmaneuvered Cousin Peter tonight! I beat him soundly," he finished happily.

"Yes, so I see, but it is now past your bedtime. And thank you, my lord, I would enjoy a glass of sherry, but only after I've seen Wesley safely in bed. Say good night, Wesley."

"Good night, Cousin Peter," he said obediently, but looking deeply disappointed. "It was a very good battle. You took your loss most honorably."

"Thank you. You are a formidable opponent," Peter said and ruffled his hair. "Now, off you go with your sister."

Hannah dispatched Wesley to bed, and feeling fairly certain that he would stay, she returned downstairs. This time she found Peter more respectably arranged in an armchair, reading the paper.

"All done?" he asked, looking up. "I had a feeling that Wesley might be growing sleepy. His exuberance was slowing."

"He fell instantly asleep. Sleep is the only time that Wesley is ever still. You are very good with him, I must say. I think you have become a hero in his eyes; you have certainly claimed a fiercely loyal place in his heart." She sat down in the armchair opposite and pulled out her needle-point from the bag she had brought down.

"Hannah?"

"Yes?" she replied, looking up at him.

"Do you really believe that to be true?"

"Yes, I do. He has never had anyone other than Galsworthy to look up to. I think you are making a tremendous difference to him."

"In that case, I have a matter to discuss with you. I have been thinking it over the last few days. What would you think of my adopting Wesley?"

"Adopting him?" Hannah's shock occluded her brain, for she could not quite take in what that was supposed to mean. "But why?" she said stupidly.

"I would like to see his situation put to rights. If I adopted him, he would bear the Frazier name, although never the title, obviously. But I would be able to settle a property and some money on your brother upon his majority without any questions being asked. I discussed it with my solicitor the other day. Surely this is what you would want for him, Hannah?"

"Yes. Yes, of course, my lord. You are truly most generous."

"Then why are you looking as if the world were about to come to an end? This will not alter your position in the least, Hannah. You are his sister. You will stay here with him. There is no reason for that to change, is there?"

"Not if that is how you wish it to be, my lord."

"Oh, for God's sake, Hannah, I thought I had made myself more than clear on the subject."

"Yes, you have."

"Then don't create a problem where there isn't one. I've never known anyone with such an inclination toward gloom and doom. Wesley deserves a good start in life and I intend to give it to him, and that includes keeping him with his sister, even if she is mule-headed."

"My lord, I am most certainly not mule-headed, and I think it very unkind of you to say that I am. I am pragmatic, that is all."

Peter grinned. "You, my dear Hannah, are mule-headed and I see nothing unkind in pointing out the obvious."

"And you, my dear Lord Blakesford, are impossible, although I cannot be out of temper with you when you have just made such a generous offer to Wesley."

"Ah, so you accept?"

"We will have to discuss it with Wesley, for it is his future, but I think it is a wonderful idea. Perhaps in a few years the early part of his life will be nothing but a dim memory, and he will feel a Frazier through and through. But are you sure you want the responsibility?"

"I already have the responsibility, Hannah. I'd just like to give Wesley his own family name, rather than have him carry someone else's. And adopting him would put an end to any questions that might arise. Besides, it would give me a proper legal status over him."

Hannah felt like crying. She was deeply touched that Peter truly cared about Wesley to such an extent. His generosity was astonishing, for he needn't have done anything at all, and he had already been more than forthcoming by giving them a roof over their heads. And if he meant to adopt Wesley, then it also meant that he would not tire of them and remove that roof, which is what she had been secretly fearing.

He really was the most extraordinary man, she decided with a rush of true relief. Even though he was aggravating and overbearing and had no polish, he had a good heart . . . she was sure of it. At least, she hadn't seen any sign that he might be reverting to ancestral type. He had behaved most properly in that direction, despite Mary Baker's warnings about his intentions.

Hannah smiled. At the moment, it seemed that life had not only taken a turn for the better, but it looked as if it might actually stay that way. Oh, God did work in mysterious ways.

The door suddenly burst open and Mrs. Brewster appeared, wild-eyed, her hair flying in all directions under her skewed cap.

"My lord, my lord!" she panted. "You must come quickly!"

"Yes, Mrs. Brewster?" Peter replied, putting his paper down. "Is there a problem of some sort?"

"It's the messier, my lord," she said, catching her breath. "He's gone and locked Mr. Galsworthy in the wine cellar, and he won't let him out! He crept down after Mr. Galsworthy and turned the key in the lock, and then took it off and hid it. I heard the pounding on the door and realized what had happened. Poor Mr. Galsworthy has been in there nearly half an hour!"

Hannah jumped to her feet and started toward the door in alarm, for she was terribly worried that Galsworthy might catch a chill in the cellar. But Peter was at the door even before she could manage it, and they made a quick beeline to the kitchen, with Mrs. Brewster panting along behind them.

Antoine was busily humming to himself as he piped icing onto a cake, and he looked up with a self-satisfied smirk until he saw who had arrived in his domain.

"My lord! This is an honnair. You have nevair before graced me with your presence in my kitchen. Mademoiselle Janes," he remembered to add. But the brightly artificial smile dropped from his face when he took in the expression on his employer's.

"The key, Antoine," Peter said in a voice that raised the hair on the back of Hannah's neck. "Now." He stretched out his hand.

"Oh . . . Madame Brewster has told you of the little jest I am playing on the Galsworthy? It is nothing, my lord. Just a silly *blague* between us."

"Give me the key, Antoine."

Peter bit out each word from between gritted teeth, and Antoine turned the color of his icing. He reached behind him into the sugar tin and pulled out the large iron key, handing it into Peter's outstretched hand. Hannah breathed a sigh of relief. She knew perfectly well that it was no silly little joke: Galsworthy had told her that Antoine had been in a sulk ever since Galsworthy had taken charge of the key.

Peter strode down the cellar steps, Hannah and Mrs. Brewster on his heels, and quickly pulled the door open. "Galsworthy, there you are. Mrs. Brewster told me I might find you in here. Have you located a claret for this evening?"

"Ah, my lord . . ." Galsworthy came carefully forward out of the gloom, holding his candle over his head, and peered at the earl, blinking. "Not only have I found the claret, but I also believe I have just discovered a particularly fine bottle."

His composure seemed in place, but Hannah saw immediately that he was quite shaken, for the top of his head was covered in cobwebs, which Galsworthy would never normally allow, and his lips appeared slightly tinged with blue.

"Very good, Galsworthy," Peter said in an equally calm fashion. "It should be given some time to breathe before dinner, don't you think?"

Hannah wanted to throw her arms around Peter and kiss him for helping Galsworthy to preserve his dignity, his most precious possession. She turned quickly and crept up the stairs before Galsworthy had a chance to see that she had been witness to his humiliation.

"Monsieur Antoine," Peter said softly when they had re-emerged. "I will see you in the library immediately after dinner, please." He raised his voice. "Galsworthy, why don't you take the evening off? We will not need you to wait at table this evening. Miss Janes and I will serve ourselves from the sideboard, and Mrs. Brewster can clear later. We would like to be private."

Mrs. Brewster, for some reason Hannah could not immediately fathom, beamed at Peter approvingly.

"Yes, my lord," Galsworthy said with a bow, but he obviously did not share Mrs. Brewster's sentiments. Instead, he managed to look severely disapproving.

Hannah could just imagine what he was thinking, for to Galsworthy, "private" screamed of an illicit liaison. It had been one of her mother's favorite words. But she smiled at him reassuringly. "We can manage, Galsworthy, really we can."

"Indeed, Miss Hannah. I know you are all that is capable. It is his lordship whom I was concerned about."

"But I am accustomed to helping myself, Galsworthy. I am not entirely as inadequate as I might appear."

"Precisely, my lord," Galsworthy said gloomily, and he shuffled off with the bottle of claret in the direction of the pantry.

Peter made an indistinct noise somewhere in the back of his throat that sounded suspiciously like a smothered laugh, and Hannah caught his eye, smiling at the wicked amusement she saw there. Peter grinned in return, and Hannah could see that he had thoroughly enjoyed the entire incident.

It had put Peter into an exceedingly lighthearted mood, and he had her holding her sides as he did a scathing imita-

tion of Antoine once they were safely back in the library.
And during dinner he didn't bother to behave, since Galsworthy was not there to disapprove, and she was too
amused to bother. He aped everyone from the village vicar
to Mrs. Brewster.

". . . So I came downstairs, feeling like a fool after having
introduced myself to a corpse, and there was Mrs. Brewster,
under the impression that I was the undertaker." He did a
perfect imitation of the conversation they'd had, and Hannah nearly fell off her chair, she was laughing so hard.

"Peter, please," she said, choking. "Oh, please stop, or
someone will have to call an undertaker to take me away."
She gasped for breath.

Peter took the napkin off his head that he had been using
as Mrs. Brewster's cap. "Don't you want to hear the rest?
What about the part where the vicar refused to have him
buried in the churchyard, and I ended up having to do it
myself out in the back woods?"

"No—oh, *no*. It can't be true; I don't believe it!"

"Believe it. Why do you think I was in such a state that
night? I'd just come from digging a grave and installing my
cousin in it."

"Oh, Peter, I am sorry . . ." Hannah burst into a fresh
storm of laughter. She covered her face with her hands until
she'd recovered. "I . . . I'm sorry. I can't help myself," she
said, tears streaming down her cheeks.

"Don't be sorry," he said, grinning. "It's nice to see you
laughing. You should do it more often. It becomes you."

"Does it?"

"Yes, it does. I thought as much when I first met you,
but you haven't shown me that side of yourself since." The
amusement faded from his face. "Hannah, if I ask you a
question, will you be honest with me?"

"I will try to be," she said, slightly alarmed to see how
seriously he was regarding her.

"Good. Tell me this, then. Do you think you are going
to be happy here?"

"Oh, yes! Why? Have I given you the impression that I
am unhappy? I have not meant to."

"It is not so much that I've felt you have been unhappy.
It is more that you have been very distant, not at all the
person I first met. I would like to know why."

"Oh," Hannah said, not exactly sure how to reply to that, for she wasn't sure herself that person even existed.

"Is there a reason?" he asked, pressing her. "Have I said or done anything to cause you to dislike me?"

"Oh, no! It's not that at all . . . perhaps it's because I have felt we are such an inconvenience to you. I thought that you only put up with us because of Wesley's connection to you."

"And tonight you know better?"

"Tonight I suppose I feel easier at heart because I know that you truly do want us here, that you want us to stay."

"You were afraid that I was going to ask you to leave?" he said with surprise. "Good God, Hannah, how could you ever have thought such a thing for a moment? I thought I had made my intentions perfectly clear to you."

"Yes, but intentions can change. It has happened before."

"Yes, that is true. I suppose my cousin taught that lesson well enough. But it honestly hadn't occurred to me that you were worried I might do the same and turn my back on you. In fact, I thought the problem was that you resented being forced to live here. I do realize that I gave you no choice but to come."

"How could I possibly resent you for that? I do not know where we would be without you."

"And yet you are proud, Hannah, is that not also true? Come, you can be honest. There is no one to hear."

Hannah bit her lip. "Yes. Yes, it is true. I have always been too proud for my own good, or so my mother continually told me. I imagine she was probably right, but sometimes when one has nothing else, one's pride becomes an anchor to hold on to."

"Yes," he said. "I do know what you mean, not that it did me any good at the time."

"I don't understand," she said, frowning.

"Hannah, I have had my troubles too, you know. My life hasn't been one smooth, uninterrupted line of pleasantries and diversions, if that is what you think. I have done some idiotic things, and I have also had my share of pain and disappointments."

"And yet you are able to laugh at everything. I wish I were better at that, for you are right: I take things far too seriously. You are so good at being absurd."

Peter regarded her gravely, and there was nothing amused in his eyes at all. "Is that how you see me? As a master of the absurd?"

Hannah colored, for there was something about the way he was looking at her that went straight through her and turned her bones to water. "No, I don't see you as a master of the absurd," she said softly. "I think that underneath all that laughter there are far more complicated things, things that run very deep in you. I don't know what they are, exactly, for you are very good at hiding them. And I have probably only had glimpses because I have seen you put in very difficult circumstances. I imagine you usually keep yourself well concealed from the rest of the world. You make a fine clown, Peter, but then you know what is said about clowns: they carry the pain of the world."

Peter winced. "I suppose I asked for that. But then you and I are not so very different. It is just that you use a different method to conceal yourself."

"What do you mean?"

"I may choose to play the clown, for it does make the world an easier place to bear. But you, you shield yourself behind an impenetrable wall of respectability, as if that will protect you from all the potential evil out there. In truth, Hannah, all it does is to shield you from yourself."

Hannah swallowed, wondering if that self had anything to do with what happened in the garden. "Really? Do you really think so?"

"Yes, I do, or I wouldn't have said it. It is only fair to trade honesty for honesty. You and I both know that there is far more to you than this straitlaced spinster you like play. It's effectively daunting, but there is no need to play the game with me."

"But . . . it is not a game. And how would you have me behave? Like a light-skirt?"

"Certainly not like a light-skirt," Peter said with exasperation. "I'd have you be yourself. You needn't carry the weight of the world on your shoulders any longer, Hannah, for despite how flimsy you might think them, mine are actually quite broad."

Hannah smiled. "I have had firsthand experience with the breadth of your shoulders, if you remember. I did not find them lacking. I found only that they did not belong to the person I had thought."

"A name does not change one's essence, Hannah. I am the same man. Forgive me for not being the simple commoner you believed, but it was near enough the truth, was it not?"

"It was near enough the truth. And had you told me then that you had come from burying the man you'd just succeeded, I should have thought you addled in your senses." She shook her head and laughed. "Looking back on it, a great many things you said to me that night make perfect sense."

"I am glad, Hannah, for I spoke honestly to you, perhaps more honestly than I could have done to anyone else. Maybe the fact that you were a stranger helped, and that you too were experiencing a certain distress helped also. I took comfort from that night, I truly did."

"I did also," she said.

"Yes, so you said at the time." He smiled at her, and Hannah's heart caught in her chest at the expression in his eyes.

And you wonder why I've been guarding myself against you ever since, Hannah thought, her heart pounding erratically. But she kept her silence, dropping her eyes to her plate and feigning an interest in her food.

Peter said nothing more. His attention also returned to his meal, but the silence between them was heavy with unspoken things. Hannah was beginning to realize that where she could manage Peter quite well in the daylight, the night could be another matter altogether. Something happened— her guard dropped and the other Hannah came out, the one who kissed strange men in gardens and liked it.

Her eyes crept up. He was just taking a sip of his claret, and her breath caught in unconscious memory of the taste of his mouth on hers. And as she watched his hand lower the glass again, she remembered the feel of that hand moving in her hair. It was a masculine hand, and she could not help but admire the strong and yet finely honed structure of his fingers. He had touched her with that hand. He had moved it along her face, and gripped her back with it . . . had pressed her against his chest, and she could still feel the hard strength of his body full against her.

Heat started to rise in her at the very thought, and she pushed her hand against her throat, trying to still the absurd pulse that had started a hard, dry beating there. What was wrong with her? Here she was, sitting at Peter's dinner table, thinking—thinking carnal thoughts about him. She was disgraceful, a true example of her breeding. What would Peter think of her if he knew?

He glanced up just at that moment. "I thought tomorrow I might take Wesley . . . Hannah . . . what is it? What is wrong?"

"Nothing. It is nothing," she said, feeling panicked that he might have read her mind. "Something caught in my throat for a moment. It is gone now. Please . . . please excuse me. I find I am tired." She jumped up from the table. "Good night, and thank you for being so kind to Galsworthy tonight. You were most understanding about his self-respect. And . . . thank you about Wesley, also. You are very kind."

She kept herself from running and managed a sedate enough pace as she exited, but by the time she had reached the refuge of her bedroom she was a shaking wreck.

Peter sat quietly for a few minutes after Hannah had left. Something had happened just then, although for the life of him he could not think what it had been. They'd had a fairly personal conversation, but he hadn't said anything that could have upset her, had he? He had only been honest with her, and she had acknowledged what he had said, or at least he thought she had, for she had been honest in return. He was damned grateful, in fact, to have the Hannah of the garden back, for he found that he had missed her. Oh, it had been good indeed to see her laugh so freely, to smile at him with warmth in her eyes.

Still, something had happened to send her fleeing, and he was damned if he knew what it was. Here they'd had a nice, amiable evening together, the first, really, since she'd arrived. There had been no Galsworthy to accommodate, she hadn't given a single thought to his manners, nor to hers, and best of all he hadn't had to do battle with a thorn bush. In fact, he'd thought that for once he was going to emerge from the evening unscathed. And then without warning she had popped up from the table like a cork from champagne and fled, looking as if he had just suggested that they disport themselves under the table. And this when he had been impeccably behaved! Look at the care he had taken not to allude in any fashion to that extraordinary kiss they had shared. The way Hannah went on, one would think it had been an evil twin who had kissed him so fervently and nothing to do with her at all.

Women were the most unpredictable creatures, and Hannah had to be the most unpredictable of all. And he had thought that Amelia had been the champion in that. But that reflection he immediately dismissed, for there was only trouble in that direction. In any case, he had more immediate things to do. He rose and went to ring an extremely loud peal over Antoine's head.

9

It seemed to me pretty plain, that they had
more of love in them than matrimony.
——Oliver Goldsmith,
The Vicar of Wakefield

Hannah could not sleep. She tossed and she turned and
finally decided that there was no point in continuing to lie
in bed. It was too cold to go outside; the wind had been
howling for half the night and it would be foolish to give
herself a proper cold on top of everything else. Although,
she considered, pulling on a wrapper, maybe a bad cold
would give her something else to think about other than
Peter Frazier.

"He is not Peter Frazier," she muttered. "He is the Earl
of Blakesford, and one does not have lewd fantasies about
earls. One does not have lewd fantasies at all. Oh, Hannah,
what is wrong with you! You know better than this!"

She lit the candle on her nightstand and pulled on her
slippers and wrapper, and then took the blanket off the
bed, wrapping it around her shoulders for good measure.
She headed down the hall and down the stairs. Had there
been a chapel she would have gone there, but there was
not, so she went instead to the portrait gallery. She thought
maybe a good dose of looking at fine ladies would remind
her of how one should think and behave at all times. At *all*
times.

The cold bright moonlight fell through the long windows
that ran all along one side of the gallery, giving off a ghostly
light. People in all sorts of dress, dating back as far as the
fifteenth century, she guessed, looked down at her from
their positions high on the wall. She moved slowly along
the wide hall, looking back up at them. There were ladies

aplenty, an attractive assortment for the most part. There were ladies with children, ladies with their husbands, and the one that Peter had referred to, the lady in the green velvet riding habit with two dogs at her feet. Hannah was quite sure that she had not hung about her horse's neck. In fact, Hannah was sure that she had sat beautifully on her saddle, her little dogs running behind as she cantered off into the distance, her husband watching her with admiration.

Well, perhaps not, given that her husband had been the old earl. Hannah was certain that he was not the sort of man to admire his wife. It was a shame, as she had a pretty face, even if it did look a bit sad.

Hannah admired the way the countess sat, one delicate hand resting on the dog's head. She had a kind face, Hannah decided. Sarah, Peter had said she was called. No doubt Sarah had been a perfect countess, distributing bounty around the land, ministering to the sick, charming her friends and relations, bearing her husband's brutishness with fortitude. It was just as a countess ought to behave. But given her boorish husband, Hannah wondered if she had taken a lover. It would not have been far off the scenario Peter had created . . . Sarah meeting her lover, perhaps tearfully bidding him farewell when she realized she could not neglect her duty to her family, her children. They would have kissed—

"Oh, *stop* this!" she cried. "Stop this right now, Hannah Janes, or God shall strike you down where you stand!"

She wrapped the blanket more tightly around her, but sank to the floor just in case the lightning bolts started to fly. The wall was cold and solid behind her back and she pressed against it, regarding the painting from this angle.

Sarah, she decided, was far too pure to take a lover. She had no doubt suffered her husband's attentions in silence, as was her duty, and she'd given him two sons, as was also her duty. Sarah had not had impure thoughts about anyone, ever. Sarah had not attracted lascivious attention to herself. Sarah had gone straight to heaven when she had died, lightly born up on the wings of angels. When it was Hannah's turn, providing she did not go straight to hell, the angles would find her a much greater burden. In fact, she could see them struggling with her now, heaving and hauling, their wings practically breaking under the strain. God would have to send two very large, burly angels to get *her* to heaven.

"Whatever it is you find so amusing, Hannah, I am pleased to see you smiling again."

Hannah jumped half out of her skin and had to stifle a cry. Peter stood above her, a candlestick in his hand, and he was regarding her quizzically. She started to scramble to her feet, but he stayed her with a hand on her shoulder.

"No, don't go," he said, dropping down next to her. "What are you doing up and in the gallery at this hour, conversing with a painting? I thought you were tired."

Hannah gave up the thought of escaping, for she could see that he was determined to keep her there. But she did wish he would move away, for she was most uncomfortable having him so close to her. "I was not conversing with a painting," she said. "I was looking at Sarah. Lady Blakesford, I mean. I thought . . . I thought if I came to know the person inside the habit, something might rub off on me when I wore it next."

"Oh? Such as what?"

Purity, Hannah thought, but instead she said, "Skill. Lady Blakesford does not look like the sort of woman to be afraid of anything. I am sure she rode beautifully. And what are you doing up and in here at this hour, my lord?"

"I was on my way upstairs, and I saw the light. I thought I would investigate, thinking it might be Wesley off on one of his adventures. But I am glad I found you, for I have been concerned about you since you left the dinner table so abruptly. Did I do or say something to upset you, Hannah? If I did, I apologize, but I wish you would tell me what it was."

"Oh no, it was nothing you said! It was nothing at all."

"Oh? And that is what led you to regard me as if I were a gargoyle?"

Hannah could not help but smile. "I did nothing of the sort."

"But you did. I can't help this face—it is one of those things one has no control over, and my mother was such a kind woman, she loved me anyway. But I must tell you, it is unnerving to be looked at as if one has struck horror into the heart."

"My lord, you are being extremely silly."

"And there is that, too. It is a difficult thing being a mindless creature."

"And now you're being excessively silly and should be ashamed of yourself, given what you said to me earlier. And you ought not be sitting on the floor with me."

"Why not, Hannah?" he asked innocently. "I enjoy sitting on floors; I've done it all my life. But tell me why it worries you. You're sitting on the floor as well, so it can't be that. Perhaps it is the late hour and the fact that you are in your night shift?"

"My lord, you mustn't allude to such things! It really is most improper! And how do you know I am in my night shift?" she added suspiciously. "I am completely wrapped in a blanket."

"Which I wish you would be generous enough to share," he said wistfully. "It is rather chilly."

Hannah hadn't noticed he was shivering. He was wearing only trousers and a linen shirt, the top buttons of the shirt undone and exposing his throat to the night air. "Oh . . . I suppose you would be cold." She moved over and gave him one side of the blanket but she stayed as far away from him as possible.

"Thank you," he said, pulling his end of the blanket about his shoulders. "So tell me, what did cause you to look at me with such alarm at dinner?"

"But I didn't . . . oh, please don't go on about it. It is painful to talk about." What was she meant to say? She could just imagine Peter's expression if she blithely said, *I was actually thinking about your making love to me, my lord.* And that thought only served to make her realize just how very close he was to her now. She shifted even farther away from him, pulling on the blanket until it was stretched tightly between them. A coin would have bounced nicely on the wool.

Peter shot her a sidelong glance, but he said only, "I did not intend to bring up anything painful, Hannah. I regret that I did. I know so little about your previous life and so it is hard to know when I have said something tactless or upsetting."

"But you didn't."

"Didn't I? Then why did you go running from the table as if you had all the hounds of hell after you?"

"I . . . I did no such thing."

"Oh, yes, you did. And you did so immediately after regarding me as if I were the devil himself, when all I'd been doing was eating my dinner and minding my own business. I don't believe I stuck my fork in my ear or drank from my finger glass, did I? No, I am sure I did not. Perhaps I forget something vital?"

Hannah colored. "No, you did not. Your table manners are quite adequate. In fact, I am sure they are improving daily."

"How reassuring. So. Why don't you tell me the truth of the matter? I thought we'd agreed to have honesty between us."

"But I can't," she said squirming. "Not to you. It would be most incorrect."

"Oh, for the love of God, Hannah! Surely we had agreed that there were a few moments out of the day when I did not have to play at being the earl, at least not with you? I have to tell you, dealing with Antoine tonight gave me more than a full measure of that role. The man is unbelievably tedious."

"You did a commendable job of dealing with him," Hannah said, relieved to have a distraction immediately at hand. "I thought you sounded most authoritative, quite as if you had been playing the part for a lifetime. But why do you keep him? Was not locking Galsworthy in the wine cellar worthy enough for dismissal?"

"No, that was only enough to bring him a severe tongue-lashing. He won't be trying that again. Antoine will be under control soon enough. His biggest problem is that he's been allowed to become a tyrant. Once his wings are clipped, he'll settle down or he'll leave."

"But do you trust him?"

"Trust him? Certainly not. But I learned a valuable lesson from my father. When people in one's employ are creating problems, it is wiser to keep them where you can see them. That way, when there's trouble, one knows about it. And if the troublemaker leaves of his own accord, then he is less likely to create trouble for one elsewhere from sheer vindictiveness."

"Oh," Hannah said. "Oh, yes, I do see. Your father sounds a wise man."

"He was. I admired him tremendously."

"You mentioned that yours was a separate branch of the

family," Hannah asked tentatively, not wanting to pry, but curiosity compelled her. "How was it exactly that your father fit into the family?"

"Now that," said Peter, "is a most interesting question. It is also not an easy one to address, for there was much bitterness involved."

"You need not tell me if you do not wish . . ." Hannah offered reluctantly.

"What, after I have spent the last few days dragging all sorts of things out of you that you would have preferred to keep to yourself? That would be most unfair of me. But if I'm to explain, then I should start at the beginning." He stood and offered her his hand, and Hannah took it, letting him help her to her feet. "No, you keep the blanket," she said when he held it out to her. "I am perfectly warm."

"Thank you," he said, wrapping it about his shoulders. "I left my jacket downstairs, thinking I was going straight to bed. Come over here." He walked down the room a few feet and pointed up at a pair of portraits.

Hannah found herself looking at two separate paintings of a young boy slightly older than Wesley. He was dressed in a blue coat and breeches, and he had a devilish gleam in his eye and a wicked tilt to his mouth. Or at least, the first portrait of him had. The other was more somber, sweeter of expression. "The artist must have decided to paint another side of his character, for the one on the right has a gentler feel to the face," she observed. "Who is he?"

"You are most astute, Hannah, but slightly misled. The boy on the right is my grandfather, Charles Frazier. The boy on the left is his brother, Stephen. He became the eighth earl."

"Oh! They were twins," Hannah said, fascinated by the extraordinary resemblance between them.

"Yes, which was the root of all the problems that ensued. You see, they were so closely identical that no one, not even their mother, could tell them apart. So the first to be born was tagged with a red ribbon about his wrist, and the younger was given a blue ribbon. Unfortunately, the nurse inadvertently removed the ribbons when bathing them and then couldn't remember which belonged to which. It only remained to toss a coin to decide which had been christened Stephen, and which Charles. There was an earldom at stake, you must remember."

"You cannot be serious! An earldom was decided on a coin toss?" Hannah did not know whether to be scandalized or wildly amused.

"It was, and the story was kept very much in the family. But since it was such an arbitrary process, their father decided that although the earldom must be passed onto Stephen, who had won the toss of the coin, the income from the estate must be divided evenly between them, and the same provision passed on to their first sons. Stephen, as you have already noticed, was not quite as steady of character as Charles, and he had a fine old time running about in a debauched fashion, while Charles stayed home and minded the place. And then both twins married within a short time of each other and produced sons. The sad thing was that Charles and his wife died of the pox shortly after their son, my father, was born. That left Stephen to bring my father up along with his own son, Henry."

"Oh, dear," Hannah said, her hand creeping to her mouth. "Your poor father."

"You do grasp a point quickly, Hannah my sweet. My poor father, indeed. He had inherited his father's gentle nature, just as Henry had inherited the diabolic nature of Stephen. My father was bullied, tormented, and generally treated extremely badly. He never spoke of it as such, but it wasn't difficult to divine the truth behind his words."

"And then what happened?" Hannah asked, her heart breaking for the poor boy who had lost his parents and then been subjected to such torment. No child deserved to be treated in such a manner.

"What happened was dictated solely by greed. Stephen died shortly before his son turned twenty-one. That gave Henry perfect freedom to do as he wished. The estate was now dictated by Henry's discretion alone, and he chose not to honor the agreement made concerning the division of the income. Henry cut my father off without a penny and turned him off the property. There is an obscure clause in the details of entailment that legally justified his actions. They concerned my mother. Henry decided that he did not approve of her background. Her father had been in trade."

"Oh, Peter," Hannah whispered. "How very dreadful. . . ."

"Not just dreadful, but sad and terribly unfair as well. My parents decided that they would rather leave England

behind and start anew somewhere else. My father thought
Jamaica sounded far enough away, so they went there."

"But what did he do with no money and no family to
help him?"

Peter paused for a moment, looking slightly uncertain,
Hannah thought, and her heart went out to him. "You
needn't be embarrassed," she said kindly. "I don't mind in
the least."

Peter smiled. "Of course you don't. He took a job as . . .
as a sort of guide for ah, for visitors to the island."

Hannah had visions of a man leading people through the
jungle, cutting a path as he went, fending off wild beasts.
"I see," she said. "So he turned his back on everything that
England represented?"

"No, not everything. Jamaica is a part of the British Em-
pire," he reminded her. "Life is definitely more relaxed in
the islands, though."

"Relaxed. Yes. Yes, of course. It must have made quite
a change from living at Longthorpe. Perhaps your father
cast off his background to keep from remembering?"

"Oh, he never forgot. He never forgot. He rarely spoke
of Longthorpe, for it pained him to do so. But on the rare
occasions that he did, he spoke of his concern for the people, for he knew that Henry, like Henry's father, would
neglect them. As it turns out, Henry managed to outstrip
his father in debauchery and corruption. I am glad that my
father did not live to know of it."

Hannah moved toward him and placed her hand on his
arm. "Peter, I am so sorry," she said softly. She hated to
hear the deep sadness in his voice, to sense the quiet anger
that lay beneath it. And yet it explained so much to her.

"Never mind," he said, pulling his eyes from the two
portraits. "It is finished now, isn't it? At least my mother
and father married for love and lived out their lives in that
happy condition. Look at what happened to Henry. He
lived an ill-begotten, miserable life, and I doubt he ever
gained much pleasure from anything or anyone, much less
gave any sort of pleasure back. If anything, I would think
that he gave nothing but misery."

"Most likely," she said bitterly.

"I am sorry, Hannah," he said, covering her hand with
his own. "I had forgotten about your mother and her

involvement with the man. He brought you your share of misery, too."

"It is not important. It really isn't. We were talking about your family, not mine. My mother was only an interlude in your cousin's life and one of no real consequence."

"Save for Wesley," he pointed out. "It is sad that a woman must bear the full burden of an unwanted child. In your case, it has been your burden also."

She shook her head adamantly. "No. I love Wesley and I would not change what happened, for I cannot imagine life without him. But I would have taken my mother's suffering away if I could have. It had started long before your cousin appeared, but still, it was distressing seeing what happened to her after he deserted her."

"And what did happen to her?"

"After he left her, she was deeply unhappy. Her health failed and she slowly wasted away until she died. I . . . I hated the Blakesford name, and I wished terrible things on the earl all of the time. I wanted him to be as miserable as he had made my mother. When you told me that his sons had died, I felt awful, almost as if I'd been responsible by willing his misery. I cannot imagine how painful it must have been, losing his children."

"Hannah, you were not responsible." He turned her by the shoulders and looked into her face. "We all have ignoble thoughts at one time or another. You had more reason to think them than most, given the little you have told me. But I severely doubt that you caused Rupert's dysentery, which is what killed him in the Peninsula, nor did you sweep James off a boat into the Ionian Sea. In any case, I don't think my cousin cared a fig for either of his sons, so I doubt very much he was made the least miserable when they died. I believe his only misery was caused by knowing that I would inherit everything he had tried so hard to keep from my father."

She bowed her head. "Nevertheless, I did have wicked thoughts. I wished your cousin ill."

"And I wished him to perdition. Do you think I succeeded?" He smiled at her.

"I hope you did," she said in a small voice. "I hope he is roasting."

"So do I. And furthermore, I don't feel the least shred of guilt over hoping it. Why should I?"

"I suppose you're right," Hannah said with a sigh. "He has caused you more trouble than anyone deserves. And even though it is too bad that his sons had to die, I am happy that you are now the earl and not one of them."

"Are you? Well, I am delighted that someone is happy about it. But what makes you happy that it is not one of them?"

"Because Mary Baker told me that they were just as disreputable as their father. She said that they took advantage of the village girls, charming them with their good looks and winning ways, then leaving them in trouble. It would have been awful to have that continue."

"You've been spending a good amount of time with Mary Baker, haven't you?" Peter asked. "It appears that Wesley is not the only one to have found a friend."

"I like Mary. She's sensible, when she's not being superstitious. She's very superstitious."

"All the village people are superstitious from what I've been able to gather. Most especially about me. I can't tell you the times I've seen them make the sign against evil when I've approached. They don't even bother to be subtle about it."

"You mustn't feel so glum about them. It will all come right once they have learned to trust you and they've seen how much you can do for them."

"Yes, well it now appears I can't do much of anything until I acquire a wife. That damned clause I told you about has cropped up to create trouble again and until I marry, I have no access to the Blakesford funds, which are considerable. I have some money of my own, but most of it is tied up in the shipping business. I have enough at hand to make a start of things, but I can't just pull out the rest of my funds at whim, not without adversely affecting a number of other people."

"Oh . . . oh, dear. Well, you had better find a wife quickly then," Hannah said with a sinking heart, for she had not really given the matter of Peter's marriage much consideration. She found the idea rather alarming.

"Yes, I know. And the worst part is that I have to find someone suitable or it's no good. Do you know what 'suitable' means, Hannah? It means I am to choose a woman of impeccable credentials, who will no doubt do all the impeccable things and bore me to tears. Her family will jump about with joy that their little darling made such a fine catch and expect me to support them, and the little darling will no doubt expect to spend most of her time in London, socializing with her friends, or holding enormous house parties. I doubt very much she will have any interest in Kirby or its people. Oh, God, *why* is this happening?"

Hannah bit her lip, thinking that if the girls she had been at school with were any example, then Peter was probably correct in his assessment. "I don't know. But maybe you will meet someone wonderful," she said doubtfully. "Maybe it will all work out happily."

He looked at her impatiently. "You no more believe that than I do, and don't try to make me feel better, Hannah, because it won't work. I don't want to feel better. There's no point in deluding myself."

"All right. I won't try to make you feel better, but there's also no point in feeling sorry for yourself, either."

Peter took her by the arms. "Oh, and how would you feel, Hannah, if you were forced to marry against your will, to create your children in some loveless conjoining? I can't think you'd like it very much, not given the passion in your nature."

"What p-passion in my nature?" Hannah asked nervously, trying to pull away. "I am sure I don't know what you're talking about."

"Ah, for God's sake, don't go all correct on me now. You know precisely what I mean. You don't know how fortunate you are, able to marry when and whom you please with no obligations hanging over your head. You can marry for love, Hannah. Do you have any idea what a luxury that is? I don't think I even realized just how much of a luxury it is until the option was taken away from me."

"But I do not think to marry at all, my lord," Hannah said softly.

"What a load of poppycock! Of course you shall marry. It would be an enormous waste if you did not."

"A waste of what?" she said, her heart beginning to pound erratically, for Peter's eyes were blazing into hers and his hands burned through her wrapper into her flesh.

"A waste of this . . ." He let go of her with one hand and touched her hair. "And of this . . ." and his hand brushed her cheek. "And of this . . ." His finger came to rest on her lips and stroked across it, and Hannah's heart felt as if it might jump completely out of her chest. She couldn't help herself—her lips began to part against the feel of his touch. And then she found herself abruptly released, and unprepared, she stumbled backward.

Peter's hands came out to catch her under her elbows. "I am sorry," he said, his voice thick. "But I think I made my point."

"Your point?" she said, feeling dazed. "Was there a point?"

"Yes. And as you are by no means stupid, I think you know exactly what it was. Good night, Hannah."

He removed the blanket from his shoulders and handed it to her, retrieved his candle, and left the gallery without another word. Hannah stood absolutely still, staring after him, her hand covering her mouth with dismay. She did not move for a long time, and then, realizing that she was cold and suddenly very tired, she too picked up her candle and made her way to bed.

Galsworthy, seeing that Hannah was safe and back in her bed, and that the young earl had gone to his own bed where he properly belonged, moved away from his post in the shadows and took himself off to his room for some well-deserved rest.

Some people needed protecting from themselves, that was all there was to it.

10

And e'en his failings leaned to Virtue's side.
—Oliver Goldsmith,
The Deserted Village

Peter went out early the next morning, saddled his gelding, and went for a very hard ride. He had not slept well the night before, although it was little wonder. It was hardly his fault. It wasn't really Hannah's fault, either, for she couldn't help being a temptress any more than he could help being tempted. But how was a man expected to live side by side with a woman he'd just discovered he wanted as violently as a starving man craved food?

Peter pulled his horse in and dismounted. He looked down from the top of the hill over Kirby. Frost hung in the air, and at this hour there was very little activity. Thin wisps of smoke curled up from a chimney here and there. He thought about the inhabitants, the women laying the fires, putting bread on the table for their children. He thought about the few men left, most of them too old for the mines, and those not too old lamed or injured in some way. He shook his head, feeling quite sick at what his family had done. It had to be changed.

He'd already drawn a large draft on his bank. Any more and he'd have to speak with Edward, for he'd need to borrow on the business, a practice neither of them subscribed to. But he had little choice, and he could pay the money back immediately when he had found someone to marry. But Edward, he knew, was busy at Seaton with the spring planting, as he would soon be, so that conversation would have to wait. It was not the sort of thing that he wanted to put on paper.

As for what he was to do about Hannah, that was a

different matter entirely. Peter drew in a deep breath of the
sharp air. It made no sense: here was a woman who not
only insisted on carrying the responsibility of the world
around with her, but who also insisted that the world behave according to her rules. She infuriated him. She was a
contradiction unto herself, one thing one minute, something
completely different the next. How was a man supposed to
deal with that? It was enough to drive one mad. And yet
he wanted her desperately: the force of his desire was
enough to send his senses reeling. It defied all reason.

He had just finished telling her that she was secure at
Longthorpe. It was no good moving her into her own house
and anyway, what about Wesley? No, he would honor his
promise to them both, but how he was to continue day in
and day out with Hannah immediately under his nose, he
didn't know.

Peter's gaze wandered over the church tower. It was Sunday, he realized. Perfect. He would drag his entire eccentric
household off to morning services for a strong dose of religion. Maybe a strong dose of religion would bring him to
his senses. Maybe God would hear his plea and perform a
spiritual castration. He shuddered at that thought. Well . . .
maybe not. Maybe instead God would perform a small miracle and Peter would find himself back in Jamaica, with
everything just the way it had been before, but perhaps with
Hannah there too, and no reason why he couldn't take her
immediately to bed.

The pale sun came out from behind a cloud, glistening
on the fresh snow. Peter reached his hand down and
scooped up a handful, balling it into his fist.

Duty. It was beginning to feel exactly like death.

Hannah had been startled by Peter's curt command when
she'd come down for breakfast, but she'd done her best to
gather everyone together. She inspected her brood as they
stood in the courtyard waiting for Peter to bring the carriage
around. Mrs. Brewster was done up in her Sunday best, her
hat an extraordinary concoction of feathers and fruit, which
somehow suited her. Her cloak was worn and threadbare,
but carefully brushed for the occasion, although it appeared
to be missing a button. Antoine was an entirely different
matter. He looked as if he were on his way to court. His
cane had a silver handle, his beaver hat was of the finest

quality, his coat was made from a thick worsted wool, and he had a decidedly sour expression on his face.

"I find it most absurd, this," he said, his nose in the air. "It is not right, being commanded to attend the church or lose my job. I nevair attend the church. Nevair!"

"Maybe something will brush off on you then," Mrs. Brewster snapped. "It's about time you repented your sins, and there's no better place for it than church. But I'll be sorely surprised if half the village girls don't take flight when they see you. Maybe God will strike you down with a lightning bolt before you can step inside and frighten them all out of their wits."

Antoine gave her a filthy look, but he only sniffed and turned away. Hannah looked down at the ground, trying not to smile, but that was a mistake, for she could not help but notice Antoine's feet. They were unusually small, and encased in boots which sported both tassels and spurs. She had to squeeze her eyes shut and pray for self-control, for the sight of Antoine adorned as a dandy was too much for her.

Galsworthy, on the other hand, was dressed in his usual somber manner and was unadorned. He stood off to one side, well away from Antoine: matters had not improved in that direction in the least. Peace was a tentative thing at best, and Hannah could only wonder when the next explosion would be. As for Mrs. Brewster, gone were the clothespins in her cap, and her dress had undergone a noticeable improvement: Hannah wondered what Galsworthy would do if he ever suspected Mrs. Brewster's interest in him. Knowing Galsworthy, he would run fast and furious in the opposite direction, for he considered it most improper for servants to engage in matters of the heart. It was a good thing that he had no idea of what was transpiring in his mistress's bosom, for he would be truly shocked. But that was a matter she intended to keep to herself. Still, it was most appropriate that she was being sent off to church, and given what Peter had implied about her ungovernable nature, he clearly thought she was in need of cleansing. He was absolutely right.

She was pulled out of her reverie by the sound of the carriage pulling up, Wesley happily ensconced on the box next to Peter, and she gathered the little group together and herded them off for their dose of religion.

* * *

The parish church of Kirby was a warm, cozy structure, an amalgam of architectural styles. They entered through the church porch and Peter led them directly up the stairs to the loft, which led Hannah to believe that Galsworthy must have whispered a word in his ear, for she had neglected to mention that there was most likely a private family box upstairs. It was not the sort of thing Peter could be expected to know: she doubted there were many churches in Jamaica, certainly not any with private family boxes, for who would there be to sit in them?

She and Wesley and Peter sat in the front pew, looking down over the nave, and Galsworthy, Mrs. Brewster, and Antoine sat behind them. The bright winter sun streamed hazily though the leaded glass windows, and as Hannah's eyes adjusted, she could make out various monuments and statutory tombs placed along the arched walls. She realized that they most probably contained the remains of past members of Peter's family, and she saw that he must be thinking the same thing, for he was looking at them with an expression of displeasure.

It was a most attractive church: there was a wonderful painting over the stone pulpit of the Last Supper, and in the west corner was a Norman font. The pews were boxed, and mostly full, and Hannah could instantly see the level of poverty to which Peter had referred, for the people were shabbily dressed and most were thin. She saw heads turn and look up, and she smiled warmly, hoping they were giving the impression Peter had desired. She knew that there would be no question of their identity and wondered what the villagers could possibly be thinking.

There was a rustle of robes and the vicar appeared, an older man with deep lines in his face and thin gray hair through which his scalp showed a shiny pink. He immediately began the service, and Hannah relaxed into the familiar ritual.

"The Lord is in his holy temple: let all the earth keep silent before him. . . ."

The words washed over Hannah, and she automatically made the correct responses, but her mind was on other matters, for exactly a week ago she had been installing her family at the Red Lion, certain that their life together was at an end. It had been a week since she had first laid swollen

eyes on Peter Frazier and lost her senses. It had been a
week of pretending that she hadn't, that she felt only as
grateful as any poor relation would feel toward her benefac-
tor, that she was interested in nothing more than teaching
him how to be an earl. It was all lies, of course, and both
she and God knew it.

"Almighty God, who seest that we have no power over
ourselves to help ourselves: keep us both outwardly in our
bodies and inwardly in our souls . . ."

That was the perfect prayer, thought Hannah, praying
very hard. Even now she could feel Peter's presence beside
her, the warmth of his body radiating into hers. She stole
a look over at his bowed head. It was a mistake, for all she
wanted to do was reach her hand out and touch those silky
golden strands, rest her head against that strong, broad
chest.

What had happened to the Hannah who tried so hard to
be virtuous and pure of thought? She seemed to have gone
to some other place, leaving behind this wanton version. It
was really no wonder—perhaps it was inevitable. Hannah
had inherited her mother's nature, that was all there was to
it.

She'd only just realized how serious the situation was,
how deeply she'd been hiding these terrible tendencies from
herself: look at how much she secretly looked forward to
her riding lesson, despite how much she loathed the actual
process. It was obviously because despite her fear, she antic-
ipated the moment when he lifted her onto Justine's back.
She waited for the feel of his hands encircling her waist,
lifting her effortlessly into the air. She was always too emotionally fraught by the time the lesson was over to feel anything but relief when he lifted her down again. But it did
not take her long to recover, for every evening she looked
forward to placing her hand on his arm and walking to the
dining room with him, feeling the subtle movement of hard
muscle under her fingers.

"Dearly beloved brethren, the Scripture moveth us, in
sundry places, to acknowledge and confess our manifold sins
and wickedness. . . ."

Hannah began privately confessing for all she was worth,
and by the time Absolution rolled around, she was more
than ready for it. "Please, Lord," she silently entreated.

"Please help me to control my baser nature. I truly don't mean to feel this way, but I cannot seem to help myself."

She tried hard to concentrate during the sermon, but she quickly realized that the vicar, for all of his good intentions, was inclined to ramble on in an obscure fashion. Not all vicars were born to be orators, she knew, but it was a pity that this one didn't realize his limitations. She automatically reached her hand out to quiet Wesley's wiggling, which seldom worked for long, but she noticed that when Peter shot Wesley one very long, eloquent look, he instantly stilled, gave Peter one long, equally eloquent look in return, and grinned that irresistible toothless grin.

"As most of you are aware . . ." the vicar said, leaving off his scholarly drone and assuming a normal tone of voice, and Hannah's attention returned to the pulpit, ". . . the ninth Earl of Blakesford is dead. I do not like to mention his name in this sacred place, but as he has a successor, who is here with us today," and thirty-odd necks craned to look up at them. "I make an exception. The new earl assures me that there will be changes made. Some of you have already met and spoken with his lordship in his daily travels about the countryside. He has been to many of the farms and seen the state of things. He particularly asked me to tell you that he wishes to offer work to any of you willing to apply for a position. I urge you to search your hearts and attempt to find forgiveness in them for the past sins his family has committed, for his lordship says he is dedicated to improving your situations. Now, to move on. . . ."

Hannah stole another look at Peter. His face held no expression, but there was something in the way he was sitting, the set of his shoulders, that told her he was deeply uncomfortable. It was little wonder. The poor man was entirely unaccustomed to being on display. He would have to become used to it, though, or he would never go on in society. And then there was also the fact that the thirty-odd pairs of eyes fixed on him were not precisely what could be called warm.

When the service was over they filed out into the March sunshine and shook the vicar's hand. Peter attempted to speak to a few of the people, but most turned away, avoiding him altogether. It appeared that the vicar's plea had fallen on deaf ears. Mrs. Brewster went off to chat for a short time while they waited to one side, and then they all climbed back into the carriage and returned to Longthorpe.

"Only four women applied for work, my lord," Galsworthy pronounced dolefully, entering the library with his silver tray. "I took the liberty of hiring a maid for Miss Janes, over her protest."

"Very good, Galsworthy," Peter said, looking up from his papers. "What was Miss Jane's protest, may I ask?"

"She felt that as she had not previously had a maid, she was not in need of one now, nor does she have an extensive wardrobe to justify the extra help."

"That will be remedied shortly," Peter said. "I am delighted that you prevailed."

"I always prevail in matters of correctness, my lord."

Peter smiled. "I imagine you do, and it is my good fortune to have you here to see to such matters."

Galsworthy cleared his throat. "If you do not mind my speaking, my lord, there is one small matter I wish to address."

"Certainly, Galsworthy," Peter said, accepting the glass of sherry that Galsworthy had poured for him. "Speak away."

"There were inquiries made, my lord, regarding Miss Jane's presence here."

"Inquiries, Galsworthy?" Peter said, raising one eyebrow. "What sort of inquiries and by whom?"

"By the women seeking employment, concerning your arrangement, my lord. There is a certain amount of skittishness. I was able to offer reassurance that all is correct. However, the situation is delicate . . ." Galsworthy trailed off.

"What would you have me do, Galsworthy? I cannot see any other sensible solution than to have Miss Janes here. I realize that it might look a bit odd, but as I intend to marry some suitable woman or another, it will shortly become a moot point."

"Ah . . ." Galsworthy said, considering this. "I see."

"How very astute of you," Peter said, trying to curb his annoyance, for it was not Galsworthy's fault that people had a prurient curiosity. He supposed a certain amount of it was justified, given the habits of his late relative. Nevertheless, the general reaction after the church service that morning had bothered him, and he hadn't been able to shake his frustration.

"Tell me, Galsworthy, did suspicion of my character drive all of these applicants away again, or do we now have a skeletal staff?"

"We are possessed of a chambermaid, a housemaid, and a laundry woman who will also work as a scullery maid. I trust your lordship approves. Mrs. Brewster observed the proceedings and pronounced the women of good character."

"I imagine she considers them of far better character than myself. I tell you, Galsworthy, legacies are not all they're cracked up to be. It's a damned inconvenience taking on someone else's reputation. The people need work desperately, and yet as you've seen, most of them won't come near the place, nor speak to me. I did, however, manage to hire a groom, two stable-hands, and a footman. The groom is aged, the hands are no more than children, and I am afraid the footman is without a foot, but I am sure you can help him along. It appears that we are going to continue to be shorthanded until the village decides that I am not a pariah. And that will not be until I find some way to dispel the lingering impression my cousin has left. Galsworthy, sit down for a moment, will you?"

"Certainly not, my lord. That would not do at all."

"Very well, stand. I should like to ask you something, for your observation might prove useful in this matter. You knew my cousin, did you not? Miss Janes has told me of the arrangement her mother had with him, so you need not feel you must be tactful."

"I would not say that I knew him, my lord. I opened the door and served at meals."

"And looked after Hannah, and later Wesley."

"Miss Janes," Galsworthy said, "was sent away immediately after Mrs. Janes began her association with his lordship. His lordship did not care for Miss Janes's presence."

"Oh?"

"Miss Janes was rather outspoken in her opinion of the arrangement, my lord."

"At the age of nine?" Peter said with a degree of surprise.

"Yes, my lord. Her attitude did not sit well with the earl."

"I see," Peter said with a grin. "No, I cannot imagine it did. Well, that explains a few things. So Hannah was banished from the house. Was she happy at her school, Galsworthy?"

"I cannot exactly say, my lord. I did not see Miss Janes again until she returned home to help her mother in her time of need. She never spoke of her experiences away."

"And when she returned? What was it like then?"

"It was a delicate situation, my lord."

"I congratulate you, Galsworthy. You dodge questions very well. I can see where Hannah has learned the art."

"I do not feel I am at liberty to speak of personal matters pertaining to my previous employer, my lord."

"I understand. However, given that Wesley is a child fathered on Mrs. Janes by my cousin without benefit of wedlock, I believe we can dispense with delicacy and go straight to the facts. Tell me, what was your opinion of my cousin's character?"

"If you must have an answer, it was very low, my lord, although it is not done for servants to form opinions of their betters."

"Oh, for the love of God, Galsworthy, please let us drop all this correctness just for a few moments, shall we? I get enough of it from your mistress. I am trying to extract some necessary information from you, and you are making the process very difficult."

"Very good, my lord, but one must fall into good habits, which only come with practice. However, if you insist that I speak candidly, I will tell you that the previous Lord Blakesford was not a nice man, nor was he generous. Mrs. Janes lived in dread of him once she realized what he could be like and the cruelties of which he was capable."

"What sort of cruelties?" Peter asked, playing with a paper knife.

"Suffice it to say that he broke Mrs. Janes's spirit, my lord. She was a vivacious woman, not possessed of a contemplative nature. She was most distressed when her husband died, and when she discovered that she had spent what he had left her, she did not know how to go on. The earl led her to believe that he would keep her well. He did, for a time. And then he began to accuse her of things in bouts of petty jealousies."

"And?" Peter said impatiently.

"In short, my lord, Mrs. Janes was often unable to go out of the house for days at a time for fear of showing her face."

"I see," Peter murmured calmly enough, but his face had darkened ominously. "Go on, Galsworthy."

"Mrs. Janes discovered she was with child. It is a miracle that she stayed that way, given what happened when she told his lordship. But after that night, Lord Blakesford never came again. Nor did any money."

"And what happened? How did Mrs. Janes make ends meet?"

Galsworthy looked extremely uncomfortable. He went so far as to shuffle one foot along the top of the carpet.

"Come along, man. Very little surprises me, and it will go no further."

"Mrs. Janes was a woman who needed companionship, my lord. As I said, she was of a vivacious nature, and gentlemen enjoyed her company. But as the years passed, times became more difficult, and the gentlemen did not come by as often. Mrs. Janes became despondent and found her solace elsewhere."

Peter rubbed his brow. "Mrs. Janes did not die of a wasting disease, then."

"Mrs. Janes mistook the French window in her bedroom for the door, my lord."

"Oh, dear God. Oh, dear, dear God." He leaned his face into his hand for a moment, then looked back up at Galsworthy. "Hannah was there at the time?"

"She was, my lord. It was unfortunate that she was the one to discover her mother's body on the pavement. It was not an easy time for her. But then, life for Miss Janes has never been particularly easy."

"So I am gathering. But that will change. I swear that will change. Hannah deserves a great deal more, and I shall see that she has it."

"I imagine that Miss Janes will make you a very fine housekeeper, my lord."

Peter gave him a keen look. He had the feeling that despite being shortsighted, Galsworthy was too observant by half, and yet he was stung by the unspoken insinuation. It seemed that even old Galsworthy thought him some kind of moral degenerate. "Must I explain to you as well that

Miss Janes will come to no harm at my hands? I have the highest regard for her and want only what is best for her."

"Forgive me, but what is best, my lord, is that her reputation remains unsullied in every way. Next to that is her happiness. I would not want her to lose the first in order to have the second. It has been known to happen."

"Galsworthy, what are you saying?" Peter asked sharply.

"You have better eyes in your head than I, my lord. I can only hope that your good sense prevails."

Peter, shaken, was about to take Galsworthy's head off, and then chose to keep his peace, for he really was not sure what Galsworthy had meant. "Have I? I begin to wonder. And speaking of eyes, I think a pair of spectacles would be in order for you, Galsworthy."

"Spectacles, my lord?"

"Indeed. I am sure they will improve your eyesight tenfold. Take yourself down to the doctor tomorrow and have him see to it. He can send me the bill."

Galsworthy bowed. "You are most thoughtful, my lord. I have not been able to afford spectacles."

"Mere practicality, Galsworthy. If you are to supervise a staff you ought at least to be able to see what you are doing."

"I can see what is under my nose. But as you say, my lord."

"Exactly, Galsworthy. As I say."

"And when does the footman begin, my lord?" Galsworthy said, effectively silenced on the subject.

"He ought to be arriving at any time. I don't think he will be able to serve at the table, for he uses a crutch, but there are other things he can do perfectly well. He went back to Kirby to collect his things. A room will need readying downstairs, for I don't think the attic quarters will do for him."

"Very good, my lord." Galsworthy left as quietly as he had come.

Peter scowled, feeling like a small boy who had just had his hand slapped when it had strayed too near the sweet tray. And deservedly so, for where he had not yet done anything truly improper, it wasn't as if he hadn't thought about it more times than he could count. He could see that it wasn't going to become any easier, living with Hannah. Church hadn't helped one iota, for instead of having saintly thoughts, he had found himself concentrating on the sweet lithe body seated next to him. He wondered what God had thought about that and found he didn't much care.

But he was concerned about what Galsworthy thought, and it seemed that Galsworthy must have realized that he was mightily attracted to Hannah. Galsworthy was right: it was not in any way fair to Hannah to risk her happiness just because he was a man tempted by her fire. If Galsworthy could see it, then who was to say who else might? He would have to put an end to the situation, and short of sending Hannah away, the only solution was to stay completely away from her, for both their sakes.

There were the fields to be tilled and sown, and fences and roofs to be mended, and paperwork—there was all sorts of paperwork that needed doing. That would take up a good portion of time just by itself.

And then in April he would go to London to find a wife. And while he was at it, he would find a husband for Hannah. Now there was an idea—that would put an end to any temptation for once and for all. A nice correct vicar, perhaps, or a steward—yes, that was it, for he needed a steward desperately. She could go off and live in a cottage with her steward, and they would only see each other very correctly on Sundays at church, or maybe every now and then just in passing.

Peter groaned and pressed his forehead into his hands. It sounded like a life made in hell.

"My lord, it is not right, I cannot go on like this, *absolument pas*! It is more than I can bear!" Antoine minced fretfully about the library, waving his hands about.

Peter sighed heavily, for he really didn't know if he could go through this exhibition again. It was being given for the third time in as many weeks, and he had the performance down exactly. He wondered if Antoine deliberately greased his hair for these scenes, or if he always wore it so.

"Monsieur Antoine," he said wearily, "I have explained it to you. As I often do not come in from working on the estate until late, and as I then have further work to do, I prefer to have a simple meal on a tray in here. I cannot contend with all this rich food you like to produce."

"And the mademoiselle?" Antoine said, pulling himself up indignantly. "It is necessary that she must eat in her chambers, or in the nursery with the child? I am to live the rest of my days preparing the rice pudding and bread in milk?"

"Where and what Miss Janes decides to eat is entirely up to her."

"Bah! She eats like a little bird. I send the food up, most of it comes down again. The only one who eats properly is the boy, and I was not trained to cook for infants. As for the Galsworthy and the others, they eat what Madame Brewster orders, and it is plain, plain, plain! *Alors*, his lordship, now there was man who knew his food." Antoine drew a deep breath, but Peter was just not prepared to go through part two of the recital.

"Monsieur Antoine, I am sorry if you feel unappreciated. Maybe when I acquire a wife your talents will be better utilized. Then again, maybe not. I have no intention of stuffing myself like a Christmas goose until I can no longer move of my own accord, which is how you would have it. And while you are in here, I would thank you to cease stirring up trouble with the staff. We need every one of them, and throwing insults about only creates disharmony. It is also unnecessary to mock young John about his infirmity. He does his best to get about and do his job, and I think you might try to be more charitable. I really will not tolerate willful cruelty: ridiculing John is exactly that. And I do not want to hear one more time that you have hidden Galsworthy's spectacles. Aside from it being an idiotic thing to do, he needs them for his work. You know perfectly well that he is as blind as a bat without them."

"Bah, the Galsworthy has been carrying tales again. He does not understand the *blague*. He is a stuffy old man. If he is so blind without them, then he should not take them off when he rests. And as for Madame Brewstair, I would have you know the woman is a witch, always bent over her cards and potions. It is evilness, my lord. She torments me with stories of blackness and misery in my future."

"Monsieur, I really do not want to hear any more of this tonight. I really do not. Please remove yourself so that I might return to my work."

"As you wish, my lord, but I warn you now, I cannot suffair much more ill-treatment. One day you will look up and Antoine will be gone. Poof!"

"That's fine with me," Peter said, bending his head back to his work. There was one loud sniff, and Peter was left alone.

He picked up his pen, then put it down again and rose, walking over to the long window. The narcissus had come up and they spread over the lawn as far as the eye could see. During the day they made a cheerful display of yellow and white, but now, as dusk drew down, they appeared almost ghostly. Brilliant streaks of red and violet marked the sky and the evening star shone brightly against the sapphire. A lake glistened in the distance, and beyond that one could see a small pagoda perched on the hillside. It was a most attractive view, and one he had grown accustomed to admiring alone. He had, in fact, become accustomed to doing a great many things alone, and although he had never needed other people around him for entertainment, he found that all this solitude was beginning to wear on his nerves.

Oh, he took pleasure in Wesley's company and their occasional travels around the estate as Wesley helped him see to things in one capacity or another. Wesley had taken instantly to the steady little pony Peter had bought and went everywhere on him. Fortunately for Peter's peace of mind, Wesley had quickly learned to ride, unlike his sister, who could scarce tell one end of a horse from another.

If he were to be completely honest with himself, that was really the cause for his feelings of isolation. He missed Hannah. He missed her silliness and her prim conversation that usually ended up veering in completely the other direction. He missed the delight she took in small things, and her completely natural behavior—when she wasn't remembering to be a lady. He found himself aching for her and did his best to disguise the fact on the occasions that he did see her. He had tried to behave in a casual fashion, to be polite, slightly distant, just as he ought. Galsworthy had relaxed his constant vigil, which meant Peter must be doing the job correctly.

But it was not easy. It really was not. From where he stood he could see the flower beds where Hannah had been working earlier. He had gone immediately in the opposite direction. He often went out of his way to circumvent her on the occasions that he spotted her in time. It was growing ridiculous. But April was nearly with them, and with it came the Season. Where he had not looked forward to finding a wife, he was now beginning to think it might be his only hope for sanity.

11

I'm now no more than a mere lodger
in my own house.
——Oliver Goldsmith,
The Good-Natured Man

The end of March brought the promise of true spring, but
the pleasure Hannah usually took in this burgeoning season
was not with her this year. She did not know exactly what
was wrong with her, only that she had not been feeling quite
herself. If truth be told, she had been on edge and snappish
and thoroughly miserable.

It had rained earlier, a heavy downfall, and Hannah had
to pick her way around the puddles that had sprung up
everywhere. She hadn't been to visit Mary for a number of
days and she felt guilty. Instead, she had stayed close to
Longthorpe, digging in the gardens, hoping for a glimpse of
Peter. But she had not been rewarded. It was not surprising—she rarely saw him anymore.

She knew he was distracted, and she could not blame him:
there were the fields to plant, and although the villagers came
out to help, they did so with heavy suspicion. Peter was trying
to manage the process practically single-handed. On top of
that, she knew there was his shipping business and the matter
of a large and valuable cargo that had just come in, which
normally he would be overseeing himself.

It was just that she missed him. She hadn't realized how
much she had come to enjoy his company, his teasing, his
lighthearted laughter. There was a void in the house without
it. Hannah picked up her pace as if she could walk Peter
out of her thoughts.

"Johno is nearly back to his old self, Hannah, and isn't
it one of God's miracles?" Mary hung the kettle over the

fire, then carefully lowered herself into the kitchen chair. "Every day he looks better, thanks to the medicine, bless his lordship's good heart. And the food you've been bringing doesn't hurt."

Hannah smiled. "The children have already put on weight, and you're looking better yourself, Mary. That new baby that you're soon going to have will be all the healthier for your eating properly now."

"Yes, indeed, and I'm grateful for that, although it seems to me that you have lost some weight, my girl, and the bloom is off your cheeks. And you haven't been to visit me for a full week. So what have you been doing? How are things really, up at the big house?" She propped her elbows on the table and prepared to listen. She wasn't about to tell Hannah that Eunice Brewster had been by twice already and gleefully filled her in on the progressive decline of both Lord Blakesford and Hannah.

"Well, let's see. Nothing much has happened. Mrs. Brewster follows Galsworthy about like a devoted dog at the heel, and he doesn't seem to mind the attention. Actually, I think it is good for him. He's been looking after other people for so long that it's time someone paid attention to him. Antoine is being his usual tiresome self, but everyone just tries to ignore him. The staff have been wonderful."

"And Eunice tells me that the house is coming right back to life."

"Yes, we have nearly the whole place open now. It's been quite amusing, actually. We go from room to room like a royal procession, with Galsworthy at the head, me behind, then Mrs. Brewster, and finally the housemaids. I listen while Galsworthy prescribes, and Mrs. Brewster issues orders to the maids. Galsworthy is very happy. He's quite accustomed to grand houses, you know, as he was in service at one for years. I think he's thrilled to be back in a position worthy of his talents. Really, why he's put up with us for so long is beyond me, as there was nothing grand about our house, and certainly nothing proper once the earl appeared."

"Well, it's a lucky thing for his lordship that Mr. Galsworthy has come to Longthorpe. I've heard the word about the village that he's a fine and respectable man."

"And a storehouse of knowledge. It's been fascinating, learning about some of the pieces and the paintings. And what Galsworthy doesn't know I can look up. The library is full of books on the subject. Mrs. Brewster said the old lord thought of nothing else but adding to his collection of objects. Do you know, Mary, I have become very fond of Mrs. Brewster. She's as odd as they come, but she is very caring."

"Eunice has a good heart, she has. I'll tell you, Hannah, there were times she kept a family from starving, slipping food away from the house right under the earl's nose. I think it gave her pleasure to cheat him, he was that dreadful to the poor countess."

"I cannot think why she stayed on after Lady Blakesford died," Hannah said, pouring the boiling water over the herbs that Mrs. Brewster had sent along for Mary.

"Eunice says she stayed only to look after the two boys," Mary explained. "But it didn't do any good. Their father treated them something dreadful, and the one ran off and joined the army, and the other ran away to the Continent somewhere, just as soon as he could. It didn't surprise a soul when the first died and then the second. It all started with those twins being mixed up, they say, one an angel, the other the devil. The devil won out, and life hasn't been the same in Kirby since."

"Well, just so you know, this Lord Blakesford is descended from the angel, who was his grandfather. Lord Blakesford told me all about it."

"Is that so?" Mary gazed at her with great interest. "Now, that's news that people will be wanting to hear. They've been wondering just what the connection was. Eunice was not clear on that point herself."

"Well, I wish you would tell her and everyone else, for the poor man is at his wit's end with trying to help people who won't be helped, and even when they do accept his help, they haven't a nice thing to say to him about it." She strained the tea and set a cup before Mary.

"Thank you," Mary said, then went straight back to her recital. "It's true that evil is a hard thing to break free of, and it's been that all right. People are superstitious around these parts, and rightly so." She lowered her voice. "Did anyone tell you what happened the night the old lordship died?"

Hannah shook her head.

"The sky lit up with thunder and lightning and then the

hail came down, heaven's wrath to be sure. After that not a single soul would go near Longthorpe, and the vicar wouldn't let the body pass over the church wall. And then do you know what happened?"

Hannah shook her head with sheer amazement.

"On the third day the body just plain vanished. No one knows how. Eunice told me when she brought the chicken that night. 'Mary,' she said, 'it was the devil come to take away his handiwork.' And Eunice would know if anybody would, for she knows all about that sort of thing. Protected by the good Lord she is. And Billy Hubbins and his sister swore they saw the devil's carriage riding across Milton Field that evening, carrying his lordship away."

"Really," Hannah said with fascination.

"Indeed. Eunice said she's heard of it happening before. We had a celebration that night, we did, for at long last the earl was dead, and to anyone's knowledge, there weren't any more of them. But then the new lordship shows up the next morning, just like clockwork, and what are people to think? You can't really be surprised they haven't come leaping around to the idea. Now mind you, it doesn't hurt that he's been three Sundays in a row to church now, and you and young Master Wesley and the household with him. And it also hasn't hurt that he's given money to the church, for the work started this week on the tower that cracked—and there's another thing. Do you know when it cracked?" Mary paused for dramatic effect.

"No, when?" Hannah responded politely.

"Hit by lightning the day the twins were christened. Now how is that for showing you the way things have been?"

"It is interesting. But still, Lord Blakesford has nothing but Kirby's good at heart. . . ."

"That may be, but you need to learn patience, my girl. Like I keep telling you, it will take time for people to believe in him. You can't undo overnight the mischief that's been in the making for fifty years. Now, they do say his lordship has the common touch, riding about and inspecting the lands. No lordly airs and graces, and I found it so myself, the day he came to visit and I didn't know who he was. I give him the benefit of the doubt myself, and I've told you that too. Look at my new roof! A blessing that, I say. My Sam will be most surprised when he comes home and finds there is no gale blowing through the house. Now what I am wanting to know is how you are brushing along with his lordship? Anything new on that front?"

"No," Hannah said with a sigh. "It's all exactly the same. He's nothing but correct. In fact, I think he's half-forgotten I exist. He practically looks right through me."

"And why are you looking so downcast, may I ask? Isn't that what you wanted, a nice correct lord?"

"Oh, Mary, what am I to do?" Hannah couldn't keep her misery to herself another moment. "I'm the one who can't seem to keep my thoughts in the right place. It's disgraceful, the things that go through my head."

Mary grinned. "Sounds mighty interesting to me."

"No, I'm serious! And the worst part . . ." Hannah bowed her head in shame.

"Come, girl, you can tell me."

"The very worst part," Hannah said tightly, "is that I think his lordship knows it." She blinked back tears.

"Now, how would he know? Is he a mind reader?"

"No . . . he practically said as much. I think he believes I'm going to go the way of my . . . my mother." Hannah stared at the floor, wiping her eyes with the back of her hand.

Mary glared. "Does he indeed?" she said indignantly. "And how dare he think such a thing, may I ask? Why, you're the purest, sweetest, most virtuous girl that ever was!"

"No, I'm not. I'm not at all. Look at the wicked thoughts I have. I don't know what to do, I really don't! He's going to be marrying soon, and bringing a wife home, and I can't—"

"Marrying?" she said, cutting Hannah off abruptly. "This is news. And whom might he be marrying, may I ask?" Mary looked extremely disapproving.

"I don't know, and neither does he. He just needs a wife. As soon as the spring planting is finished he's going up to London to find one."

"What, like picking a turnip? That's the most foolish thing I ever did hear."

"Not as foolish as saying that he'd marry the first eligible woman to show up on his doorstep to save himself the trouble of looking. He made that bad-tempered announcement last week when he came in from the fields. I think the truth is that he's nervous about mingling in society, Mary, and I don't blame him. I'd be nervous too if I were in his shoes. I haven't seen enough of him to be able to give him any more pointers about proper behavior, and he's bound to make a cake of himself one way or another. He doesn't know the first thing about correct forms of address, or precedence, or even how to dance. I was to give him lessons in that as well. But there hasn't been time for it. And now he has to find a proper wife, so he doesn't have much choice but to go up to London."

"And what's the matter with you, may I ask?" Mary said bluntly.

"Me? What do you mean?"

"I mean that he could marry you, couldn't he? You're eligible, and you're not just on the doorstep, you're already inside the door. He'd save himself more than trouble."

Hannah paled. "Mary, what can you be thinking? He couldn't possibly marry me. Not possibly! What a ridiculous notion!"

"Why? It's clear as day that you're in love with the man."

Hannah put her cup down with shaking hands. "What would make you think such a thing?"

"My dear girl, it's written all over your face. Now, don't go taking a start over the matter. What did you think it was that's been worrying at you? Indigestion?"

"Oh . . . oh, no. Oh, you don't really think . . . Oh, Mary, that's even more wicked than just having lust!"

"Hannah, girl, there's nothing wicked about it. It's the most natural thing in the world to be thinking this way about the man you love. Do you think I don't feel the exact same way about my Sam as you feel about his lordship? Why, I've been pining for him all these months he's been gone. It's just what I told you when we first met, Hannah Janes. There's not a thing wrong with wanting, just so long as you have a ring on your finger before doing."

"But . . . but you don't understand! Peter can't marry me. He knows that as well as I do, not that the idea has crossed his mind, but even if it had, which it wouldn't, there are things he doesn't know, things that would make it impossible."

"Such as what?" Mary said, fixing her with a stern eye. "Come now, Hannah, out with it. You haven't been silly and gone doing things you shouldn't?"

"Oh, no," Hannah said, coloring. "No, of course not. It's nothing like that."

"Well, then. That's all that matters."

"But it isn't, Mary," she said, moving quickly away from the subject. "He has to marry well, a proper lady. It is part of his obligation. I am just saying that I would not be suitable in the least."

"I think that's a load of piffle. And anyway, look how he was raised, you told me so yourself."

"Yes, but he has come a long way since then. I am sure he will have no trouble at all finding a wife. After all, he is handsome and titled and he is rich."

"And you speak as if the man has no heart, nor the right to a wife who loves him."

"Oh, Mary I don't mean to; it is only that he must be sensible. He knows where his duty lies. And it is very wicked of me to have fallen in love with a man who is soon to be someone else's husband."

"Wicked, my foot. If I know anything about it, he's probably pining just as bad as you are."

"In that you are very wrong, Mary," Hannah said, managing a smile. "I told you—he pays me no attention in the least. And when he does, he is bad-tempered and abrupt. I don't think that is the behavior of a man who is pining."

"And that shows just how little you know," Mary said, but her words went unremarked, as Wesley came bursting in through the door with Frankie just then, and some plea about a baby sparrow that had fallen from a tree, and Wesley absolutely had to take it home.

"Oh, please, Hannah, it can live in the day nursery," Wesley panted.

"The mother won't be taking it back, miss," Frankie pointed out. "It'll just waste and die, or some critter will get it."

"Yes, all right, Wesley," Hannah said. "Put it in my basket then, and cover it with the cloth. I had best be on my way, Mary. I don't want to be getting lost in the dark."

Mary grinned. "You see, you need to master the horses. How are the lessons coming?"

"Oh, it's the same old thing every day. Justine is brought out, the groom helps me on, we walk around the courtyard while I clutch at her mane and say prayers, and then I climb down again, no better for the experience. I cannot believe old Hopkins hasn't given up on me, but he is determined that I shall learn. He says that Peter has commanded it."

"It will be easier on you than walking this distance all the time."

"I don't mind, Mary. At least when I'm on my own two feet I know I am not going to run away with myself."

"I don't know about that, my girl. It seems to me that you've been running in all sorts of directions, and most of them in circles. Mind what I said to you now. And don't you go being a stranger, Hannah Janes. Frankie, go upstairs and see if your brother is awake. Miss Janes has left a cup by the hearth for him, and you can make sure he takes it."

Hannah said good-bye and left. But as she walked home she heard almost nothing of what Wesley was saying to her as he hopped along beside. She was so deeply wrapped in her confusion that she almost did not notice the carriage that bowled along the main road, nearly knocking her into the ditch.

Hannah, startled, looked after it for a moment, then looked down at her cloak, which had caught the worst of the mud sprayed from the passing wheels. She sighed heavily, then realized that Peter would probably not even notice, even if he were at home. Love? How could she possibly be in love with a man who hardly knew she existed? The entire idea was absurd. She called Wesley out of a puddle and continued on her way.

"Now, Pamela, my pet, you just be sure you mind yourself when we arrive," Lady Chandler said, adjusting her bonnet as the carriage moved down the Longthorpe drive. "You have a tendency to prattle when you're nervous. Just let me take care of the excuses. We've left it late enough in the day so that his lordship will be forced to offer his hospitality. After all, he cannot expect us to go on to Lincolnshire at this hour, now can he?"

"No, Mama," Pamela said, fiddling with her bodice. "Oh, look, here we are now. Oh, dear me, it is magnificent. Oh, but Mama, are you quite sure we are not overstepping ourselves?"

"Nonsense, child. A Chandler never oversteps. Where is your confidence? I declare, my pet, you cause me dismay. Now chin up, you are about to meet your destiny."

The destiny to which Lady Chandler was referring had

just at that moment come out of the front door, and Pamela
had a terrible sense of déjà vu, for her last target had appeared similarly from his house and had worn the same
expression of disbelief on his face when he had seen her.

"Miss Chandler?" Peter said slowly, as she descended
from the carriage. "What, may I ask, are you doing here?"

"Oh, la!" said Lady Chandler, descending after her
daughter and pushing her to one side. "Lord Blakesford!
Oh, you poor dear man, how horrid for you, we did think
we ought to stop and offer our condolences. Oh, my apolo-
gies, for we never expected the roads to be quite so bad. I
meant to say, here we were on our way to Lincolnshire to
visit my sister and thought only to pass by to offer you
support in your time of trouble, and what should happen
but we became mired and now the hour is impossibly late!
Of course you will be able to put us up for the night, but
isn't it always the way? Oh, how I do wish they would do
something about the roads. You remember my daughter,
Pamela, of course. Now, my dear boy, you must tell me
everything, for it must have been the most awful shock,
learning about your cousin and the sudden succession. And
here you are, with all in your hands. Oh, dear, dear, and
so unprepared." She took him by the arm and steered him
back through the door. "My dear boy, where is the butler?"
she asked querulously, handing her cloak to Pamela. "I am
desperately in need of refreshment . . ."

Peter could not quite believe it. He really could not. Of
all the people in the world that he could not bear, Pamela
Chandler took the prize. Lady Chandler managed to eclipse
even Pamela, not an easy feat. And now here they were in
his front hall at five o'clock in the afternoon, uninvited and
entirely unwelcome, and there wasn't a blessed thing he
could do about ejecting them.

"Please, won't you come into the library where it is
warm?" he asked as civilly as he could manage. And seeing
that Galsworthy had emerged from the back he said, "Galsworthy, would you take the ladies' cloaks? And if you
please, bring some . . . some refreshments?"

"Would you like me to speak to Monsieur Antoine about
dinner, my lord?" Galsworthy asked, his face unreadable.

"Oh, yes, I suppose so. And you'd best tell Mrs. Brewster

to have two bedchambers prepared. Lady Chandler and her daughter will be stopping for the night.''

"Very good, my lord." Galsworthy moved away, and Peter went into the library with as much enthusiasm as he would feel facing a firing squad.

"Oh, it is such a pleasure to see you again, dear Lord Blakesford," Pamela trilled, as if their last meeting had not been an unmitigated disaster.

"Is it?" Peter said dryly, leading them into the room. "I really don't know what to say. Lady Chandler, perhaps you would like to take the seat nearest the fire?" He noticed that Pamela had instantly gone to inspect the paintings hanging on the walls. Knowing her, she was more impressed with their value than their beauty. "Miss Chandler?" he said. "Won't you sit as well?"

She started, and Peter was delighted to see a momentary flash of embarrassment. "Oh, yes, thank you so much, Lord Blakesford," she said, simpering, and Peter felt quite sick. "You have always been more than considerate. I shall sit just here, near my mama. Oh, what a very pretty marquetry desk you have. Such fine work is not often to be seen." She removed her bonnet and delicately arranged her blond curls as she spoke. "Goodness, it was a horrible journey. The roads are simply appalling."

"What a shame," Peter said without inflection.

"Now," said Lady Chandler, who had finally finished her own grooming. "You must begin at the beginning, Lord Blakesford. We were all so surprised to see the announcement in the paper, naturally, and you must have been equally unprepared. What exactly was it that happened? I had no idea your dear papa was ever in line . . .''

Peter gritted his teeth and wondered just how long he could go on without saying something unforgivable. He could not afford to offend Lady Chandler, for the news of that would be all over town in a matter of hours, and he needed his reputation intact, at least for the moment. He endured sitting there while Lady Chandler and her daughter polished off the tea that Galsworthy brought in, and he knew he'd have to last at least through dinner, but any longer than that might create serious problems. One could only hold one's tongue for so long.

And then the door flew open, and he saw the answer to his prayers. Wesley stood there, a small, chirping, feathered thing held close in his hands, his sister standing behind him in the hall, facing the opposite direction and wiping mud and rain from her face and cloak. He wanted to collapse with laughter. Nothing could have created more of a pleasing contrast to the artificial Pamela and her impossible mother.

"Look, Peter!" Wesley said with satisfaction, not noticing either visitor. He gingerly uncovered his hands. "Frankie and I found a baby bird, and it is to be mine, Hannah said so. I brought it home in a basket, and I am going to make it a nest in the nursery. What shall I feed it, Peter? Do you know what they eat?"

"I don't, although you might ask Mrs. Brewster, for she tends to know about that sort of thing. But I do think you ought to take it upstairs quickly and make a warm place for it."

Wesley, still oblivious to the two women, who were staring at him with astonishment, dashed away. Hannah did not have the same luxury. She turned as Wesley scampered around her legs, only to see Peter standing there, grinning at her. That made a change, as he hadn't given her a single real smile since the night he had accused her of having passion.

"Good evening, my lord," she said with as much dignity as she could summon. "I trust you are well this evening." She mopped at her face again.

"Well?" he answered quizzically, trying terribly hard to contain his amusement, for the streaks of mud on Hannah's face struck him as being adorable. And she looked so indignant, a mood that he knew was dangerous, but a mood he had become fond of despite himself. Hannah had turned indignation into a positive art. Oh, lord, how he had missed her. It had been hell staying away. It would continue to be hell to stay away. But in this moment, under these circumstances, Hannah appeared a godsend, and he could not help but feel a large measure of delight.

"Yes, well. 'Are you well?' That is the usual polite greeting, or are you staring at me so because of the state of my clothes? I had thought you didn't mind the sight of mud. It was something to do with wallowing with pigs, I believe."

Peter burst into laughter. "Hannah, you are incorrigible."

"And you were not nearly run down by a speeding carriage and splattered from head to toe. I have only the one cloak, my lord, let alone one life, and I thoroughly resent your amusement."

"I beg your pardon," he said, attempting to sober.

Hannah was about to grant him that pardon when a face appeared behind him, a most familiar face. It was a face that had caused her extreme unhappiness and one that she had hoped never to see again. And yet there it was, gazing at her stonily and with negative intent.

Pamela Chandler had not changed over the years, Hannah thought in that dreadful frozen moment of recognition. She had merely hardened. And Hannah could see that she had hardened far beyond the cruelties she had been capable of perpetrating at the school they had attended together; indeed, from the look in her eyes, Pamela looked capable of true violence. Hannah drew in a long slow breath, trying to gather her wits about her, knowing the attack was imminent.

She was right. Pamela emerged from behind Peter's left shoulder. "Goodness, who ever would have thought it," she said. "Why it's . . . let me think. Ah, yes. It's little Hannah Janes, isn't it? And you haven't changed a bit, now have you?" She looked Hannah up and down, and Hannah knew exactly what she was thinking.

"Hello, Pamela," Hannah said in as controlled a fashion as she could manage.

"The two of you know each other?" Peter asked in surprise.

"Oh, yes," Pamela cooed. "We were at school together, isn't that right, Hannah, dear?"

"Yes, that is right," Hannah said, the memories flooding back unbidden, unwanted. The torment that Pamela and her group of friends had rained down upon her had been something she'd sworn she'd forget once she'd left the school. But it had stayed with her nevertheless, the belittling, the nastiness, the malicious gossip, most of which was true.

"I find myself amazed," Peter said. "Hannah, Lady Chandler and her daughter will be joining us this evening."

"Will they?" Hannah said through the stone that had settled in her chest.

"Yes, we are, and if my bedchamber is ready, I should like to change my clothes," Pamela said, brushing at her skirts. "I am sure that I must be the most frightful sight, stained with travel as I am." She deliberately cast a look of disgust at Hannah's cloak. "Perhaps you will be so kind as to show my mother and myself to our rooms?"

Hannah took her cloak off and handed it to Galsworthy, who had magically appeared at her side. "Certainly, Pamela," she said. "I would be pleased. If you will just bring your mother along, I shall take you up straightaway."

"The blue stateroom and the green-and-black bedroom have been prepared, Miss Janes," Galsworthy murmured. "I shall have your cloak attended to immediately."

"Thank you, Galsworthy," Hannah murmured in reply, astonished that she could speak at all. But she squared her shoulders and set her chin. She'd just have to find a way to get through, that was all there was to it. But she could only hope that this was not to be a protracted stay. She really did not know how much she could bear of Pamela Chandler and the bitter memories she brought along with her. And she also didn't know how much Pamela was capable of keeping to herself.

12

Was there ever such a cross-grained brute?
—Oliver Goldsmith,
She Stoops to Conquer

"Really, Mama, can you believe it, that dirty little Hannah Janes, here at Longthorpe? It is simply too much. I wonder how she ever found the position? I will wager his lordship doesn't know anything about her disgraceful past." Pamela fussed with the silk flowers at her waistband.

"I cannot say, my pet, but I shouldn't let it worry you in the least. You can dismiss her immediately you are married. Yes, that is perfect," she said, examining her reflection with satisfaction. "Who knows, perhaps old Lord Blakesford took her in—he'd finished with the mother, why not have a romp with the daughter?"

"Oh, Mama!" Pamela gasped, one hand flying to her mouth in scandalous delight. "You don't think . . ."

"How am I to know? Now come along, dear. Let us not dawdle. Lord Blakesford is sure to be waiting anxiously. I thought he looked most pleasantly surprised to see you." She looked around the handsomely furnished room with its antique brocade draperies, state bed, and tapestried walls. "Yes, this will do nicely when I come to stay, my pet, although I do think the hangings need replacing. I would prefer them in pink, I think, or perhaps lavender. I shall have to think on it. Do come along, Pamela dear. We have only tonight to make an impression, and we ought not waste another moment."

She sailed down the hallway with Pamela hurrying along at her heels.

"Oh, but the sauces your chef produces are beyond one's wildest dreams, my lord," Lady Chandler said, stuffing a

mouthful of prune soufflé covered with a brandy cream into
her mouth. Peter, watching, thought that mouth might
never close, full of food or no. She had devoured virtually
everything that had been brought to the table, rolling her
eyes and smacking her lips and shoving food into her mouth
as if she would never eat again. She was the most disgusting
person Peter had ever had the misfortune to observe at the
table, and he wondered what Hannah was thinking.

But Hannah had no intention of letting anyone see what
she was thinking. She kept her eyes down through the entire
meal, and as Pamela and Lady Chandler had completely
ignored her in favor of fawning over Peter, she was not
pressed into conversation.

"And then I said, 'Why, Duchess, you are so droll. Do
tell us all another, for I haven't laughed so hard in an age,'
and she obliged. . ."

It did seem fairly apparent, Peter thought, that Hannah
had no fondness for her old schoolmate, and as far as he
was concerned, that only reflected Hannah's good taste. But
he didn't like seeing her so pale and drawn. Thinking about
it though, she hadn't looked well for some time now. There
were new hollows in her cheeks and dark smudges under
her eyes as if she hadn't been getting enough sleep.

"Pamela and I spent the month of March at Hapslong
Abbey with Pamela's dear friend Caroline Fox-Lyons. She's
now the Countess of Roxbury, of course, although I worry
that the marriage was ill-advised, as Roxbury is so much
older . . ."

And just what she deserves, Hannah thought, remembering Caroline Fox-Lyons very well. She and Pamela might
have been twins, for they were two of a kind, petty and
nasty. Caroline had been the one to take the scissors to her
own Sunday dress and blame it on Hannah, who had been
severely punished and lectured about jealousy in front of
the entire school. She glanced over at Galsworthy, who was
staring into space, but she could tell by the expression on
his face that he thought Lady Chandler exceedingly vulgar.
The woman had not given Pamela a chance to open her
mouth, so Galsworthy had not yet had a chance to see that
the daughter had inherited most of the mother's sterling
qualities.

"You really must come up for the Season, Lord Blakesford. Lady Jersey is giving a ball in a fortnight, and from

all I have heard, it will be the most enormous crush. We have received our invitations, naturally, and are in the throes of planning what to wear. Dear Pamela has always looked so attractive in pink, don't you think? It is quite her favorite color, isn't it, my pet? Now I have always been better suited to blue . . ."

Peter looked over at Hannah, wanting to laugh, for she had an expression of supreme resignation on her face. She was not attending any more than he was. In fact, she seemed to be lost deep in thought. It was just as well, for Lady Chandler made one's brain ache. He found it hard to believe that she was as well-connected as she was, although he seemed to remember that she came from one of the Stavordale branches—or was it the Strathspays? He never could seem to keep these things straight. And of course Chandler was with the foreign office, and quite well liked. Peter couldn't help but feel sorry for the man, being saddled with a wife and daughter such as these two.

Lady Chandler continued to move her mouth, and the words kept pouring forth, but since they had no real sense or substance, Peter simply nodded his head, drank the very good claret that Galsworthy had produced, and wished for the morrow when he could watch their carriage barreling away.

"And how is the dear marquess?" Lady Chandler trilled. "Lord Blakesford?"

"I beg your pardon?" he said, jerked out of his ruminations. "The marquess? What marquess?"

"Why, Seaton, of course, silly man."

Peter's back stiffened with alarm. This direction of conversation could only lead to trouble, and he foolishly hadn't thought to anticipate it. And sure enough, Hannah's head had shot up, and her eyes were fixed on him with definite curiosity.

"As far as I know he is well, thank you. And your husband, Lady Chandler? I haven't inquired after him. He is well?"

"He is as busy as usual. But then you would understand that well enough, given your own father's career—"

"Indeed. And how is your sister, Lady Chandler? She is well?"

"Oh, how kind of you to ask! Alicia is ailing, I am afraid.

Ague, you know. She has always been plagued by it. The Lincolnshire winter brings it on."

"I am so sorry. I find the cold difficult to tolerate myself. Perhaps she will improve now that the warmer weather is here."

"There is that, and then the Season cheers her up enormously. I always wonder how I survive the rest of the year, although I must say, the autumn was considerably enlivened by the news of Seaton's secret marriage. We were all so surprised to hear of it, and the fact that he had a child. Well!"

The woman was like a dog with a bone, Peter thought with an internal groan. She could not be shaken. "I am sure there will be many more interesting things to come along, Lady Chandler, than that."

"Oh, I daresay, although you must remember that Eliza was Pamela's companion, and so dear to us, so we take a keen interest, naturally. Now tell me, how is dear Eliza? I haven't heard a thing since Pamela was up at Seaton with you—when was it? Ah yes, back in February." She beamed.

Hannah slowly put down her fork. She had been doing her level best to ignore Lady Chandler's prattle and Pamela's insidious looks, but this last piece of information regarding Peter sent her head spinning. Seaton? It was one of the largest estates in Great Britain. And Peter had been there with Pamela? She couldn't understand it—it made no sense. He didn't move in those circles at all, knew almost nothing about them. But Lady Chandler clarified everything practically in the next breath.

"Pamela had such a wonderful time, did you not, my pet? She told me that dear Eliza was expecting again. How perfectly thrilling. And will you stand as godfather to the child?"

"I have no idea," Peter said with a dangerous glint in his eye. "I haven't been asked."

"Oh, but I thought you would be the perfect choice, seeing that you and Seaton are as close as brothers."

"This seems an extremely personal topic of conversation, Lady Chandler."

"Nonsense. There's no need to stand on formality with me."

"Formality, Lady Chandler?" Peter asked, wanting very much to tip his wineglass into her ample lap. "I would hardly call asking you to refrain from discussing my personal life standing on formality."

"Now, now," Lady Chandler said, looking up and down the table to see if there was any delicacy she might have missed. "There's no point getting top-lofty with me, my boy. Don't forget that I knew your father, and never a nicer man, I've always said. He was never overtaken with his position, and he gave the loveliest parties. Do you remember the ball he had at Government House when we were passing through Jamaica on our way to Honduras for Freddie's posting? I remember how you waltzed with dear Pamela—"

"Lady Chandler!" Peter roared, putting his glass down so hard that the wine splashed up and over the side. "If you please! Could we keep to the weather or someone's health?"

"Why, Lord Blakesford!" Lady Chandler said with astonishment. She turned to her daughter, who was staring at Peter with wide blue eyes, her hand over her mouth. "Pamela, my pet, now don't upset yourself. I am sure Lord Blakesford did not mean to be rude. It is just that his nerves are overset. No doubt it is his recent bereavement."

Pamela was not the least upset. It was just that she had had occasion to be at the receiving end of Peter's temper once before and had no wish to repeat the experience. "I think, Mama, that it might be time to withdraw," she said in a whisper. "Perhaps a nice game of whist would be the thing?"

"I beg your pardon," Peter said icily. "It has been a long day. I think I would rather retire. But please, do entertain yourselves however you wish."

"Oh, la, you are so kind, Lord Blakesford. Come along, Pamela, dearest. Perhaps you would ask the butler to bring in the tea tray? My compliments to the chef. Superb, simply superb. But you could use a few footmen, my boy. Your butler is slow on his feet. And I really don't think you ought to have your housekeeper sitting at your table. It isn't fitting in the least." She rose with an effort and sailed out of the room in the same grand manner as she'd sailed in, Pamela behind her.

"Hannah," Peter started to say. "I am sorry about that . . ."

Hannah just stared at him. She couldn't have moved in that moment if she'd tried.

"Lady Chandler is a bit much to take, I do know. But not to worry, she will be going away again tomorrow. Hannah? What is it? You look upset."

"Upset?" she said, struggling to get the word out, but once she had started, the words came pouring out, along with a torrent of anger and hurt. "Upset, my lord? Oh, not at all. I am not upset in the least. Why should I be? I have only been lied to, misled, made to look like a complete fool. Why should that upset me? I should be quite accustomed to it by now."

"Oh. That. Hannah . . ." Peter felt quite helpless, for he really did not know what to say. "I have not meant to mislead you in any way. Truly, I haven't."

"Shall we call it an error of omission, then?" she said, glaring at him. "Or perhaps you needed some amusement— yes, that must have been it. You thought to amuse yourself by playing the ignorant provincial. But you did not grow up with the pigs, my lord, did you? Far from it. You were dancing away the nights at Government House, weren't you? And what, may I ask, was your father's illustrious position that he was giving balls there?"

Peter rubbed the corner of his mouth with one finger. He had a treacherous desire to burst into laughter, for the situation was truly ridiculous. "He was, ah . . . he was the chargé d'affaires for the Crown."

"He was the *chargé d'affaires*? Oh . . ." Hannah swallowed, trying to recover from this extraordinary piece of information.

"Yes. He was."

"In which case," she said, her anger incited to flash point, "I am quite sure he would have taught you to use your cutlery properly. I am also sure that he would have taught you all the correct forms of address."

"Yes, naturally."

"Which you would know in any case, given that you've been rubbing shoulders with marquesses for half your life."

"Seaton is my business partner," he said. "We became friends at Cambridge."

"Cambridge? You went to Cambridge?" Hannah's head was reeling.

"Yes, and before that I was at Eton. I was miserable there. I think I indicated that to you some time ago."

"Yes, but I thought . . . I thought you must have been referring to some school in Jamaica . . ."

"There were none, or at least none that would have done, and so I was sent to England for my later schooling."

Her eyes turned to stone as something else occurred to her. "I suppose you speak French," she said, thinking of how she had corrected him in that as well.

"As it happens, I do, fluently. It is useful when one is involved in international trading. It is Mrs. Brewster who can't wrap her tongue around the language."

"Oh . . ." Hannah said, her hands gripping the edge of the table so hard that her knuckles had gone white. "Oh, you are truly monstrous."

"Why, Hannah? Why does that make me monstrous? It is not as if you ever asked me."

"But you let me think . . . Oh, why, Peter? Why have you played with me so?" She angrily wiped away her tears with shaking fingers.

Peter stood and came around to her chair. He took her by the shoulders and turned her to face him, tilting her chin up to meet his eyes. "I have not been playing with you, Hannah. If you remember, it was you who leapt to the conclusion that I was a barbarian, you who announced that I would have no idea how to go on as an earl. I am at fault for not having corrected you immediately, but you were so determined to believe the other. And I confess, you were so sweet about offering to help that sheer curiosity compelled me to go along with you."

She just shook her head.

Peter took her hands and lifted her to her feet. "I did not ever outright lie to you, although I must confess that your misassumptions did give me cause for amusement, and I badly needed a distraction at the time. But Hannah, I was never amused at your expense, and quite honestly, I'm not sure I would have been able to convince you to come and live here if you hadn't thought you could be useful in that particular fashion. I never meant any harm by it, I swear it to you." He took her face between his hands and stroked the wisps of hair off her cheek with his thumbs. "Please believe me."

Hannah wanted to—she wanted to with all her heart.

And then the door burst open and Peter abruptly released her, but not before Pamela had seen them.

"Oh!" she cried. "Oh! I just came to get my shawl! I think I left it on my chair; I'll just take it . . . Oh, oh dear. How perfectly appalling!" She grabbed up her shawl and went running out of the room, white-faced, but with two angry red spots on her cheeks.

"Oh, hell," Peter said softly.

Hannah looked at him and then at the empty doorway as the truth finally hit home. She felt as if she had been hit in the stomach, for she suddenly wanted to be sick.

"Please excuse me, my lord," she said and started to turn away.

"No, Hannah, wait." He reached out for her arm, but she wrenched away from him.

"I would thank you to let me go," she said quietly. "And I would also thank you not to touch me ever again."

"Hannah, for the love of God—"

But she was gone. Peter picked up the nearest glass and flung it against the wall, and at least it gave him the satisfaction of shattering into a hundred tiny bits.

Hannah reached the safe harbor of her room, but once she was there she didn't know what to with herself. She was cut through so deeply with pain and humiliation that she had to concentrate just on breathing. Her thoughts were in turmoil: it wasn't just that Peter had deceived her, had allowed her to think he was one thing when he was something else entirely. It wasn't just that; what was almost worse was Pamela.

She walked over to the window and looked out across the vast stretch of lawn, her arms holding tight around her waist as if that might stop the sickness inside. It was more than obvious that he had invited Pamela to visit with the intention of making her his wife. He might not like her particularly; that much she had been able to divine, knowing him as she did—or had thought that she did. But he didn't care whether he liked his wife or not. All he cared about was expediency. Well, let him have his expediency and regret it for the rest of his days, for Pamela Chandler was going to make his life a sheer living hell, and her mother would merely provide the sauce. Hannah would laugh herself silly watching his misery, and well deserved it would be.

Peter would be a rich man with a noose around his neck so tight that he'd wish he had never heard of the earldom or Pamela Chandler.

Hannah flung herself on the bed, not even bothering to take her dress off as any proper lady ought. What did she care about being proper? She was nothing more than a silly little fool in Peter's eyes. It really didn't matter anymore. And anyway, he'd find out about the rest of it from Pamela fast enough. Pamela had always taken great delight in slandering Hannah to anyone who would listen. And from the expression on Pamela's face, Hannah was going to pay and pay dearly for the near-embrace that Pamela had witnessed.

She buried her face in her pillow and cried her heart out.

Pamela waited inside the library door for Peter to emerge. Her mother had gone to bed, thinking there was no use staying up if Lord Blakesford was not going to be up with her. Pamela had had the same thought and had only thought to collect her shawl before retiring. And then she had stumbled across that disgraceful scene in the dining room. It was more than obvious to her what had been going on under everyone's noses. It was absolutely appalling, and oh, how typical of Hannah. Well, if Hannah thought to snare Lord Blakesford she would have to think again. It would not happen. Pamela would see to that. Lord Blakesford would be put in the way of things soon enough.

Peter came out of the dining room more than ready to put an end to the disastrous day when he heard his name softly called across the hall. He looked over only to see Pamela lurking in the shadows. Peter crossed over to her. "Yes, Miss Chandler?" he asked wearily, not really up to another scene, but thinking he might be able to avert some gossip Pamela might attempt. "Is there something you need?"

"Lord Blakesford, I must talk with you. It is urgent."

"My dear Miss Chandler, if this is regarding what you just saw, let me assure you—"

"Please, my lord. I cannot speak of this in the hall. Will you come into the library with me? I would not want to be overheard. It is a private matter."

Peter sighed and held out his arm, letting Pamela go ahead of him. He left the door halfway open, then walked over to the fireplace and looked down into the flames, his back deliberately turned to her. "Very well, Miss Chandler, speak. But make it short. I am tired, and I would like to go to bed. You and your mother have already prolonged the day by arriving on my doorstep, and without an invitation, I might add, which seems to be a habit of yours." He turned and looked at her coldly. "And since you have seen to it that there is no one else to hear, then let me say this to you. If you have come to Longthorpe hoping to spin your wiles on me, then I might just as well tell you that you have wasted a trip. I thought I made my feelings about you and your tactics perfectly clear two months ago when you arrived at Seaton to make mischief between the marquess and his wife."

"Yes, you did," Pamela said, flushing uncomfortably. "But this time it was my mama's idea, and I could not dissuade her."

"That much I believe. So. What was so urgent that you had to pull me in here alone at this late hour? If you intend to cry seduction, it would be a very grave error."

"Oh! No, that was not it at all," Pamela said, but wishing she had thought of it. "It is about Hannah Janes," she said.

"About Hannah. And what do you think you can tell me about Hannah that I do not already know, Miss Chandler?"

"A great deal, I imagine, for I doubt she has told you the truth about herself. Hannah Janes was the talk of the Ladies' Academy. It wasn't just her appalling behavior. It was the other situation." Pamela pursed her lips and cast her eyes down in an effort to appear modest.

"What are you going on about now?" Peter asked impatiently. "If you are trying to tell me that Hannah's mother was my cousin's mistress, I know all about it, Miss Chandler. I know all about Hannah's past."

"You do?" Pamela was completely taken aback.

"Yes, I do. And I am surprised that you would bring up such a thing at all—not that it is any of your business."

"Well, it is not as if it wasn't absolutely shocking, but I suppose it was to be expected, given her mother's history. But I ask you, sending the daughter to the Academy to mix with decent girls? It was a miracle we weren't all tainted, it really was."

"Oh, really? Actually, I think it a small miracle that Hannah managed to escape being tainted by you. I am sorry to disappoint you, Miss Chandler, but you have failed to shock

me despite your best efforts. Wasn't that the purpose behind this little talk?"

"I thought it was my duty to let you know what you have
taken in," Pamela said, flushing angrily.

"Actually, Miss Chandler," Peter said tightly, "I know
very well what I have 'taken in,' as you so kindly put it.
And I am very happy to have Hannah here, as it happens.
She and her brother have given me a great deal of
pleasure."

"Her brother?" Pamela said, her hand creeping over her
mouth. "What brother?"

"Her brother, Wesley Janes."

"But . . . but Hannah has no brother. I am quite certain
of it."

"He is only seven, Miss Chandler. He would have been
born after Hannah left the Academy. You cannot be expected to know everything."

"Oh, my word!" Pamela said, her mouth falling open.
"So it was true after all. . . ."

"What was true?" Peter asked, completely fed up with
the conversation but wanting to be sure he had wrung every
piece of gossip out of Pamela so that he would know what
to forestall.

Pamela sank into a chair. "Oh, my lord! This is most
terrible! I should have realized that Hannah would do
nearly anything, but I cannot believe that she has deceived
you this badly."

"Miss Chandler, what are you babbling on about?"

"Hannah has lied to you most grievously."

"I beg your pardon?" Peter said, just about at the end
of his rope, but alarmed by the expression on Pamela's face,
for he saw that she was truly shocked. "And how has Hannah lied to me, might I ask?"

"But . . . but . . . oh, dear. Oh, dear, how very awkward
this is. Hannah—you must know that she was sent home
from the Academy. There was talk about what had happened, for one of the girls had listened at the door when
Hannah was called into the headmistress's office. And we
all knew that she had not been well for some time, but no
one thought anything of it until the other happened. And
then . . . well."

"Well, what?" Peter said in a biting tone.

"Hannah had been seen coming out of the stables a num-

ber of times, and everyone knew how terrified Hannah was
of horses. It was a great joke about the school that she
might hate horses, but she didn't mind the keeper. Like
mother, like daughter, they said. You could see it in the
way she walked, the way she looked, as if she was just
waiting for an invitation. It was positively shameful."

"Miss Chandler, I really do not think I can tolerate another one of your ramblings. Please. Just get to the point."

"The point? But I told you. It was Hannah's lewd behavior with Perry Deacon, the stable boy . . . I suppose it was
really no surprise that she should get with child, although I
was never completely sure of the story until now. I thought
she must have been sent home simply because her behavior
was so disgusting."

"Get . . . get with child?" Peter said incredulously. "Are
you out of your mind?"

"I know it is shocking, my lord. But that boy Wesley is
no more her brother than I am."

"Miss Chandler," Peter said, barely containing himself,
"I would normally not bring this up, but if it is the only
way to still your tongue about Hannah, then I shall. You
already know of the arrangement between my cousin and
Hannah's mother. Well, Wesley is the result of that relationship. That is why he is here. Hannah brought him to
me when she could no longer support him herself."

"Oh, how wicked of her to pawn her child off on you!"

"I beg your pardon? Did you not hear what I just told
you?"

"Well, of course I did." Pamela's eyes narrowed. "And
thinking about it, I'll wager that's the same story the two
of them fabricated to pull the wool over everyone's eyes.
Selina Janes would have claimed the child was hers to protect Hannah from disgrace. After all, Selina was already
disgraced, wasn't she, so what difference would it make to
her? And now Hannah thinks to take advantage of the old
deception and pass the boy off as a relative of yours so that
she can worm her way into your house and bed. No doubt
she wants the same arrangement with you as her mother
had with your cousin. It is a disgrace!"

"And that is the last straw, Miss Chandler," Peter said,
his eyes snapping with hard anger. "You will leave. You
will be gone from this house first thing in the morning, for
I do not have the stomach for you and your wretched gossip

another minute. I really haven't. Please, remove yourself from my sight before I do something I regret, such as strangle you." He turned his back on her, his fists clenched by his side.

He heard only a little gasp, then running footsteps and the sound of the door banging closed. He put both hands on the mantelpiece and bent over, breathing hard. It took him a few minutes before he had enough command of himself to straighten.

He felt like a man twice his age, his bones heavy and cold, his heart sick. He wouldn't believe it. He couldn't believe it of her, that she was even capable of doing something so deceitful. Not Hannah. It was Pamela Chandler, after all, who had come up with the story, and she was as malicious and unreliable as they came. And yet a seed of doubt had been planted in his mind, and he could not shake it loose.

Peter sat down very carefully, going over everything Hannah had said and done since he had first met her that fateful night—that one night when she hadn't known who he really was. She had been so sweet, so responsive, and she had given herself in full measure to that shared embrace. Had that been the behavior of a virgin? Or, more to the point, had it been the behavior of a woman of experience?

Thoughts of Amelia came crowding into his mind. Amelia the beautiful, with a complexion like a rose and a sweetness to match. Amelia the faithful, who had sworn undying love to him, who had lain in his arms night after sweet night and stolen his heart along with his soul. Amelia, who had promised to marry him until her husband had come to fetch her and bring her back to England. Oh, yes. Amelia had wept and begged to stay, but he'd had no choice but to let her go. It had taken him a long time to recover from Amelia.

And Hannah? He wasn't quite sure why it hurt so very much, the thought that she might have betrayed him. It wasn't as if there had ever been anything between them. He had been so careful to see to that. Perhaps that was it— it was because he had been so damned busy minding his duty this time around, careful to do the right thing, that he felt so devastated. Was it really possible that she had been deceiving him all along? The pieces were there if one chose to look at them in that light—the contradictions and her erratic behavior at times.

And yet he was suspecting her without giving her a fair chance to explain. He would have to confront her, of course. He could not adopt Wesley unless he knew the truth, although if she had lied to him so successfully up until now, who was to say she would not continue to do so?

But as much as he hated to admit it, what almost bothered him more was the idea that Hannah had been in another man's arms, had given herself to him. That he found acutely painful, that she had given someone else what he wanted himself so desperately, that she had kissed someone else as she had kissed him that one time, that she had . . . Peter ground his teeth and squeezed his eyes tightly shut. It just hurt too much to think about, all of it. And yet, even if Hannah had not lied to him, even if she had never lain with another man, one day she would. And he would have to accept that fact.

The clock chimed three, and Peter started. He hadn't realized he had been sitting there for so long. The fire had grown cold, and he found that he was shivering.

He pushed himself to his feet and made his way upstairs, thinking that it might have been a great deal easier to be dead instead of alive and only feeling like death.

13

I find you want me to furnish you with
arguments and intellects too.
　　　　　　—Oliver Goldsmith,
　　　　　　　The Vicar of Wakefield

Mrs. Brewster was not happy. She hadn't been happy when
she had been informed of the arrival of the visitors, and she
was even unhappier now, for she had read the cards twice,
and they had said the same thing both times. In fact, if
anything, this morning's reading was even worse than that
of the night before. She'd been so sure that everything had
been progressing according to plan, so what had gone
wrong? And why was that silly little blond chit getting in
the way of what should have been the closing chapter on
full-blown love? Star-crossed, that's what they were, those
two.

She looked again at the cards and muttered to herself,
tapping them and moving them across the table. Imminent
disaster, that's what they said. Disaster, pain, and suffering.
It did not look good at all. There were certainly all the signs
of difficulties and contradictions, and the nine of spades
signifying deceit—who was deceiving whom, that's what
she'd like to know. And what the king of diamonds was
doing coming up in a spread like this—well, that was another thing she'd like to know. A dark man, nothing too
surprising in that, and honest, too. That made a nice
change. But the card sometimes meant a heritage to come,
and she was quite sure there was nothing like that afoot,
for it had already happened, hadn't it? On the other hand,
it could signify advice to be followed. Well, if people would
listen to her, they could avert all this nonsense.

The king of hearts had come up again, of course, but

with his house in shambles. Oh, that nine of spades was a terrible card, sitting where it was just next to him. Mrs. Brewster pursed her lips and wrinkled her brow, then turned up the card on the other side of the king. And here was the queen of diamonds. Now that was nice, for she was a steady one, the lady of the manor, bountiful and kind and virtuous, and levelheaded to boot. They could use some of that around the house, couldn't they just. And seeing as she was sitting right next to the king of hearts, well that meant that she was well disposed toward him, and a good counselor. Someone needed to counsel the boy, for he couldn't see what was under his own nose, God love the lad.

Well, despite the appearance of those diamonds, the cards were heavily laden with bad omens. Deceit and despair, imminent disaster, that's all there was to it. She'd have to wait and see, just wait and see. Perhaps she shouldn't be surprised, given what today marked. But that only made her feel more gloomy.

She pushed the cards together and put them in the pocket of her apron, then went to make Mr. Galsworthy his morning cup of tea. He had been most melancholy last night, and a nice cup of tea might cheer him up. "My lady!" Mrs. Brewster said with surprise as Lady Chandler came barreling into the kitchen. "Is something amiss?"

"I would like to speak to the chef, woman, and privately if you please. Leave us."

Antoine turned from the stove, where he had been sulking over the evening's soup. "You wish to speak to Antoine, madame?" he said, his little button eyes brightening. "Perhaps you have come to discuss the brilliance of my talent? You enjoyed the masterpiece I created out of nothing, with no advance notice, *non*?"

Lady Chandler lowered her voice. "It was the finest meal I have had in many a year," she said. "Absolutely inspired, monsieur. Now, I wonder if you and I could not come to a little agreement. I am sure I can better the salary his lordship gives you. What would it require to tempt you away from your position here?"

"Three hundred guineas a year," Antoine said, instantly seizing the opportunity to extort.

"Three hundred . . ." Lady Chandler made a strangled noise in her throat. But she calculated quickly, desperate to whisk this prize away from the unappreciative earl, who had had the temerity to refuse her daughter. Pamela's tearful appearance in her room last night had sent her into such a state of shock that she'd had a nearly sleepless night. The thought that owing to Pamela's incredible stupidity she might not sample Antoine's food ever again had been almost too much to bear. But then inspiration had struck.

"Three hundred guineas," Antoine repeated. "If you cannot afford me, madame . . ." He shrugged eloquently.

"I am thinking, monsieur," Lady Chandler said. After all, since it was all Pamela's fault, she would cut the silly girl's dress allowance in half . . . yes, she could find the funds. "It is done," she said brightly.

"And a trip to France once a year for my inspiration. It is very important, this."

"Yes . . . yes, very well, a trip to France."

"And I must be appreciated," Antoine added for good measure. "I have not been appreciated in my present post. It has been most distressing for my nerves, you understand."

"But of course, monsieur. You shall be idolized!" Lady Chandler clutched at her bosom passionately. "All of London will beg to come to my table!"

"I must be in command, madame. Antoine must rule absolutely, yes?"

"Yes, indeed, monsieur. You shall be king, le roy." She batted her eyelashes

"That is *le roi*, madame," Antoine said disdainfully. "Please. My ears cannot tolerate the mangling of *le français*. *Et maintenant*, I must be accommodated in luxury. My clothing must be of the finest. I have my own tailor, naturally, who will send you his accounting quarterly. And my shoemaker, he is in Paris . . ."

Lady Chandler's head nodded automatically as bills danced before her eyes. She blinked rapidly as Antoine went on categorizing his requirements, and she forced herself to remember the magnificence of his cooking and the supreme jealousy she would inspire in her friends. "Yes, yes!" she finally said, cutting off the recital. "You shall have whatever you require. Now, come along, come along. My carriage is waiting. Pack your things and do not dawdle. We head to London instantly! The Season awaits!"

Antoine regally inclined his head. "I will be with you

momentarily. I have no need to make my farewell to these fools. I bid farewell instead to pudding de riz, to boiled eggs, to . . . to unsauced chickens!" He pranced off gleefully, and Lady Chandler, who felt that she had just scored the culinary coup of the decade, marched out to the carriage, her bosom swelled with pride. Lord Blakesford would be sorry he had crossed her. Just wait until he discovered that she had stolen his brilliant chef. He would pay for having turned down her daughter. No one crossed a Chandler.

Mrs. Brewster came out of the pantry, her little face wreathed in smiles. So that was what the cards had meant by deceit and loss. She sighed happily. There was nothing disastrous in that, save for what was going to happen to that dreadful woman, who was going to be cheated blind and have her cellars drunk dry. And she deserved every minute of it, if what Mr. Galsworthy had reported back to her from the dining room the night before was true. She picked up her skirts and danced a little jig, then went to find dear Mr. Galsworthy to tell him the good news.

Hannah pulled on her cloak, which thankfully had been brushed clean of mud, and went out the door, her basket on her arm. She intended to collect eggs to bring to Mary, for she was in need of some good advice.

Wesley had gone off at the crack of dawn with Frankie, something about a fishing spot they had found, so she knew he would be occupied for most of the day, and she could have a nice long talk without fear of interruption. But she was surprised to see a carriage sitting in the courtyard, and she instantly recognized it as the one that had nearly run her down the day before. She should have known it had belonged to the Chandlers.

"So!" Pamela said, coming up behind her. "If it isn't the harlot of Longthorpe. I see you've taken your nasty deceitful ways a few steps up in the world. The earls of Blakesford are so popular with your family."

"Oh, please," Hannah said, not willing to be dragged into any sort of conversation with Pamela, most particularly not one of this variety. "I am in a hurry, Pamela. Can't you just leave me alone for once?"

"I will be pleased to leave you alone," Pamela retorted. "For your information, I am departing. I was on the point of accepting his lordship's offer, but instead I have declined. I spoke with his lordship last night. I am leaving, naturally, to spare any awkwardness."

"What . . . but why?" Hannah said, astonished, but almost faint with relief.

"I am surprised you would even ask such a thing after your performance last night. I was disgusted."

"But Pamela, you misunderstood what you saw. It was nothing at all. I was upset over something, and his lordship was being kind." Hannah couldn't think why she was even explaining. She certainly did not want to change Pamela's mind.

"It is no good playing innocent with me, for I know your game too well," Pamela said, her nose shoved up in the air.

"I don't know what you are talking about!"

"Oh, don't you? Well, to be perfectly plain, I have no intention of living under the same roof as my husband's mistress."

"His mistress?" Hannah said, taken aback. "I am not his mistress, nor will I ever be!"

Pamela gave her a look loaded with skepticism. "Hannah, really—don't tell me you have been so stupid as to hope he would offer you marriage. Earls don't offer marriage to one such as yourself. You should have learned that lesson from your mother. The tenth Lord Blakesford only wants from you what the ninth Lord Blakesford wanted from her. If you think anything else you are deluded."

"He wants no such thing!" Hannah said, close to tears.

"Oh, doesn't he? Odd then, isn't it, the way that he looks at you, the way he touches you?"

"N-no! We are friends, that is all!"

"Trust me, Hannah, that is not how gentlemen behave toward their female friends. You could light a fire with the looks he gives you. Don't think I didn't notice the minute you walked in and the way he watched you all during dinner. If he hasn't made it clear to you yet, he will soon enough. And if you are waiting until he becomes so hungry that he makes you an offer just for the satisfaction of bedding you, forget about it, for he won't. The only offer he is planning on is to make you his lover. He can't afford to do anything else."

Hannah slowly shook her head from side to side, waves

of shock sweeping through her. "No . . ." she choked. "It cannot be true. You must be lying."

"Why would I lie? I would be perfectly content to be the Countess of Longthorpe. It is everything I ever hoped for. But I would not be a laughingstock, sharing my husband and my house with his whore. I have my pride. I will not be part of such an arrangement."

"But . . . but I don't want an arrangement," Hannah said. "I don't want anything at all but to be left in peace."

"Well, if he wants you for his mistress, that is his business. But if that's not what you want, then you should pack up your bags and that . . . that boy, and be gone, because if you stay, that is what it will come to. Surely you must realize that he cannot possibly marry you? Poor Hannah. You have such high expectations for one of such low birth. Do you know, I am almost sorry for you." She turned on her heel and marched triumphantly past Hannah to the carriage. Hannah almost did not register the fact that Antoine's self-satisfied face looked out from the window. Pamela disappeared into the interior, the footman put the steps up, and the carriage clattered away.

Hannah watched until it was nothing but a small speck in the distance, then dropped her basket, picked up her skirts, and ran all the way to the Baker farm.

"Mrs. Brewster, what are you doing?" Peter asked, looking up at the little woman, who was perched high on a ladder, putting a ribbon of black silk rosettes on top of Lady Sarah Blakesford's portrait. It was the last thing he'd expected to see upon entering the gallery, but nothing much surprised him anymore, and certainly not after the revelations of last night.

"It is the anniversary of my angel's death, my lord," Mrs. Brewster said. "I always commemorate my angel's death. Next I shall go to the churchyard to cover her stone in flowers and sing hymns over her blessed grave."

"Oh, I see," Peter said absently. "That is very nice of you, I am sure," he thought to add. "I don't suppose you have any idea of where Hannah might be?"

"Well, let me see. She did not take any breakfast this morning, and Master Wesley left at daybreak, so she's not with him. We did not have our usual morning consultation as to the affairs of the household, and more's the pity, for the messier has packed his bags and departed, my lord, not that we shouldn't be celebrating."

"Antoine is gone?" Peter said with surprise, but delighted to hear of it. "Where has he departed to! And when?"

"That's the better news. He departed with that Chandler woman. Came barging into the kitchen not two hours ago, she did, and the next thing I know, the messier has his bags in hand and is out the front door with the promise of riches beyond compare. Good riddance, I say, to him and to her and that sly-boots of a daughter. Never a more demanding miss have I have the misfortune to come across. And I hope you haven't anything foolish in mind, my lord, for if ever there was one to give you misery, she would be it."

"Mrs. Brewster, I assure you that I wish nothing more than to stay out of Miss Chandler's matrimonial path. You needn't worry yourself on that score. I'm delighted to hear about their departure, and I am equally pleased to hear that Monsieur Antoine has left with them. I hope they enjoy each other tremendously, for they are extremely well suited. But I do need to know where Hannah is. I've looked high and low since I came in an hour ago, and there's no sign of her."

"It is my guess, my lord, that she is upset, if crying herself to sleep is anything to go by."

"She cried herself to sleep?"

"She did indeed, the poor lamb, for when I came up with some nice warm milk I could hear the sobs through the door, no matter how she tried to pretend otherwise when I went in."

"And do you know why she is upset, Mrs. Brewster?" Peter asked, not sure he even wanted to hear the answer.

"Well, no doubt it was the thought of you marrying that woman, and I'm sure I would feel the same if I were Miss Hannah."

"But I'm not *going* to marry the blasted woman!" Peter shouted in frustration. "Believe me, the thought never crossed my mind!"

"Well, then see that when the thought of marriage does occur that you point it in the right direction," Mrs. Brewster said tartly. "I'm fed up with all the misery running about this house. Now when my lamb is upset, she usually goes to visit Mary Baker. So if I were you and wanted to find

Miss Hannah in a hurry, which is how it looks to me, I'd take myself off down there."

He was gone without another word, and Mrs. Brewster gave a little cackle. "Well, well. And isn't it just about time?" She gave Sarah Blakesford's glazed cheek a little pat. "You see, my angel? There will soon be someone to fill your dear shoes, see if there isn't. Goodness, sometimes I think the good Lord gave all the sense to females. Well. At least we don't have to worry about the sly-boots stepping in and making a bumble broth of all our plans now do we?"

She climbed down off her perch, placed her bonnet on her head, and went off to tend to her angel's earthly resting place.

"Oh, Miss Hannah, Miss Hannah!" little Susie Baker cried, looking quite white-faced but relieved as she opened the door and saw Hannah standing there, half-bent over, her hands holding her sides. "Come quick—my mum, she needs you!" She grabbed Hannah's hand and pulled her into the dark interior. Hannah, completely out of breath, hurried as fast as she could. She could hear moans coming from the back bedroom, and the little girl stopped at the door, pressing herself against the wall. "My mum's in there," she said and stuck her thumb in her mouth.

"Thank you, Susie. Why don't you go outside now and play? I'll look after your mother. I'm sure there's nothing to worry about." Hannah waited until the child had left, then cautiously opened the door, frightened half out of her mind at what she might find.

"Mary?" she said, approaching the bed, where Mary was hunched over on her side. "Mary, what is it? What is wrong?"

Mary opened her eyes. Her face was covered in sweat and her brow was knotted. "Oh," she gasped. "Oh, thank the good Lord you've come, Hannah. The baby's coming right quick, and I don't think the midwife will be here in time."

"The baby—oh, Mary!"

"Now don't you go worrying. It's the easiest thing in the world; just get some linens from the chest and my sewing box. And you might put on some water for washing—ah!" She put the piece of knotted cloth back in her mouth and clenched down on it hard.

Hannah set straight to work, trying to be efficient, for she knew if she gave in to her panic, all would be lost. She put the water on, found the linens and the sewing box, checked the cradle to be sure it was ready to receive the infant. She squeezed her eyes shut for a moment, then forced herself to focus. She washed her hands, then wet a rag and brought it to Mary, wiping her forehead with it.

"There," she said soothingly. "There you are. It will soon be over."

Mary nodded, then let out a long low groan of pain. Hannah smoothed the wet hair off Mary's forehead and held her hand, almost crying out herself when it felt as if it would be crushed under the force of Mary's grip.

A half hour went by, and Hannah said prayers that the midwife would come, for she really wasn't at all sure she could manage on her own. But she had to be brave for Mary's sake, put a good face on the matter so that Mary would feel safe. But when the banging came at the door she jumped up from the bed and ran, wrenching the door nearly off its hinges. Only to see Peter standing there. "Oh, no," she said, her heart falling along with her hopes.

"Oh, no?" he repeated sharply, tying his horse to the hitching post. "Is there a reason that you do not wish to speak with me?"

"Yes! I . . . I mean, no. Oh, not now!" she cried. "I have to get back to Mary—she's having her baby, and there's no one to help, and I haven't the first idea!" She turned and ran back inside.

"Good God," Peter said, following her straight back into the bedroom.

Hannah looked up in astonishment when she saw him. "You can't come in here," she said.

"Can't I? I hardly think this is a time for your blasted proprieties, Hannah." He went directly over to the bed. "Mrs. Baker," he said soothingly. "It is Lord Blakesford."

Mary licked her lips. "Good afternoon, my lord," she said faintly.

"How close is the child to arriving?" he asked her.

"What, and now you're going to play at being a doctor?" Hannah asked with disgust.

"Hannah, hold your tongue. Mrs. Baker?"

"Soon," Mary said from between gritted teeth. "It . . . will be . . . soon."

"Would you like me to leave, Mrs. Baker? I am no midwife, but I can try to help."

Mary attempted a smile. "Then by all means stay. Between the two of you, someone should be able to work it out." She closed her eyes as the next contraction swept over her.

Peter waited until it had passed, then turned to Hannah. "Hannah, pay close attention, for you are going to deliver this child following my instructions."

"And what makes you think I can't manage by myself, my lord?" Hannah asked, her anger toward him resurfacing now that she did not have to worry about being alone.

"Oh, and are you now saying that you have had previous experience, Hannah?" he asked coldly.

"No . . . no, naturally I haven't, but I am a woman. I should be able to reason it out. Somehow," she added doubtfully. "Anyway, I cannot think you know the first thing about it!"

"I would hope that I know more than you, unless you have been keeping things from me."

Hannah glared at him. "I don't know what you mean."

"The devil you don't," he said, his teeth gritted nearly as tightly as Mary Baker's. "But this is most certainly not the time to discuss the matter."

"And you are one to talk, as if you haven't been keeping essential things from me, you . . . you cad!" She sponged Mary's forehead again, but her eyes blazed with fury. His mistress indeed.

"I did not get a child with a hired hand at the tender age of sixteen and lie about it," he said coldly.

"Oh!" Hannah said, the blood draining from her face. "Pamela . . . Pamela told you?"

"So. It is true," he said, his face darkening.

"Yes," Hannah said furiously. "It is true. And I suppose that has changed everything about me in your eyes?"

"I was not unmoved by the revelation, Hannah. Naturally it changes the way that I perceive you. What would you have me do? Carry on as if nothing is different?"

"Certainly not, my lord. I learned last night that you were not the person I thought you to be. It has only been confirmed for me today."

"*I* was not the person *you* thought?" he said in disbelief. "That is incredible, coming from you."

Mary, who had been largely ignoring them, shifted. "I think it is time, Hannah. The child comes."

"Oh, I beg your pardon, Mary," Hannah said contritely. "Oh, dear, what do I do now?"

"Be quiet," Peter said as Mary took a deep breath and pushed with all of her strength.

As Mary had never taken very long to have her children and had always done it with a minimum of fuss, it was not long at all before the baby was ready to make its entry into the world.

"Peter . . ." Hannah said, looking helplessly at the top of a tiny head beginning to appear. "What am I supposed to do?"

"Wait," he said, peering anxiously as the head crowned. "It will come on its own. And when it does, just support the neck and the rest will come." He closed his eyes and prayed.

Hannah was overcome. She had never seen such a sight before. The indignant face emerged and then the soft, pliable shoulders, and all at once she was holding a tiny, pink, wriggling little body in her hands. The infant gave a squeak, and then burst into full voice.

"Another boy, Mary!" she cried. "Oh, he's so beautiful! Oh, what a fine job you did! He is quite perfect . . ." She gazed down at the newborn in awe.

"Then just hand him up here," Mary said with a laugh, "and let his mother have a look."

Peter handed Hannah a blanket and she covered the child, then gave him to Mary, who took her new son and admired him happily. "Aye, he's not bad, is he? He has a look of his father about him."

"Um, what do I do about this?" Hannah asked, looking at the long twisted cord that still attached mother to child.

"You cut it," Peter said impatiently, and Mary gave a peal of laughter.

"It's what the sewing kit is for, my girl. You tie off the cord, then take the scissors and cut. There's no hurt to either of us. Go ahead now. He can't be attached to his mother forever."

Hannah swallowed, and Peter raised his eyes to the ceiling. He took thread from the basket, made two ties, and cut between them.

"And a fine father you'll be, my lord," Mary said.

"Where did you learn such things, might I ask? Most men wouldn't go near a birthing room, let alone know what to do once they got there."

"I have a friend who pulled me along to help with one of his mares."

"Well, good for him," said Mary. "There's nothing like a man who cares for his animals."

"Yes. He is a good man." Peter looked at Hannah. "His name is Edward Seaton."

Hannah, who had been admiring the newborn, looked sharply around at Peter.

"It surprises you, Hannah, that a marquess might be so pedestrian? But then, according to your rules, we peers are not meant to behave in such a fashion. We are meant to be snobs, to ignore the common people in favor of our elevated, superior selves."

"I never said that; I only wanted to help you, Peter! And you were laughing at me the entire time."

"Hannah, you took my behavior and twisted it to suit your own perverse ideas. Because I have never chosen to behave like a self-indulgent fop, you made the assumption that I had no idea how it was done."

"That is not fair, my lord. You led me on."

"And you led me on, Hannah, in a far worse way. But we will discuss this later outside, not in front of Mrs. Baker."

Mary gave them both a wry look. "I must say, it's the first time I've given birth while a lover's spat raged over my belly, although I didn't mind in the least—it took my mind off the pains. In fact, I found the two of you high entertainment."

"I am delighted we amused you," Peter said tightly. "If I am no longer needed, I will go outside. Hannah, I will wait for you to finish up in here, and then we are going to have a talk." Peter congratulated Mary on her son, then went out, quietly shutting the door behind him.

"And what was that all about?" Mary asked, putting her child to her breast and helping him to nurse. "It sounds to me as if you two have had a falling-out."

"A falling-out? It's far worse than just a simple falling-out, Mary. But now is no time to talk about it, not when you've just delivered a baby."

"Nonsense. There's no time like the present, and I've nothing better to do. Little Jamie here isn't going to say a word, now is he, and neither of us is going anywhere. Go on, girl, tell me all about it. Best to get the whole thing off your chest. It's what you came for in the first place, isn't it?"

So Hannah did. She told Mary the entire story about her parents, or at least what she knew about it herself. She helped deliver the afterbirth as she explained about Pamela Chandler and the school and the rumors and teasing. She told her all about the earl and everything that had happened since as she carefully washed the infant. She told Mary about Peter and the hoax he had put across on her, and finally, as she changed the sheets and cleaned everything up, she arrived at that morning. She left nothing out, despite how painful much of it was to speak of.

". . . So you see, Mary, it's all very terrible, and I do not know what I am to do!" She finished brushing Mary's hair and tied a ribbon in it. "There. You look very pretty."

"Never mind how I look, although I thank you, Hannah Janes. You've been a good friend to me today, helping me in my time. And despite what you might think of his lordship just now, it was good of him to be here too. A man has to have a brave heart to deal with women's work. Now, how the two of you have managed to get in such a muddle is beyond me, but I think you'd better go out there and get it sorted out. Neither of you has exactly been honest with each other. I don't know what's to be done about it now, not with all the water that's gone under the bridge, but you had better make a start, Hannah, before there's any more trouble."

"I don't know how it could possibly get any worse than it already is," she said miserably.

"But you still love him, don't you, child?" Mary said gently.

"Yes, of course I do. I mean . . . oh, I don't know, Mary! I can't see that it makes any difference how I feel, and I can't really blame him. Perhaps I ought to have told him everything at the beginning instead of leaving Pamela Chandler to do it and make it sound worse than it is—if that is possible. And now, now to know that he thinks he can make me his mistress, just because of that. Oh, Mary!"

Mary planted a kiss on her baby's downy head. "I'd stop worrying about it and go and do what you can to mend matters. And you can tell the children that they can come in and see their new baby brother."

"But what about your dinner? Who's to look after you and the children?"

"Don't you worry about us, Hannah. There's bread on the table and yesterday's stew on the fire, and our Susie is old enough to ladle it out for me and the others. I'll be up and on my feet in an hour or two, right as rain. Take heart, Hannah, girl. It will all work out somehow."

"I pray you are right, Mary. I pray you are right." She kissed Mary's cheek, admired the baby one last time, and took her leave. But despite her bright smile, her heart was heavy and there was a terrible ache in her chest as she went out to face Peter.

14

Friendship is a disinterested commerce between equals;
love an abject intercourse between tyrants and slaves.
—Oliver Goldsmith,
The Good-Natured Man

Peter paced outside the cottage, waiting for Hannah to
emerge. He was so angry he scarce knew what to do with
himself. Hannah had admitted her deception with nary a
blink, as if it had been nothing at all. She'd had the almighty
effrontery to be angry with him for a small piece of foolishness on his part, yet tear into him for questioning her on
her own appalling lie! It was almost beyond credit. But then
he'd learned that Hannah was a woman of contradictions,
a chameleon who was capable of changing from abbess into
seductress, a woman who could bring him to his knees with
frustration and leave him there dying of desire. Really, why
should he be surprised at this last piece of audacity?

The thought only made him pace the harder. He finally
fetched his horse and pulled him about with him, for poor
Rhubarb hadn't had enough proper exercise of late, and
Peter reckoned that he might just as well have company in
his pacing.

Peter had worked himself into a filthy temper by the time
Hannah emerged into the daylight. He waited while she
went to fetch the children, and he patiently waited while
Hannah herded them inside. He thought himself admirable
for his restraint as he gave her the time to settle them and
explain matters. By the time Hannah emerged for the last
time, he was ready to strangle her, for he was quite certain
that no man had ever been so badly used.

He dropped Rhubarb's reins and turned to face her

squarely, his arms crossed against his chest. "So, Hannah. What have you to say for yourself?" he demanded.

"What have I to say for myself, my lord?" Hannah, seeing his temper, which reincited her own, squared off against him. "I have only to say that you are guilty of going against your word."

"My *word*? You say this in the face of what I have just learned about you? And yet despite all of that, I have done nothing to go against my word. Not one thing!"

"But you have considered it, have you not?"

"Yes," he said with complete honesty. "I have considered it. How could I not?"

Hannah looked at him. She saw the golden locks, the sapphire eyes that had first captured her attention. She saw the man who had stolen her heart with no effort at all, and she also saw the man she now knew him to be. Pamela, despite all of her glaring faults and conniving ways, was right. Hannah had to leave if she was to escape the fate he had planned for her. And yet the thought of leaving made her feel as if she wanted to die.

"Hannah, you have the nerve simply to stand there and say nothing? I find your behavior extraordinary."

"Why?" she asked. "Do you expect me to fall on the ground and beg your forgiveness for something I could not help? I cannot do that. I will not do it, Peter, most certainly not to suit you. And you are not so pure nor saintly yourself to go about judging other people. In fact, I think you are cast in the exact same mold as your ancestors!"

"Hannah, I never claimed to be saintly, nor pure for that matter."

"Maybe not, but I did believe you were a man of your word! Just because you have discovered something about me that you find disagreeable, it doesn't mean that you can go and change our arrangement."

Peter shoved his hands on his hips and glared at her. "Hannah, I cannot credit what I am hearing! You speak as if I should take this piece of information completely in my stride, as if I should in no way be shocked or upset that you misrepresented yourself to me."

"I did no less than you, my lord, by omitting certain facts about myself."

"And yet you accepted my hospitality, you paraded your-self about as a woman of impeccable virtue, you let me believe that I had an inherent responsibility to Wesley. I would not compare the two things. I merely neglected to tell you I had been raised perfectly adequately."

"But what has Wesley to do with any of this?" Hannah said, completely thrown off the argument by Peter's last statement.

"What has Wesley to do with . . . Hannah, for God's sake!" Peter looked as if he might go for her throat at any moment. "Were you waiting for the adoption to go through before you told me the truth, when you thought it would all be safe and set in stone? And then how was I to feel? Or perhaps you were never planning on telling me: perhaps you intended to keep me in the dark. Was that it? Did you truly think I would never learn the truth of the matter?"

"What truth?" Hannah said, not sure she was comprehending anything correctly. She felt as if she were underwater and everything had distorted. "I don't understand!"

"Ah, Hannah, and you play the game so well, so damned well. I should congratulate you. But don't you think it is a bit late now to make a show at innocence when you admitted your folly earlier, no doubt in the confusion of the moment? Come, Hannah. It is a bit late for maidenly protests. You lost that right eight years ago."

Hannah stared at him, her blood running hot and cold all at once. "What . . . what are you saying?"

"I am saying that eight years ago you conceived Wesley in some torrid encounter in a stable. Need I be plainer than that? Hannah, come. It is past time for lies. Let us at least be frank with each other."

Hannah did not stop to think. She took two steps up to him, pulled her arm back, and swung as hard as she could. Her palm met with his cheek in a great crack, and the force of the blow sent Peter staggering backward.

"You wretch!" she cried, hurt beyond belief. "You idiotic blockhead! Do you believe the lies Pamela pushed down your throat because they are convenient for you? Is that why you think you can do as you please with me, since you assume I have already fallen so far?"

"What in God's name are you talking about?" Peter said, astonished by her sudden rage.

"Don't play the fool with me now, you unprincipled rakehell!"

"Unprincipled rakehell? I have done nothing . . . nothing

to earn that sobriquet, my dear girl. If anything, I have gone to great lengths to be honorable."

"Honorable!" Hannah gasped. "H-honorable?"

"Yes. Honorable. And why are we talking about my honor, when it is yours that is being called to account?"

"Oh! You are truly despicable! Very well, then, if you are so honorable, perhaps the truth of the matter is that you have decided that you want us gone, and you can think of no other way out of your promise but to accuse me of such an abhorrent thing. Well, you have nothing on the latter part to worry about, my fine lord, for Wesley and I shall be gone by morning and shall never darken your miserable door again!"

"Hannah—"

"No. I don't want to hear another word. I have been badly wrong in my judgment of you from the first, but you have opened my eyes to your true nature. I should have known; I should have been alerted by your behavior when we first met that you will play any game to work your way into a girl's heart and then take your advantage. Well, not with me, you won't. Despite what you may think of me, or of my poor mother, I will never follow in her footsteps. I will be no man's trifle. And just so you know, Wesley is indeed my brother *and* your cousin. Not that it makes any difference. Not anymore." She turned away and stormed off, hot tears pouring down her face.

"Hannah, stop," he commanded. "Hannah, wait. We have not finished."

She stopped only long enough to turn and give him a withering look. "Oh, we have finished, my lord. We have most certainly finished, for now and all time." She started off again, sick at heart and angry and violently confused, but knowing she never wanted to lay eyes on him again, not ever, not after what he had just accused her of. Oh, Pamela had done her dirty work, but Peter had found it convenient to believe her. She stumbled, scarcely able to see through her tears. And then she heard Peter coming after her, and she knew he would be upon her at any moment, for she could not outrun him.

She panicked and did the only sensible thing she could think of. She ran and grabbed his horse, who had peacefully wandered off to graze and was just ahead of her. Somehow she managed to put her foot in the stirrup and pull herself astride. She grabbed the reins up and kicked the horse for all she was worth, and the startled beast took off with a leap.

Hannah heard Peter's cries behind her, but they faded quickly, as did her momentary lunacy. She could not think what had come over her: she was atop a horse who, far from obeying her and slowing down once she had reached a safe range from her pursuer, had gone into a headlong, completely terrifying flight. They tore through the woods, branches scraping at her, her body thrown from side to side as she struggled to keep her precarious position. There were no stirrups to give her purchase, for Peter's were far too long for her legs to reach. She was not accustomed to sitting astride, nor to anything other than a gentle walk. But far worse than all of that was her terror, the mind-numbing terror that occluded everything else.

Hannah knew she was truly going to die, for there could be no other finish to this nightmare. She knew now that she'd had good reason to intuitively fear horses: had they not overturned Leopold Janes in a carriage and left her mother without a husband? And now this horse was going somehow to overturn her and leave Wesley without a sister. Her heart pounded as fast as the horse's hooves against the dirt. She did not know how much longer she could hold on. Her legs felt like rubber, and she knew she was slipping.

Hannah dropped the reins and buried her head against the gelding's neck, saying every prayer she'd ever heard and making up others to suit the occasion. And then they broke from the woods onto the main road. Hannah was about to breathe a sigh of relief, thinking they would surely stop, when she realized that the moment they had hit the flat surface the horse only picked up his pace and was now running full out for home.

"Oh, dear God!" she cried. "Please! Please help me!"

Instead of help, God sent a carriage clattering down the road behind them, which only inflamed the horse more. His nostrils flaring, saliva frothing from his mouth, the gelding shied violently, and Hannah went flying off his back. She landed hard on her side, her leg twisted under her, and she heard a horrific snap even before feeling the searing pain. She had the extraordinary sensation of all the air leaving her body, and she could not seem to pull it back in again. And then it came rushing in her nose and mouth and she heard screaming, and she wondered where it was coming from. She wished it would stop, for it went on and on and made her head ache. Her head felt most peculiar, light and dizzy, and everything seemed to be quite hazy. In fact, she thought she might be floating and it was not unpleasant.

The last thing she recalled was hearing voices over her, concerned voices, asking her questions she could not really understand. She managed to say "Longthorpe," not because it had been asked, but because it was the only word that occurred to her.

And then she heard some more screaming and decided it was too tedious to listen to, and besides, she was very cold, so she went to sleep instead.

"Oh, dear blessed Lord above!" Galsworthy wrung his hands as Hannah's still body was carried through the door on a plank by four strange footmen in livery. "What has happened? Please tell me, sir, what has happened? Surely she is not dead?"

The gentleman turned his attention from the injured girl to the distraught butler. "No, she is not dead. She was thrown from her horse and has sustained some injuries. This woman is a member of the household?"

Galsworthy nodded vigorously. "She is Miss Hannah Janes, a relation of Lord Blakesford."

"*This* is Hannah Janes?" The gentleman looked even more distressed. "I see. How dreadful. I am Seaton. Where is Lord Blakesford?"

"I do not know. He went out earlier." Galsworthy was about to expire with shock.

"Then summon a doctor, my good man, and do it instantly. Use my carriage. My wife will see to Miss Janes's immediate care. Please direct her to the appropriate bedroom. My footmen will carry the litter. And the moment Lord Blakesford returns have him sent up."

"Yes, my lord," Galsworthy said, and hastened to comply with every particular.

"Eliza, just how serious is her condition?" Lord Seaton asked his wife as soon as Hannah had been put into her bed and Eliza had the freedom to examine her.

"It is not good, but it could have been far worse, Edward." Eliza looked up at her husband gravely. "Obviously her femur is fractured, and she is certainly in shock, although I haven't detected any other injuries. Thank God she fainted when she did, for I think the pain must have been extreme. I suspect part of the bone might be pressing against a nerve. It must be set immediately. I don't suppose you've done such a thing before?" she asked hopefully. "I have never set a bone on a human."

"My dear wife, you seem to think me a positive magician when it comes to these matters. I too have set bones on animals, but I am as untried in this situation as you are."

"Well, then we shall set it together," Eliza said decisively. "An animal cannot be so very different from a person. A bone is a bone, after all."

"Yes, Eliza, I do realize that," Edward said with the shadow of a smile. "But you are with child, and I do not think you ought to overtax yourself. It takes considerable strength to set a bone—you know that."

"Edward. Stop being so foolish, for there is no time to waste. You will do all the pulling. I will merely apply the splint, but first we must find something suitable to make it with. Let me see . . ." Eliza looked about and soon located a small wooden chair, which Edward immediately pulled the legs from. Eliza found some linens in the cupboard and tore them into strips to hold the splint in place. And then Edward applied traction to Hannah's leg, slowly turning it from its misshapen position until it appeared straight. Eliza carefully placed the splint and bound it, and then she piled blankets on Hannah's torso in an effort to warm her.

"I cannot think of anything more to do," Edward said, standing back and looking down at Hannah's still, pale face. "I hope we have done enough, for if anything should happen to Hannah Janes, I suspect that Peter is going to be very unhappy—that is, if one can judge by his letters."

"I suspect you are right," Eliza replied. "How interesting that you divined the same thing as I did. He has eliminated all but the very briefest of mention of Hannah, while going on at great length about everyone else in the household, including Hannah's young brother."

Edward nodded. "Precisely. Alas, poor Peter. He has tried so hard to elude love after that disaster with Amelia Lasherby. Could it be that once again it threatens, and he is running as fast as he can in the opposite direction?"

"We shall see," Eliza said. "But you might be right, Edward, for I do not understand all this nonsense of going to

London to find a ready-made wife. That is not like Peter at all. He is a man of great sensibility, as hard as he tries to disguise the fact."

"That is exactly the point. Peter feels things very deeply, and his heart is unusually vulnerable. I have seen him in pain before, first when his parents died, his father so soon after his mother. And when Amelia left him, I have to tell you—that is not something I want to witness again. He has matured since then, of course, but I don't think he feels things any less intensely. It doesn't surprise me that he keeps himself at a distance."

"But still, Edward, a marriage of convenience? I cannot bear the idea!"

"Nor can I, and I will do everything in my power to prevent him from making such a mistake. I am no expert on love, but I know this much," Edward said, putting his arm around his wife's waist. "He is not the right sort of man to make a loveless match. It would go against everything in his nature, and eventually it would probably break his spirit, for he is also not the sort of man who would take a mistress for companionship on the side. Peter has too much integrity. Oddly enough, it is his greatest problem, his integrity. Peter expects so much of himself he is likely to drive himself over the edge."

At that moment the door crashed open, and they both looked up in surprise as a small person came flying through in a near blur and halted at the bed.

"Oh, my lamb, my poor darling lamb! It was just as the cards said, disaster! And on the very same day as my poor angel died—what are we to do!" The woman wrung her hands frantically, then stopped for a moment as she took in Edward and Eliza standing at the foot of the bed. Her eyes narrowed. "Oh. And I suppose you are the ones who did this to my pet? A fine thing to go mowing innocent people down in the middle of a public road. As if some dolt didn't try to do the very same thing only yesterday. Some people think themselves too good for the rest, don't they just, think they own the road, don't they?"

"I am very sorry that the accident occurred, ma'am," Edward said, instantly recognizing the woman as Mrs. Brewster from Peter's hilarious descriptions. "But although our carriage startled her horse, we did not strike her. She fell. With luck, Miss Janes will recover."

"It's going to take more than luck, my man, make no mistake. Now what have you gone and done to her, may I ask? What's her leg all bandaged up for?"

"It is a splint, Mrs. Brewster," Eliza said, moving over to the little woman. "I thought it best to set her leg immediately, as it did not seem wise to leave it as it was."

"And what do you know about such things, may I ask? And how do you know my name?" She regarded Eliza with extreme suspicion.

"Lord Blakesford is a good friend. He has often written to us since he arrived at Longthorpe. He has been very . . . descriptive. And as for Miss Janes, I have had some experience with looking after injured animals, as has my husband. Miss Janes has broken her limb halfway between her knee and her hip, but the break appears clean. From my examination I do not believe she has any other serious injuries, but we shall have to wait until she regains consciousness for her to tell us."

"Humph," Mrs. Brewster said succinctly, marching over to Hannah and looking down at her. She took her forefinger and thumb and pried open Hannah's unseeing eye, then put her finger on Hannah's neck and felt the pulse there. "Shock is what I'd say, and who could be surprised? Well, I am rarely wrong in these things, and I say she will live. I shall make some compresses instantly and a nice healing broth for when my lamb comes around." Mrs. Brewster started out the door, then paused and turned around again. "The cards said you were coming, but they didn't say a thing about that red hair," she said, looking at Eliza doubtfully. "And I certainly wasn't expecting my lamb to be run down like a rabbit in the road by two people who are supposed to be sensible. But never mind, what's done is done. The cards said disaster, not death, so there's no point worrying overmuch. I suppose you'll be staying?"

"Yes, if you please," Eliza said, trying not to laugh. "We will only require one bedchamber, so do not go to any extra trouble."

Mrs. Brewster gave them a long look. "Well, it's not the least bit fashionable, but why not? You brought along enough servants to make extra work as it is."

"I beg your pardon if we have put you out in any particular," Edward said with a completely straight face. "However, my staff is most obliging, largely to please their mistress. I am sure that if you ask them they would be happy to help."

Mrs. Brewster gave a sharp nod of her head. "As it should be. Now I must be off, for dear Mr. Galsworthy is fit to be tied, quite sure Miss Janes is off to the angels. Now that I've seen for myself that she isn't going anywhere for the moment, I'll just go and soothe him. And don't expect anything fancy for dinner. The messier took off today with no notice, and may that Chandler woman live to suffer violent indigestion for the rest of her days."

"The . . . the Chandler woman?" Eliza asked, aghast. "Surely not Pamela Chandler?"

"Oh, you know the sly-boots? Well, she and her god-forsaken mother dropped onto the doorstep last night without so much as a by-your-leave. They set off this morning leaving nothing but trouble behind them, for my lamb was badly overset and his lordship was in a state, and last seen he was off to find her. And that's the last heard of either of them until this calamity. And I for one would like to know where his lordship is."

As if she had summoned him with a wand, Peter came tearing into the room, thoroughly winded. "Edward, Eliza . . . what in God's name has happened? Galsworthy said Hannah had been crushed half to death . . ." He went over to the bed, his face as white as Hannah's. "Oh, God. Oh, please . . . Hannah? Hannah, wake up!" He took her limp hand in his and put his other on her brow, pushing the hair off her face. "Hannah?" He looked about as frightened and desperate in that moment as a man could.

Eliza gently touched his shoulder. "It is not as bad as it looks, Peter. Hannah has been injured, yes, but not necessarily beyond repair. It will be some time before we know for certain, but I feel that she will come through this."

"Oh, she'll come through," Mrs. Brewster added, "providing no one upsets her, if you catch my meaning. She'll be needing all her strength. A broken limb is quite enough without adding a broken heart to it." With that statement Mrs. Brewster took herself off.

Peter, frowning, looked after her for a moment, then turned to Edward and Eliza. "This is my fault, you know. I drove Hannah to it."

"You drove her to it?" Edward said. "And how did you do that? How could you possibly have driven Hannah and her horse onto the road just as our carriage came along, Peter? If anyone feels responsible, it is us, for her horse would not have shied had we not come along just then."

"It wasn't her horse, it was my horse," Peter said, pushing his hands through his hair. "Hannah took my horse: you know, the new gelding I told you I bought in Oxford. He's still fairly skittish, and Hannah can't ride to save her life." He winced. "I suppose that is all too appropriate an expression in this case."

"What happened?" Eliza asked, taking his arm and looking up into his face with deep concern.

"What happened? I don't know exactly. We had an argument. There were some angry words exchanged. I said things that perhaps I oughtn't to have. I don't know . . ." He rubbed at his forehead. "In any case, the next thing I knew she had jumped on Rhubarb's back and taken off. It could only end in disaster, I knew that. Hannah—she was like a frightened child around horses. He would have sensed it, of course, that and the fact that she had no mastery. He instantly ran away with her."

"Then it is no wonder that he shied when he saw our carriage. Oh, poor Hannah. It must have been dreadful for her."

Peter nodded. "Yes. Dreadful. I ran after her, of course, but I knew there was no hope of catching them. I just arrived home, only to hear the news. Oh, dear God, what I am going to do? Is she going to come through this, Eliza? She looks like death." He picked up Hannah's cold hand again and pressed it against his lips.

"I hope so, Peter. There is no way of telling for the moment. I imagine that she's lost some blood, and there is that to consider."

"Blood?" Peter said, going even whiter. "Where? How?"

"Internally. It is normal with a break of the femur. But with luck the bleeding will have stopped by now, as the bone is back in place. At least, that is how it tends to happen with animals. And then you keep them warm, and give them plenty of water and rest, and you let them heal." Eliza did not add that she had lost as many beasts as she'd saved, but it was harder with animals, she reckoned, for one could not reason with them as easily as with people. "The doctor should be here shortly," she added, for Peter did not look reassured in the slightest.

"Perhaps you would like to be alone?" Edward asked tactfully, for Peter did not seem to be paying much attention.

Peter just nodded.

"We shall await you downstairs. I am truly sorry, my friend. We feel very distressed that we should have been the inadvertent cause of Hannah's injury."

"I asked you to come," Peter said dully. "It was just bad luck that you happened along when you did. Really, it might have been anyone. Please, make yourselves comfortable. Galsworthy can see to whatever you might need."

Having said that, he turned away, all of his attention focused on Hannah. Edward and Eliza quietly slipped out.

Galsworthy sat at the kitchen table, his hands clenched in his lap. The glass of brandy that Mrs. Brewster had given him sat untouched by his elbow. It was all he could do to keep his composure. His poor Hannah—she had looked so helpless and small when he had gone up to see her, like a young child, lying so still in her bed, her leg all bound up in plaster. She still had not regained consciousness, but Mrs. Brewster told him that when the doctor had suggested bleeding Hannah, his lordship had erupted into a rage, and told the man he would have none of it and could take his leeches and cups elsewhere.

Galsworthy found it most edifying that his lordship had refused to leave Hannah's side, even during the doctor's examination—most improper, but one couldn't think about such things now. He really didn't know if he could bear losing her, he really didn't.

"Now, Mr. Galsworthy, you're not attending to a word I'm saying," Mrs. Brewster said, bustling about, directing the preparation of the evening meal. "You're not to worry, for dear Hannah will come through right as rain, see if she doesn't. I am taking personal charge of the matter."

"That is most reassuring, Mrs. Brewster," Galsworthy said gloomily. "But even you cannot ensure that broken bones will heal properly. And why has she not woken yet?"

"I am sure it is due to the pain. She'll come around soon enough. And look at his lordship's devotion, sitting there at her side, hour after hour. It's that touching."

"Devotion isn't going to make Hannah better," Galsworthy said bitterly.

"But who is to say it won't open his eyes to the obvious?" Mrs. Brewster said smartly, looking about at the other servants, who were all listening intently. "Maybe some good will come out of all of this, and the lamb's accident will knock some sense into his head. He surely looks as if he's had a bad shock." She smiled smugly. "We'll have a wedding yet, see if we don't."

"I don't know how you can be so unconcerned, Mrs. Brewster. Anyone would think you'd arranged the entire episode for your own purposes. Well, I for one do not like it, not with my dear girl lying up there in her bed with a broken leg. And as for this business of marriage that you keep bringing up, we all know that his lordship has his heart set on marrying one of his own kind."

"And what's the matter with Hannah Janes?" Mrs. Brewster asked, planting her hands on her skinny hips.

"Not a thing. She's a good, unspoiled, virtuous girl, not that it isn't a miracle that she's stayed that way with his lordship around."

"Now, Mr. Galsworthy, you can't blame a body for having thoughts in his head. At least he's kept his hands to himself."

"And how long will that last? It's not as if he's offered to make an honest woman out of her. And speaking of that, I'm not even sure I want him marrying my Hannah. Look at the lies he told her about himself, upsetting her as he did after all her kindness in trying to bring him up to snuff, while he played the buffoon for his own amusement. And look at that . . . that Chandler person and her daughter. If that is his idea of marriageable material, then I say Hannah is better off without him. No one has a call to go looking down their nose at Hannah Janes." Galsworthy gave an indignant sniff and pushed his beloved spectacles farther up on his nose. "No, Hannah would do better to find herself a husband who is not above the common touch. There's no need for her to go about marrying earls and being made miserable. Not that he'd ask her, which is back to the point. No, he'll just make her miserable without marrying her."

"I think you're being too harsh on the lad, Mr. Galsworthy. Give him a chance to know his own heart."

"He won't do for her, Mrs. Brewster, he simply won't," Galsworthy said stubbornly.

"Not even if she loves him?" Mrs. Brewster pulled out a

chair and sat down across from him, firmly tapping her finger on the table. "You can't have missed the fact that the girl is head over heels, Mr. Galsworthy."

"And if that is so, then all she's going to get from it is even more misery, mark my words. I am telling you, the last thing the man has on his mind is marriage, at least where Hannah is concerned."

There was a general murmur of agreement from the servants, and Mrs. Brewster aimed a crushing look at them over her shoulder. "We'll see about that," she said. "And as for the lot of you, I don't know why you're all standing around listening in on a private conversation when there's a dinner to get on the table. It also won't do to let the earl's guests go hungry. A marquess, did you say?" she said to one of the Seaton footmen who had been called in to help. "Fancy. Still, he seems nice enough, as does that wife of his. Don't you go worrying anymore, Mr. Galsworthy. I won't let a thing happen to the lamb. I have a good feeling about it all. Now, where is that boy Wesley, I'd like to know? You'd scarce know he lives here these days, not that he isn't looking happy and healthy, and that's one of them, at least."

Mrs. Brewster went back to issuing orders, and Galsworthy, feeling slightly reassured about Hannah's condition despite himself, drank his brandy, then went to attend to his lordship's guests.

Hannah opened her eyes to dim light. There was a tall figure standing in silhouette by the window. She couldn't think where she was for a moment, or what had happened, but she did know that her leg hurt most horribly and her head throbbed. She stirred, then moaned as a stab of pain flashed through her thigh.

Peter was instantly at her side. "Hannah?" he said softly, sitting down in the straight chair next to the bed and taking her hand. "Hannah, you're awake. Thank God for that. How do you feel?"

"Peter, what has happened?" she asked, her eyes trying to focus on him. "Oh, my leg—it hurts so!" She tried to shift, then gasped with renewed pain.

"No, don't move, sweetheart," he said, stroking her brow. "You must stay still. You've broken the bone, and you mustn't jar it. The doctor left some laudanum for the pain, but I'm afraid you may not have any until we are sure your head is all right."

"It hurts," she said. "But I think it is fine. Did I crack it on something?"

"Do you not remember what happened?"

Hannah frowned, trying to concentrate, for everything seemed to be foggy. "I . . . I think I fell. There was a horse. Yes, that was it . . . I fell off a horse. Oh, Peter, I *knew* it would happen one day, and do you see? I told you they were dangerous."

"Yes, I know, sweetheart, but they're only dangerous when you do foolish things. You scared me half to death, Hannah. I don't think I've ever run so fast in my life. I can't tell you what went through my head, and then to come home and find you like this—" He kissed her hand. "Suffice it to say that you gave me the fright of my life. But all is well that ends well, and with luck your leg will knit perfectly and never give you another day's trouble. Thank God that Edward and Eliza knew enough to set it correctly, for the doctor said if it had had to wait until he could come, it might have been very much worse for you."

"Edward and Eliza?" Hannah said, confused.

"Yes, Edward and Eliza Seaton. I've mentioned them to you before. They were the people who came along in their carriage just as you came to the road. They saw you fall, and they brought you back here. Do you not remember any of that?"

"I remember that I was very frightened, and there was a carriage coming, and the horse—" She stopped abruptly as memory came flooding back in full, and her eyes widened, then narrowed. She pulled her hand away abruptly.

"Hannah, what is it?" he said.

"I remember," she said coldly. "Oh, I remember everything now. And I cannot think what you are doing in here, my lord, for you are not welcome."

"Hannah, I am sorry that we argued. We must talk, but not now, for you need to rest."

"We will not talk at all, my lord," Hannah said, the awful ache starting again in her chest. "And although it is unfortunate that I have broken my leg, as indubitably I will have to stay in bed for some time, I will be going as soon as I can walk out of Longthorpe. In the meantime, you can find someone else to take my place in whatever capacity it pleases you."

"Hannah, please don't be foolish. I don't want you to leave, I truly don't."

"It is not anything to do with what you wish anymore, my lord. It is what I wish. Please. Leave me, for I do not wish you to stay." She turned her face away.

"But this is Wesley's home, Hannah, as well as yours. Surely you do not mean to take him away when he has been so happy here? If I made a mistake, then I am sorry. Please do not let Wesley suffer because of a misunderstanding."

Hannah did not answer him.

"Hannah, please, sweetheart. Do not stand on your pride."

She turned her head back on the pillow and looked at him with blazing eyes. "Do not call me that; you have no right! And has it ever occurred to you that my pride is all I have left? You did your best to strip even that from me. Now leave. Leave!"

Peter stood. "Very well, as I have no wish to distress you. But I hope you regain your senses soon. I will send Mrs. Brewster up to attend to you."

Hannah waited until the door had closed behind him before bursting into tears, and she wasted only one or two of them on the pain in her leg, for the pain in her heart was far worse.

15

O Memory! thou fond deceiver,
Still importunate and vain,
To former joys recurring ever,
And turning all the past to pain.
　　　　　　　—Oliver Goldsmith,
　　　　　　　　　Song: O Memory

Peter curtly summoned Mrs. Brewster, then went straight
to his room. He had just started to pull off his jacket when
a knock came at the door, and impatiently he wrenched it
open.

"Edward. And what do you want?"

"That's a fine welcome for an old friend. I came to ask
about Hannah. Eliza asked me to inquire." He moved past
Peter into the room.

"Hannah," Peter said, slamming the door shut and throwing his jacket on the floor, "is fit as a fiddle, save for a
crack in her bone, which she mightily deserved."

Edward inclined his head. "I see," he said, giving Peter
an incisive look. "What a miraculous recovery. And what
has sent you into such a fit of temper?"

"I am not having a fit of temper," Peter said from between gritted teeth. "I am a reasonable man of even disposi-
tion. You can ask anyone who knows me. It is Hannah
Janes who is possessed of an uneven, unreasonable temperament. On top of that, she is the most ungrateful woman I
have ever had the misfortune to know." Peter's waistcoat
went the way of his jacket. "Here I've spent the last twenty-
four hours in nothing less than a state of extreme distress,
first because I was confronted with evidence of Hannah's
treachery, and then because it was necessary to confront

her with it. And when I went to do so, what should happen but I find myself delivering an infant, of all things."

"You delivered an infant? On your own? I don't believe it."

"Very well, don't believe it. However, it is perfectly true, although Hannah performed the actual delivery. I had to stand there and instruct her."

Edward grinned. "And you did not swoon? I am very proud of you. Perhaps your stomach has hardened since you became an earl."

Peter gave him a filthy look. "And I had to cut the blasted cord, for Hannah was just standing about in a moronic fashion."

"You have come a long way, haven't you?"

"I should have been given a medal," Peter said, pulling his shirt over his head and dousing his face and shoulders with water. "And then," he said over the splashing, "after waiting outside for hours while Hannah dawdled about—"

"Let me guess. It was the realization that the placenta was yet to come that caused you to flee."

"Any fool can deliver a placenta. I saw no need for my presence," Peter said curtly, looking up for a moment. "After patiently waiting all that time, prepared to hear Hannah out over the earlier matter, to which she'd already inadvertently confessed, what did she do? Did she calmly and logically answer my questions? No. Of course not, not Hannah." He reached for a towel and dried himself. "Oh, no. Instead she had the nerve to throw all sorts of unfathomable accusations at me—me, Edward, as if I had something to answer for! And if that wasn't enough, she then announced that she was leaving Longthorpe and proceeded to steal my horse. The girl has the same suicidal tendencies as her brother and is a thief on top of it!" Peter pulled off his boots and threw one across the room and then the other.

"Shocking," Edward said, folding his arms and leaning his shoulder against the wall.

"Indeed. Just think of the harm she might have done to Rhubarb. She might have broken his leg instead of her own, and I'd have had to shoot him."

"A pity I didn't think of that," Edward said.

Peter ignored him. "And then what happened? I was forced to run after her, worried out of my mind, only to discover that she'd nearly been killed, just as I'd expected."

"Quite. It was a monstrous thing to do to you."

"Precisely," Peter said, tugging at the waistband of his trousers. "But wait, for I have not yet finished. You will not believe this. Here I spend the rest of the day worrying myself sick over her, and what does she do?"

"I cannot imagine," Edward said, regarding his friend with fascination.

"I shall tell you. She has the gall to come back to her senses and proceed to throw me out of the room! In my own house, I might add!" He reached down and pulled at the legs of his trousers.

Edward watched as Peter caught his heel and started hopping about on one foot.

"Oh, damn the infernal things!" Peter shouted, dropping into a chair and yanking the offending garment off. "Women. I ask you, Edward. How is one meant to understand them? Here I have been nothing but kind and generous. I have thought of nothing but her welfare at the considerable expense of my own, I might add, attempting to behave like a gentleman against all my natural instincts. You can imagine how painful it has been, how many sleepless nights I have endured. And does she thank me for it? No, she accuses me of behaving like a rakehell! Me! Can you credit it?"

Edward crossed over to the wardrobe and found clean pantaloons and a shirt and handed them to his friend, who was sitting in the chair, clothed only in his indignation.

"It seems damnably unfair," Edward agreed, resuming his lounging position against the wall. "What are you going to do? Put her on the first stagecoach, perhaps? Or maybe a post-chaise—she does have a broken leg after all, and you are not a heartless man."

"Exactly what I have been saying," Peter said with satisfaction, pulling on the pantaloons. "Tell me, Edward. You have known me all these years. Have you ever known me to behave dishonorably?"

Edward considered. "Dishonorably? Perhaps not as often as you should have, but there have been one or two occasions. . . ."

"As if you are one to talk!" Peter pointed at one bare pectoral. "I may have sown a few wild oats, but I have never deceived a woman, nor attempted to seduce one who was anything less than willing, which is a great deal more than you can say."

"True," Edward said equitably.

"Well, then," Peter said, mollified. "I tell you, the way Hannah has been going on, you would think I had been trying to knock her door down every night! It is absurd, I tell you! I cannot help but feel deeply offended. However, despite everything, I will not put Hannah on the next stage. I will allow her to stay, for after all, there is Wesley to be thought of. As I pointed out to Hannah, Wesley ought not to suffer for Hannah's appalling behavior." He started to pull the fresh shirt over his head.

"Ah, Peter, if I might ask you one question, just to clear up a small confusion in my mind?"

"Certainly," came Peter's voice, muffled from behind the linen.

"What was it exactly that you confronted Hannah with, the thing that caused her to purloin your horse and so thoughtlessly attempt to kill herself?"

Peter's head appeared out of the opening. "I accused her of having given birth to her brother."

Edward stared at him, his mouth uncharacteristically dropping open. And then he snapped it shut. "A most interesting feat, I must say," he said dryly.

"You know what I mean," Peter said with annoyance, tucking his shirt in. "I thought she had given birth to Wesley and that her mother had claimed the child as her own in order to protect her daughter. I remember Hannah telling me that they had gone abroad at the time, and why else? Is it not what people do when they want to cover up a pregnancy? It makes perfect sense."

"Perhaps," said Edward. "But I cannot help but feel that you have somehow gotten hold of the wrong end of the stick, and the fact that Pamela Chandler was here only last night, before this entire disaster occurred, makes me wonder if you did not have help with that stick."

Peter looked uncomfortable. "Pamela, true to form, dropped by without an invitation, yes. I quickly discovered that she had been at school with Hannah, and also true to form, Pamela made no secret of her dislike of Hannah. But she did not know Hannah was at Longthorpe, so she did not come to make deliberate trouble. And she genuinely did not know about Wesley. She was clearly shocked when she found out that he was living here as my cousin." Peter quickly explained the story. "So you can see just from that why I would have my doubts, and there are too many other odd things, never mind Hannah's confession in the heat of the birth today."

"Hmm. I am going to have to think this through. If you don't mind, I will present the story to Eliza. She knows Pamela far better than we do, having spent those miserable years as her companion. Perhaps she can work this out."

"Tell Eliza whatever you please," Peter said, picking up his hairbrush and bending down to the looking-glass. "The situation cannot be any worse than it is."

"Oh, I don't know," Edward said. "You can probably manage to complicate it further if you really put your back into it."

Peter glared at him. "I have no intention of doing anything at all. If Hannah does not wish to speak to me, so be it. Let her stew in her own juice: I have better things to do. And I am not the person who is in the wrong. I have been nothing but magnanimous. Hannah is an ungrateful baggage, and I intend to have nothing further to do with her until she adopts a more sensible attitude. I don't care how long it takes—I am not backing down on the matter. Imagine, dismissing me from her presence as if I were a chattel for her to order about! She is lucky I did not take her over my knee for her insolence!"

"Your restraint is exemplary. I shall just go and dress for dinner and wake Eliza. She sleeps an absurd amount at the moment. We will see you downstairs."

Peter, left alone, sighed and went back to dressing, wondering what had happened to Galsworthy, who usually assisted him. Nothing was going right. Nothing at all. In fact, he couldn't remember having been more miserable in his life.

During dinner, Eliza carried the conversation, telling Peter about their trip to Southampton, describing recent events at Seaton, all things he was not required to make anything more than a casual reply to. He realized that Eliza had been told the entire story and was deliberately keeping off the subject, for it was also obvious that the serving staff were equally interested in their conversation, despite their attempts to appear deaf. As this included not only Galsworthy and John, the footman, but also two of the footmen from Seaton, Peter gathered that the talk had been flying in the kitchen. He could only be thankful that Antoine had departed before he could add his own particular poison to the broth.

But the moment the library door had shut behind them, Eliza turned to Peter. "Now that we are alone, I wish you would tell me what has been happening around here? Your letters have kept us very well informed, and you described the lunacy perfectly, but you said nothing of any of the rest of it. Why does that sweet man Galsworthy regard you as if he'd like to do you murder, and your footman—" Eliza stopped for a moment, trying very hard to conceal her twitching mouth behind a cough. "And your footman," she continued, "look as if he'd like to assist? Mrs. Brewster seems the only person even mildly pleased with you, Peter, which surprises me. I'd have thought you'd at least have managed to charm the chambermaid, but she didn't have anything nice to say at all. In fact she seems to think you're the devil incarnate. So I ask again, what have you been doing?"

"I have no idea," Peter said succinctly. "If I knew what I was doing, I wouldn't be in this dilemma."

"That at least is one statement that makes some sense," Eliza said. "Edward told me your brains were addled. Apparently you think Hannah has been going about bearing children, when she hasn't the first idea how to deliver one. Most women who have been through the process have a perfectly clear understanding of what needs doing. Did that thought happen to occur to you when you were forced to stand there and instruct her? Really, Peter." Eliza looked about to go off into peals.

"There is nothing amusing in this, Eliza," Peter said sharply. "I still do not know the truth of the matter, but needless to say, Hannah was very upset when I brought up the subject of her having given birth to Wesley."

"May I ask why you accused her of such a thing?" Eliza said, giving her husband a quelling look. "You of all people do not go about judging people quickly or jumping to false conclusions. You must have had good reason to doubt Hannah?"

"I thought I had. I am no longer sure."

"Well, that is the first truly sensible thing you have said, considering the fact that it was Pamela who told you the tale to begin with."

"She didn't, exactly. She started out to assassinate Hannah's general character. She had caught us in a . . . a private moment and thought she would alert me to Hannah's wicked ways."

"Oh, I see," Eliza said with a grin. "She was afraid Hannah was going to seduce you, was that it?"

"You know Pamela's drivel well enough," Peter said, coloring.

Eliza, enjoying Peter's discomfort to the hilt, said, "Certainly. And I also know exactly how she thinks. If she could not have you, which she had to have known perfectly well from the outset, then Hannah wasn't going to have you either. So. She decided to tell you that Hannah was not good enough for you, nor for anyone else."

"Yes. Exactly. And in this case I think her original mark against Hannah was that Selina Janes had taken my cousin for a lover, as if Hannah had in any way been responsible for that."

"Selina Janes?" Eliza said, a faint bell going off in her head. "Oh, wait . . . wait, let me just think. There might be something here after all."

"What? What, Eliza?" Peter said anxiously. "Do you think it might be true, after all, about Hannah?"

"Don't be absurd," Eliza said. "No, I seem to remember some story Pamela went on about at one point, and that name, Selina, it does sound familiar. It is not very common, after all. If I can just remember what set Pamela off on this particular tirade, I am sure it will come to me." She looked into the distance, her brow furrowed with concentration.

Peter watched her intently, wanting to shake the memory out of her, but he sat down instead, gripping his fingers together and placing his forehead against them, trying to be patient.

"Oh, yes!" Eliza suddenly said, looking back at him. "I remember! But she wasn't Selina Janes then, she was Selina Delaware. Oh, how very interesting."

"Hannah's mother was a Delaware?" Peter said with considerable surprise.

"Yes, she was Lord Delaware's youngest daughter. Pamela was up in arms because she had been snubbed by his grandson at some ball or other, and she went into a snit about how his aunt was no better than a whore and his grand-father no better than a murderer, and everyone knew it."

"Good God," Edward murmured. "I think I remember something about this. It was quite a scandal at the time, was it not? I couldn't have been more than eleven or twelve, but I do remember hearing a discussion about it and taking the side of the footman."

Eliza smiled wickedly at her husband. "How humane of you, considering the little beast you were supposed to have been."

"It was not that in the least. It was only that my father was defending Lord Delaware, so naturally I took the other side."

"Will the two of you please tell me what you are talking about?" Peter said, ready to tear his hair out. "What murder? What footman?"

"Well, it is only hearsay," Edward said, "but the story I heard was that Selina Delaware and the footman had a liaison. The footman was found on the side of the public highway, shot dead. It was blamed on highwaymen, but it was widely believed that Lord Delaware had not taken kindly to the idea of his daughter consorting with one of the servants."

"Oh, Edward," Eliza said, "you have left out the two most important parts! First, the story was that Selina and the footman were very much in love. Second, Selina was with child."

"Was she?" Edward said. "I hadn't heard about that, only that she had run away from home."

"Yes, and at the age of only sixteen. Thinking about it, if my father had shot my lover, I would have run away from home too. It is really rather tragic. And I do remember Pamela saying that Selina turned up married to a man some thirty years her senior only a month or two later. He claimed the child was his. Apparently he'd been secretly in love with Selina for some time, so I suppose he was willing to protect her."

"Eliza, he was Lord Delaware's bailiff," Edward said. "That much I do remember, for I was most impressed with the man's nerve. Lord Delaware never spoke to either of them again. He cut his daughter off."

"Oh, yes, that's right. And I do feel sure the bailiff''s name was Janes . . . Peter? Are you all right?"

Peter lifted his head from his hands. "Oh, yes, perfectly," he said. "Perfectly. Why should I not be? I have just learned that Hannah is old Delaware's illegitimate grand-daughter, that Delaware killed Hannah's father in cold blood, and that most of the polite world knows of the scandal. Yes, I am just fine."

"I can imagine your distress," Edward said. "But I think at least you might reconsider Pamela's accusation about Hannah. Does it really ring true?"

"I know Hannah. She is the most prickly paragon of virtue I have ever met when she remembers to pay attention to such things. The way she carries on, you'd think men had nothing else in their heads but to compromise her. Ha! You couldn't get near enough. But on the other hand, in those few moments when she does forget . . ." He frowned. "Still, even then . . . I don't know. I need to rethink the situation."

Eliza tapped her chin with one finger. "It occurs to me, Peter, that the reason Hannah behaves as such a paragon is because she would not repeat her mother's mistakes. That does not sound to me like a girl who would go cavorting about with a stable boy. It sounds like a girl who is genuinely frightened of the consequences of such behavior. It also sounds like someone who would be outraged at your suggestion that she did cavort with a stable boy and bore a child as a result—and then lied about it. I do not wonder that she ran from you, especially if she cares about what you think of her."

Peter looked away.

"May I ask you a deeply personal question?" she continued. "Do you love Hannah Janes?"

Peter's eyes shot to Eliza. "Certainly not! What would make you think such an extraordinary thing? Hannah is a member of my family, sister to my cousin, if that is indeed the truth. There is nothing more to it."

"Oh?" Edward said. "Well, that explains why you were in such a state today. Thank you for clarifying the matter."

Peter scowled at him. "It is obvious that the two of you have become besotted with the idea of love. Well, you may keep the sentiment to yourselves, for it has no place in this situation."

"Hasn't it?" Edward looked down at his old friend from his position against the mantelpiece. "How interesting that you should think so. It appears that Amelia Lasherby had a far worse effect on you than I'd realized. A pity, but then so many things are."

"Don't . . . don't bring Amelia into this," Peter said furiously. "That is long over and done with!"

"Yes, it is, and it is a good thing. Maybe Hannah will be a better choice."

"Oh, stuff it, Edward!" Peter said, jumping to his feet. "Just how far do you intend to push me?"

"As far as I need to in order to open your eyes to the truth."

"What truth? There is no truth. As I told you earlier, Hannah is a bad-tempered baggage, a millstone around my neck. I have allowed her to stay only because of her brother. And may I ask why you have suddenly decided to throw her at my head? You've never even properly met the girl!"

"No, I haven't. But I think your feelings must be perfectly clear, not only to me, but also to the rest of the world after today; I only find it difficult to believe that you can be so blind as not to see them for yourself."

"Enough! I have no feelings for Hannah, and that is an end to the matter! And even if I had, they would be entirely wasted."

"Oh? And why is that?" Edward asked mildly.

"Because if I am to lay my hands on the income that goes along with this damned earldom, I am forced to marry someone suitable. If you remember, Edward, my father was done out of his inheritance merely by marrying a merchant's daughter. If you foolishly think to push Hannah at me, then consider this: my marrying the daughter of my late cousin's mistress, sister of his bastard son, and child of a scandalous union is not going to make the solicitor jump up and exult. I couldn't give a damn about such things myself, but there is an entire destitute village that I have to consider. Do I make myself clear?"

Edward exchanged a quick but eloquent glance with his wife. "I believe you have made yourself very clear," he said. "You feel you must marry someone you do not love because you have a village to support."

Peter shoved his hands on his hips and looked down. "Yes."

"I see. I won't even begin to argue the foolishness about

the money. I will happily buy all your shares in the business if that will give you what you need to restore your precious village. I would give you the money outright for that matter, if I thought for a moment that you'd take it. I have more than I will ever need. But I know you too well. You will stand on every damned noble inch that you can find. You always have. And if someone doesn't point the fact out to you, you probably will never change."

"Why should I change? I am doing what is right, Edward."

"Do you think so? I am not so sure. Duty and obligation are one thing and cannot be entirely avoided. But if I were you, I would rethink your idea of what is right, before you go destroying your life. And it is no good looking as if you would like to take the andirons to my head. It was you who saved me from myself not so long ago. I am merely trying to return the favor."

Peter glared at him. "You do me no favor," he said tightly. "And I would thank you to keep your opinions to yourself, Edward, for I am not in need of them. I would also thank you to drop the subject entirely, as it is none of your business. Good night." He stormed from the room.

"Oh, my," Eliza said when the door had slammed behind him. "It is worse than I thought. I have never seen Peter lose his self-control before, except in hilarity."

"It is about time," Edward said. "Peter has spent his life practicing control. All this turbulence is a good thing, although it might take him some time to work through it and come out on the other side. I only hope he does not leave it too long. I would hate to see him lose what he doesn't yet realize he has."

Eliza nodded. "I think I must get to know Hannah Janes. I really think I must. I have a terrible feeling that Peter is about to make a hash of things."

"No doubt," Edward said. "and when he does, we shall just have to find a way to put it right. Come, Eliza mine. Let me take you upstairs. We have a full fortnight to work on Peter and his hash. Tonight let us think only of ourselves." He grinned and took his willing wife off to pass the night in pleasure.

Peter passed the night alone and in turmoil.

16

It's a damned long, dark,
boggy, dirty, dangerous way.
—Oliver Goldsmith,
The Good-Natured Man

Eliza spent the next fortnight with Hannah, sitting with her,
reading to her, telling her stories of Seaton, her animals,
their son Matthew, Edward's parrot Archie, anything to
keep Hannah's mind off her pain, which was severe. She
did not bring up the subject of Peter, whom Hannah had
steadfastly refused to see, for the last thing Hannah needed
was to be upset. But when Hannah brought the subject up
herself, Eliza did not miss the opportunity. Peter was more
miserable than she'd ever seen him and pretending he
wasn't, keeping it all bottled up inside. Hannah was no
better off than he, and doing exactly the same thing. And
now Eliza was leaving, and it was a last chance to try to
put things to right.

She had been helping Hannah to change her nightdress
while talking about Edward's decision to move to Jamaica
many years before, when Hannah unexpectedly chimed in.

"Lord Blakesford said he met your husband at
Cambridge."

"Indeed he did. Peter was a great help to Edward, for
Edward had a very unhappy and turbulent relationship with
his father. Peter was fortunate enough to have had a happy
family life, but he missed his home very much, and he and
Edward became like brothers to each other. So when Edward
decided to leave England, Peter suggested Jamaica,
and they went into the shipping business together. They
were young and untried, but they made a great success of
it and never looked back. In truth, I think they also had a

rousing good time. I am sorry to say that my husband had quite the reputation, although Peter was much better behaved. I never had the pleasure of meeting his parents, but apparently Peter had tremendous respect for them, so he behaved himself rather better in society than his wicked friend." Eliza laughed. "I suppose having a father who was chargé d'affaires made it difficult to misbehave."

Hannah frowned. "I never imagined Jamaica had any sort of society at all."

"Oh, indeed. It is nothing like the London Season, but there are balls and routs and all sorts of other social activities. One can easily become worn out. Jamaica is not lacking in aristocrats. Quite a few came to buy plantations. The trade is very profitable."

"Lord Blakesford never behaved as if he came from that sort of background."

"Oh? And how is that?"

"He just never . . . I don't know, exactly. I had the impression that he was concerned about assuming the earldom, for he had not been trained for it. In fact he misled me very badly on the subject, making me think that he had no idea of how to behave as an earl ought. I was to teach him."

Eliza burst into laughter. "Peter has a perfectly wicked sense of humor. It is one of the things I love most about him. And you are quite right; he had not expected it. But Peter is no greenhorn, if that is what you thought. He has been around and about every bit as much as Edward."

"Yes. I realize that now. I was very angry when I discovered the truth of the matter."

"You must understand, Hannah, that Peter has never been a man to make a fuss about himself. He has no patience for the overblown mannerisms and petty gossip and lavish parties that so much of the gentry favors."

"Then *why* would he choose someone like Pamela Chandler to marry? That is all she thinks about!"

"Where in the name of heaven did you come up with that idea?" Eliza said, astonished. She put down the hairbrush she had just picked up. "My dear Hannah, Peter cannot bear the sight of Pamela Chandler!"

"But was he not with her at Seaton? I thought that was where they had become attached. And then he asked her to visit, for he had decided on her as a wife! She was here with her mother. Did he not tell you? Peter asked her to marry him, and she turned him down."

"Someone has been leading you down the garden path, and I don't think it was Peter. And from what Peter tells me, Pamela and her mother were not invited in the least. They simply arrived. Pamela has a habit of doing just that, which is the only reason why she was at Seaton at the same time Peter was there. Edward and I loathe the woman." She picked up the hairbrush again and started to brush out Hannah's hair. "Pamela is desperate for a husband. It's rather sad in a way, although she has caused me so much trouble that I have a hard time feeling sympathetic. But let me assure you, Pamela is the last person in the world that Peter would offer for. He may have his moments of outrageous idiocy, but nothing would drive him to that sort of stupidity."

Hannah didn't answer. Instead, she bit her lip and looked out the window.

"Of course," Eliza added as an afterthought, "all men can be outrageous idiots at times, so one simply has to persevere. You would not believe some of the things Edward has done, you really wouldn't. But I love him dearly." She shrugged. "They just cannot help themselves. It is something to do with male pride, which has no rhyme or reason. One simply has to be patient and wait for them to regain their sanity, and then forgive them."

Hannah swallowed hard. "Did Peter tell you that we argued?" she said.

"No. It wasn't difficult to divine, however, and I managed to get the facts out of him. He is very upset, Hannah, although he is trying very hard to pretend that he isn't. Why will you not see him?"

"I cannot tell you. But I cannot see him, and I must leave Longthorpe as soon as I am better."

"Hannah, that seems rather extreme. He knows he was wrong."

"It makes no difference," Hannah said, trying not to cry. She'd been doing far too much of that. How could she tell Eliza that she had ceased to be angry long ago, that she had to leave because she loved Peter too much to stay? She could not even bear the thought of seeing him again, for she knew it would only open up the wound, and he would see it all for himself. And then he might never let her go, and she would end up just like her mother. She couldn't do that to herself. She couldn't do it to the wife he would bring home. She certainly couldn't do it to Peter, for in the end it would destroy the very reputation he was so desperately trying to build. There was no other solution. "I must leave. I cannot stay," she repeated.

Eliza was silent for a moment. "I see," she finally said. "And will you take Wesley with you?"

Hannah shook her head. "I have thought about it, and Peter is right. Wesley belongs here with him. This is his home, and he is happy here. Peter can provide far better for him than I ever could. Galsworthy will look after him for me."

"And where will you go? Have you made any plans?"

Hannah shook her head. She had to force the words out. "I thought I would . . . I would go to London. Surely I can find some sort of employment there?"

"Perhaps. But if you find that you truly cannot stay on here, I have a much better idea. I am in desperate need of an assistant, for with the child coming, I cannot do as much as I used to. We will be at Seaton until the autumn, and then we go to Jamaica, if you wouldn't mind that."

"Oh . . . oh, thank you, Eliza!" Hannah's relief nearly overwhelmed her. "Yes, I will do anything I can to help you! But you have already been too kind!"

"I haven't in the least. And I do know what it is to feel desperate. I would urge you to work your problems out with Peter for all your sakes, but you must also do what is right for you. I cannot see what is in your heart, Hannah, except to see that you are greatly upset. But I will not press you on the matter. You have a few weeks yet before you must make a decision. Use them wisely. Oh, and Hannah," she added, gently prompting, "if you are ready to receive visitors, half the village has been here to ask after you. Apparently you are well loved. I know you have not been feeling like seeing anyone until now, but perhaps you might be happy for the company."

"No. No, I think it is better not. Please, tell them all that I thank them for their concern. But if I am leaving, it is best if they forget me. They will have a proper mistress soon enough and their devotion should go to her."

"As you wish. I will leave you now, for Edward and Peter

should be returning for dinner shortly. But I will come again in the morning to say good-bye before we leave."

"Thank you so much for everything, Eliza. And thank you for your offer. You have no idea how much it means."

"Nonsense," Eliza said brightly. But when she left she had a great deal on her mind, for Hannah's inadvertent statement about the villagers had finally elucidated matters. Well, at least she'd seen to it that if Hannah left Longthorpe, she would be safely installed at Seaton where Peter could come after her.

It seemed that Hannah was afflicted with the same disease of nobleness as Peter, and so they were both going to have to be saved from themselves. It was time to pay a visit to Mary Baker, Eliza decided, and she would do so first thing in the morning.

Hannah took one last look around her room. It was just as it had been when she'd first arrived. She might never have lived in it. All of her belongings were packed in the one small bag she had brought with her.

She went to the mantelpiece and left a handful of letters for the people she was leaving behind. There was one for Peter, of course. In the end, there had been very little to say.

Hannah picked up her case and made her way slowly down the stairs. Eliza had arranged for a carriage to take her away, but it waited for her a short distance down the drive, for Hannah wanted no one to know of her departure until after she'd gone. Dawn had not yet broken, and it was dark as she limped across the courtyard and out through the gateway.

The footman took her bag and helped her up the steps into the waiting carriage, and then he shut the door behind her.

Hannah sat very still as the carriage started to move off. She felt completely numb, save for the ache in her leg. Something warm fell onto her hand and she reached up. It surprised her very much to discover that her face was completely wet. She wondered if it had been raining.

"My lord . . . oh, my lord, she's gone!" Mrs. Brewster burst into the library, waving a handful of letters over her head.

Peter slowly stood up from his desk, where he'd been doing the morning accounts. "What exactly do you mean, she's gone?" he asked, his voice very low, each word carefully controlled. "Who has gone, Mrs. Brewster?"

"The lamb, my lord! She's left us! Packed her things and gone, and nothing left of her but these! Not a single word to any of us, not even of farewell!"

"No. I don't believe it!" Peter was across the room in a flash. He pulled the letters from Mrs. Brewster's hand, rifling through them until he came to one addressed to him and thrust the rest back at her.

"Leave me, Mrs. Brewster," he commanded. "Leave me!" he shouted as he saw her still standing there. Frightened, she scurried out, and he ripped open Hannah's letter. It took him only twenty seconds to read the five lines.

"Damn you!" he cried, balling it up and throwing it on the floor. "Oh, Hannah, why? *Why?*"

And yet her letter had said it all. She could not stay; she had already told him why. There was nothing left to say. She was leaving him Wesley as he had requested. And she asked him not to try to find her. She was starting life anew.

That was it? After everything they had been through, that was all Hannah could find to leave him with? He bent down and picked up the paper, smoothing it out again with his hand. He ran his thumb over the place where she'd signed her name. Hannah. Just, Hannah.

And now she was gone.

He pressed the sheet of paper against his chest as if it might somehow fill the horrible void that had suddenly opened there. Hannah was gone. He had not actually believed that she meant it, that she would leave. And to go with no warning, to go without a word, with no indication of where she was heading?

Peter gripped the mantelpiece, feeling dazed. He could not quite comprehend it: it didn't seem possible that if he went upstairs her room would be bare. He would never see her again? It was unthinkable.

"Oh, Hannah!" he cried helplessly. "Don't you understand? I love you, you sweet fool! I love you! I could care less if Wesley is your child—or if he isn't! I couldn't care about any of it! I just want you back!"

He heard the words ringing hollowly in his ears, and he banged his fist on the mantelpiece. It was he who had been the fool. Edward had been right: he was a jackass. He had hidden his own heart from himself so successfully that he had ended up driving Hannah away. It was little wonder she had left. He wouldn't have wanted to have anything to do with him had he been her.

He had been a coward, too caught up in his duty to act on his feelings until it was too late. And why? Because he had known from the very start that Hannah had the ability to reach straight into his soul, and therefore the power to tear him to bits. And it was that he had avoided, telling himself that Hannah was untouchable, that he had obligations elsewhere. The fact was that he had thought to keep himself safe from the pain that such a love was capable of causing. He had been afraid of repeating his experience with Amelia.

But Hannah was no Amelia. Amelia had manipulated him—he knew that now. She had used him, lied to him, knowing all the while that her husband would come after her. She had probably expected more of a fight over her when he did come, rather than to be so immediately released. But looking back, the entire episode had been based on smoke. Smoke and passion. It was a deadly combination.

But it hadn't been like that with Hannah: she had been real. Everything about her had been real, from her ridiculous notions about propriety to her unexpected temper and her stubborn nature. She was a sweet, honest, direct woman who had been badly used in her life, and he had only contributed to that. He had treated her, if truth be told, as if she really were a poor relation. He had dictated where he should have asked. He had not stopped to consider her feelings, even to think about what they might be, any more than he had acknowledged his own, yet all the while he had been falling in love with her. And he had thrown it all away in one monumentally stupid, autocratic moment, and Hannah had nearly lost her life as a result. And now he had lost her for all time.

It was entirely his own fault. He had focused on his damnable duty; he had let other people control his decisions. Well, it would stop now. He might have lost Hannah, but he had learned one valuable lesson. He was through with doing the correct thing.

Peter went back to his desk and sat down, pulling out a

sheet of paper. He dipped his quill in the inkstand and began to write.

> My dear Mr. Nichols,
> I have come to the conclusion that I will allow no one to dictate my choice of wife, suitable or no. Therefore I am informing you that you may burn the two million pounds for all I care. I will find another way to support Longthorpe and the people of Kirby.
> Your humble servant, etc.
>
> Blakesford

Peter looked at the letter for a long moment. He folded it, sealed it, and franked it.

And then he put his head in his hands and he cried.

Galsworthy and Mrs. Brewster sat at their usual spot in the kitchen, their chins on their hands, both looking extremely glum. Nothing had been right about the house, not since Hannah had left six weeks before.

"I don't know what's left to do, Mr. Galsworthy. I really don't," Mrs. Brewster said. "The cards aren't helping one bit. Wait and see, they say, but we've been waiting, and we haven't seen a thing. The veil will unfold, they say, but not a thing has unfolded, and his lordship hasn't done a thing about going looking for the lamb. It's not good, Mr. Galsworthy. It is not good. I cannot think what could have happened to upset her so, sitting in her room all by herself for all those weeks, refusing to see anyone but Wesley. And look at him, the poor lad, heartbroken over his sister's disappearance. What could have sent her running, Mr. Galsworthy, without a word to anyone?"

"I have told you continually that it must have been something dreadful to get Hannah to take his lordship's horse and run off on it like that."

"Never mind the horse. Mary Baker has already said that they were in full battle when she had little Jamie, but something much worse happened after they had left her. My brain is too tired to go over this one more time. Where is his lordship now?"

"In his usual place, locked in the library. Tonight he's sitting there with the brandy bottle, and that's most unlike him."

"It is a pity those nice Seatons had to leave, for they would have had something to say about it. Her ladyship gave my lamb so much comfort in those early days, sitting with her all those hours. But she wouldn't see his lordship. Oh, no. She wouldn't even mention his name."

Galsworthy shook his head. "Hannah was never so unhappy. It fair breaks my heart to think of it, how she must be feeling, all on her own. And I will tell you, Mrs. Brewster. I will tell you that as much as I hate to admit it, his lordship is suffering dreadfully. I've never seen a man look so sick and pale. Here we have Mrs. Looper to cook for him, good nourishing food, just as he likes it, and he eats hardly enough to keep a bird alive."

"Well, if nothing else, at least the people of Kirby have turned around toward his lordship. They can see his heart is breaking over the girl, and there's nothing like a good love story to keep a body going. Every woman I know has her eye fixed on this house, wanting to know how it is all going to turn out. It doesn't hurt that the men have come back either, since Sam Baker put word out at the mines that things had changed. Why, just look at all the fields. It does my heart good to see them producing again. And the houses, back to looking the way they should. It's a shame that his lordship has been forced to sell things from the house to raise funds, and here we all were thinking he had to be rich as Croesus with the way the old earl hoarded his money. Never mind, at least this earl's heart is in the right place. The people can hold their heads up again. Now all we need is the lamb back and his lordship to wed her, and everything will be perfect."

Galsworthy scratched his head. "I cannot think what has gotten into Hannah. She's never behaved like this in her entire life—not that she doesn't have a stubborn streak, mind you, but this goes far beyond that. She's not unlike her mother in some ways. The woman lost her heart as a girl and never recovered from it. It destroyed her in the end. Ah, well. Pray God that will not be the case here, and Hannah will return to us safe and sound. Is there any more tea, Mrs. Brewster? A man needs his tea in trying times."

Mary Baker could wait no more. Her beloved Sam had come home for good the night before, and she had taken the time to pour the entire story into his ear. Sam, being his usual thoughtful, practical self, had listened carefully, then told her exactly what to do before tumbling her again under the covers.

Mary took his advice to heart. She put on her Sunday best, carefully put her bonnet on her head, and took herself off to Longthorpe, where she requested an audience with Lord Blakesford. She was granted it immediately, and Mary Baker, who feared no man, marched straight into the library.

"My lord," she said, slightly shocked at his haggard appearance. "I have come for some plain speaking."

"If you come on behalf of your husband, ma'am, I heard that he had returned." Peter put his pen down and rubbed his eyes. "I was planning on visiting him in the morning. The job of steward is his if he would like it. Indeed, I would be grateful for his services. I have heard nothing but good about Sam Baker."

"Oh! Thank you, my lord! Steward . . . oh, my! Sam would be happy for the job, I know he would do right by you."

"Yes, I am sure. He is perfectly well qualified, and the people trust him."

"They do indeed, my lord. Everyone looks up to my Sam. Why, look at how he stayed at the mines until he saw every last one of our boys home again. But I did not come about Sam. I came to speak to you about Hannah."

His eyes met hers with a combination of alarm and hope. "Hannah? Has she sent you with some message?"

"No, my lord. And she will not. You know that Hannah and I were close, but she has not written, other than the note she left me. It's because she felt obliged to break all of her ties with Kirby and Longthorpe. She felt it was the right thing to do, for your sake."

"How do you know this, Mrs. Baker?" Peter asked, jumping to his feet.

"I cannot say, my lord, for I promised to keep my silence about that. I can only tell you that it is so. She did not leave from anger, although that's what she wanted you to think so that you wouldn't come after her."

"Oh, dear God," Peter said, sitting down again.

"I might as well tell you that all of Kirby is crushed, for they were counting on your marrying her. Not a soul can understand why you haven't taken the girl in hand. She's hurting, you are hurting, and you go about helping everyone but yourself. Pardon me, but you are behaving like a numskull, not doing a thing about it."

"Believe me, Mrs. Baker, I would if I could. I realize I've behaved like a damned fool over the matter. But Hannah refused to tell me where she was going. She wants nothing more to do with me."

"Well, of course she doesn't. She thinks she's no good for you."

"No good for me? What in—Mrs. Baker, what are you saying?"

"I will tell you this, and don't you ever let on to Hannah that I told you. We know all about Hannah and her mother's doings, for she didn't keep it a secret, and we respected her all the more for it. But Hannah Janes is a lady, all right, the best kind. She knows how to look after those who need it, with no care for her skirts or her fine lily-white hankies, or even her health, for that matter, for she's looked after more of the sick than I can count. But she thinks she's not proper enough for you, not a respectable lady."

"She told you so?" Peter asked on a near whisper.

"Naturally she did. She loves you. She did from the start. It was as clear as the nose on my face. And what did you do but talk about bringing home a high-and-mighty wife who would suit your fine position. How was that supposed to make her feel? It was breaking her heart. She couldn't stay in a house where she was in love with the lord, watching you with your wife, seeing you going off into the bedroom at night together. And what about your going to her bedroom after you'd done your duty, what about that? She told me all about it that day of the accident, that she thought you wanted her for your mistress. Oh, I understood why Hannah left, all right. She knew she wouldn't be able to hold out against you, and that would be wrong."

"Mrs. Baker, are you sure about all of this?" Peter asked, his face strained.

"Of course I'm sure. I can't credit that you didn't think of it yourself."

"Mrs. Baker, all I ever wished was to make Hannah happy. I love her with all my heart, and I swear I would never have dishonored her."

"Humph. You might not have been able to help yourself, did you ever think of that? Well, I'm telling you now, the only way you are ever going to make that girl happy is by marrying her. But you have a fight ahead of you—that is, if you want to marry her at all."

"Yes, Mrs. Baker, I do, most desperately. I am astonished to hear the village is all behind the idea—you have no idea how much. I had thought they would oppose such a thing."

"Oppose it—why, they've all been waiting for you to prove yourself!"

Peter buried his head in his hands for a moment, then looked up at her with the faintest of smiles. "How very extraordinary. But tell me this. How in the name of God am I meant to propose to Hannah if I don't know where to find her?"

"Now, this is what my Sam said on the matter, my lord, and don't go taking it wrong that we were discussing your personal life. But Sam says when a man wants something bad enough, he should go after it. He shouldn't let anyone stand in his way, including the woman he loves, which is what you did by sitting back and letting Hannah get away. He says that if you're pining after Hannah badly enough, then you'll forget all the fine manners you've been raised with and just go and tell her how you feel, whether she wants to listen or not. And I reckon Sam is right. So I'm here to tell you that Hannah is at Seaton, my lord. I'll take my leave, and when I say my prayers tonight, they'll include you. Maybe the dear Lord will put some sense into that head of yours and give you some strength on top of it."

Mary Baker turned and walked out the door.

Peter stared after her, hardly able to believe his ears. Seaton? *Seaton?* She had been there all this time? He was going to murder someone, he surely was, and he didn't know whether to start with Edward or Eliza.

"Galsworthy!" he bellowed, jumping to his feet and going to the door. "Galsworthy, pack a bag! And call for the carriage! I'm about to behave extremely badly, and it is long past due!"

"Why, Peter," Eliza said, looking up from her ledger as Peter came storming unannounced into her study the next morning. "It is about time. I was expecting you a good fortnight ago."

"You I will deal with later," he said furiously. "Where is she? Where is Hannah?"

"My, you do look uncharacteristically testy, Peter. I suggest you calm down before you attempt to speak with her."

"Eliza. . . ."

"Oh, very well," Eliza said, smiling mischievously. "There is no need to grind your teeth at me. That is Edward's specialty. I believe she is gardening in the conservatory with Archie. He has taken a shine to her, which is an enormous relief, as I simply haven't the energy for him at the moment with the baby nearly here. Oh, how nice," she said, looking over his shoulder at the door. "You've brought Galsworthy, I see. Hannah will be so happy. She's missed you, Galsworthy. Do go along with Lord Blakesford, won't you? You can stand guard outside the door just in case he decides to do anything temperamental."

"I shall strangle you, Eliza, see if I don't."

"You most certainly will not. I did the most sensible thing I could have under the circumstances, when you were making no sense at all. You ought to thank me. And by the by, I had the entire story from Hannah about the stable boy. His mother had just died, poor thing, and he needed a friend. Hannah offered him comfort—platonic comfort. You were quite wrong, just as I thought."

"Hang what you thought! It is what Hannah thinks that I care about."

"Well, that makes a nice change. But it's not going to do you the least bit of good to go in there and grind your teeth at her, either. You might try behaving yourself."

"That is the very last thing I intend doing!" Peter turned on his heel and went storming back out again, Galsworthy hurrying along behind him, looking alarmed.

Eliza smiled, feeling extremely pleased with herself, then pushed herself to her feet and went to find Edward to alert him to Peter's most timely arrival.

Hannah was pruning the chrysanthemums while Archie watched with a sharp eye, occasionally climbing down off his tree to collect a fallen head and then carry it back up again to shred to pieces with his sharp beak.

Hannah was paying no attention to the parrot at all, lost in her own unhappy thoughts, when she realized that he had started a happy squawking reserved only for favored people. She glanced over at him, thinking that he wanted some attention, but instead she saw that he was parading up and down his branch, wings outstretched, and he wasn't looking at her at all. Instead, his beady eye was focused behind her. She quickly turned around to see who it was, expecting Eliza or Edward.

"Hello, Hannah."

"Peter!" she gasped, dropping the secateurs in her shock. Her hand crept to her throat. "No! Oh, no, please go away! Please!" Seeing his face brought her almost more pain than she'd thought possible. She'd tried so hard to forget that face, to not think about him at all. It hadn't been possible, of course, but seeing him in the flesh only brought everything rushing back in full.

"No, Hannah," Peter said, advancing toward her. "I shan't go away. And you are not going anywhere either. You are going to listen to me."

"You have nothing to say that I want to listen to, my lord. I have told you that I want nothing more to do with you at all! I find it boorish of you in the extreme to impose on me in this fashion. Why would you intrude now, after all this time, knowing that I do not want to see you?"

"Oh, be still, Hannah," Peter said. He took two steps forward, pulled her into his arms and kissed her for all he was worth, stifling her protest against his lips. He knew it had not been a bad idea when he felt Hannah's body softening against him and her mouth responding fluently to what he was trying to tell her.

"My God, I have missed you," he said when he finally released her, his breathing ragged. "Hannah . . . oh, Hannah, I've been such a damned fool."

Hannah put her hands on his chest and shoved at him. "What has come over you? You come after me when I have asked you not to, you have the temerity to kiss me like that . . . I mean at all," she amended, "and then you stand there as if everything is perfectly fine?"

"Yes," he said. "That is exactly right. I have finally come to my senses. I love you, Hannah Janes, but that is not what I have come to my senses about. I've known that for quite some time now. What I have realized is that I am much larger than you are, and you can't do a thing about tossing me out. You will have to listen to me whether you like it or not. You have made me suffer quite long enough.

So it is time to put an end to it. I am very sorry for all of my stupidity, but I will try my very best not ever to be so stupid again. Hannah? Why are you crying?"

"Because you are still incredibly stupid," she said furiously. "What do you hope to accomplish by this?"

"I hope to ask you to be my wife and have you accept," he said, picking up her hand and holding it close to his chest.

"To be your *wife?* Are you mad?"

"I love you. I cannot tolerate the thought of losing you. I have been miserable, as has everyone else who loves you. I want . . . I want to have children with you, and play the autocrat when I can't help myself, and apologize afterward. I want to make love to you day and night and day again. I want to look after you and cherish you and have you cherish me. Hannah, please, will you marry me? Will you?"

Hannah slowly shook her head, feeling as if her heart might literally shatter. "No. I cannot."

"Hannah, why not? For God's sake, why not? I know you love me."

"I am not for you, Peter," she said softly. "I am not the right sort of woman. I cannot see you lose everything you have worked so hard for. You and I both know where your duty lies."

"To hell with my duty!" Peter cried. "It is what got me into trouble in the first place! Listen to me, I have been in enough agony over the last few weeks. Nothing is worth this. Nothing. Do you remember, Hannah, the first night we met in the garden?"

"I am not likely to forget," she said, coloring.

"And I have not forgotten one moment of it myself. But I was wrong. I was wrong. I was so preoccupied with the idea of duty that I neglected what was truly important— what was in my heart." He cleared his throat. "I have to tell you this so that you can understand. There was a woman, Hannah. I was young and foolish, and I'd never been in love. She . . . she captivated me. And then I learned that she was married. There was nothing to do, of course, but to send her back to her husband."

"*That* was what you were talking about that night?" Hannah said.

"Yes and no. I wasn't talking about Amelia, but about the consequences of such a thing. Trust me, she and I did not part in any tender fashion. What happened between us—it had to do with you, not with her. In fact, you drove all thought of Amelia out of my mind. But Hannah, I didn't realize how afraid of love I'd become. I was downright terrified, if the truth be told. So I didn't examine my feelings for you. I came up with every excuse in the world for them. I stayed away from you, I pretended distance, I thought I would marry, and you would marry, and it would all go away. And then you were hurt, and I thought I would die if I lost you. And even then I didn't really understand, not until I really did lose you."

"Peter, I cannot listen to this—"

"You will, Hannah. I am determined. I ought to have broken down your door to tell you all of this instead of trying to behave like a gentleman. And then you were gone, and I had no idea where to find you. You can't imagine how terrible that was. There were times that I thought I would lose my mind."

"I am sorry," she said, looking away. "It was not my intention to hurt you."

"I know that. But to have left as you did—I have worried so about you, about all sorts of things. Hannah, your leg—how is it?"

"It is much better, thank you. There will be no lasting effects."

"Thank God. And your heart?" he asked. "How is your heart? Does it ache as badly as mine does?"

"Peter, this is impossible! I shouldn't even be speaking with you!"

"But that is where you are wrong. If you had only spoken with me in the first place, we could have avoided so much unnecessary pain. Hannah, everyone is waiting for you to come home. Please, won't you?"

"I cannot, Peter. I am so sorry, but I cannot." She wiped her eyes.

"Of course you can. I have told Nichols to go to hell. I don't need the damned money; I've managed to find it elsewhere. So if you are about to throw your supposed lack of suitability up in my face, you have no argument in that direction."

Hannah put her face in her hands. "Oh, please," she moaned. "Please do not do this to me."

"It is all right, sweetheart, it is all right. All that matters is that you love me. Can you deny that you do?"

Hannah looked up at him, not at all sure she could take much more. "It does not matter how much I love you," she managed to say. "I am still not the one for you. There are things that you don't know about me, things that make it impossible."

"What, that you are technically illegitimate? Of course I know! Selina Delaware was your mother. Your true father was a footman in the Delaware household. And? Am I supposed to care?"

Hannah stared at him, aghast. "You know? You know, and yet you would still offer me marriage? You *are* mad! You cannot marry someone who is illegitimate!"

"I am completely sane, and you are not illegitimate. As far as the world and the courts are concerned, Hannah, your father was Janes. He married your mother, he acknowledged you as his daughter. I can't tell you how many perfectly respectable children bear surnames that have nothing to do with their actual paternity. It matters not in the least."

"Yes, but that does not change the fact that my father was a footman! I am not a suitable wife for you!"

"I couldn't give a fig about the blasted footman, Hannah."

It was too much for Galsworthy, who had been quietly listening at the open door. He came forward with great dignity. "I beg your pardon, my lord, Miss Hannah, but I must interrupt."

"Galsworthy!" Hannah said with delight, forgetting everything in the pleasure of seeing his dear face again. "Oh, Galsworthy, how are you? How is Wesley?"

"He is missing, Miss Hannah, as are we all."

"Oh, and I have missed you all, too. How is Mrs. Brewster—and John, and Mary Alice, and Joan?"

"They are all well, Miss Hannah."

Peter scowled. "What is it, man? Can you not see we are in the middle of a very private conversation? What could possibly be so important as to require an interruption?"

"I am sorry to intrude, but I was standing watch outside and could not help but overhear."

"Oh, bloody likely, Galsworthy. But since you did and

have decided to comment, get on with it, for my patience is short."

Galsworthy drew himself up with all of his considerable dignity. "It is about the footman, my lord. You may not give a fig about him, but I do, and Hannah should as well. He was her father, after all, and he loved Selina very much, as she did him, from the time they were children. I tried to warn him against it, but there was no stopping either of them. Your life, Hannah, cost Martin his, and you should have some respect for him. He died defending your mother against your grandfather when Lord Delaware learned that they intended to marry."

"And how is it that you are privy to all of this information, Galsworthy, that none of the rest of us know anything about?"

"Because I was there, my lord. I was butler to Lord Delaware. And I was also Martin's father."

"Good God," Peter said softly. "Good God in heaven. Are you saying . . . you are saying that you are Hannah's grandfather?"

"I am, my lord. And I am sorry if it comes as a shock to you, Hannah, but I have not looked after you all of these years to see you make a mistake now. I taught you to be a lady, and I taught you to watch after yourself so that you didn't end up like your mother, but I am beginning to think that I taught you too well, Miss Hannah Janes. The fact of the matter is that his lordship loves you and is willing to do honorably by you. I did not teach you to be a fool, nor a snob, either. Your father was a fine honorable man, and you have no right to be ashamed of him. And there's nothing the least bit unsuitable about you, I'd like to add. You are as fine as any lady in the land, and better behaved than many, I can tell you that. So if his lordship loves you and wants to do right by you, then there's nothing at all that says you can't accept him. And he can apply to me for permission," Galsworthy finished firmly.

Peter grinned. "Then may I have the honor of your granddaughter's hand in marriage?"

"You may. And it is about time you asked for her."

"Oh . . . oh, Galsworthy," Hannah said, bursting into tears. "Why did you never tell me! Oh, why did you wait all this time?" She ran and flung herself into his arms.

"Because you had no need to know until now, Hannah."

He stroked her hair. "It was best that the world saw me only as your butler, for it kept the rumors at bay. After Martin was killed, someone needed to look after your mother and yourself. So I went away with her and saw you into this world. And now I am seeing you married, so you'd better give his lordship a sensible answer and give him some peace. No man deserves to be put through such misery, even if you thought you were doing the right thing. Which you were not."

Hannah kissed Galsworthy's cheek and pretended not to notice the tears in his eyes. "You know that I have always loved you—you have been the closest thing to a father I have ever known, and one of the finest men I have ever come across. I am proud to call you my grandfather. Thank you, oh, *thank* you for telling me."

"Never mind all of that, Hannah girl. I've given my permission, so get on with his lordship's answer. The man looks about ready to jump out of his skin." He detached Hannah from his coat, straightened his waistcoat, and shuffled carefully away.

"Well?" Peter said nervously, not at all sure what effect this unexpected announcement on Galsworthy's part was going to have on the situation. "Will you, Hannah? After all, if Galsworthy says it is correct, then surely it must be?"

Hannah looked at him, her eyes shining with sudden hope. "Do you think so?"

"Oh, yes. Yes, I definitely do."

"I am not at all sure I know how to be a countess."

Peter burst into laughter. "If anyone knows how to be a countess, sweetheart, it is you. Galsworthy has seen to that. And anyway, you come from a long line of barons and baronesses; thinking about it, it's a blessing your father was a footman, for the Delawares are terribly overbred. There's nothing like a little fresh blood, and you couldn't ask for finer blood than Galsworthy's. Oh, all that correctness, just think. You'll make a perfect countess."

"But Peter, I cannot ride—"

"I shall teach you to drive a carriage."

"And everyone in Kirby knows I am not the least respectable."

"And they love you all the more for it. They have told me so."

"Have they? Really?"

"Absolutely. In fact it seems that the only way I am to redeem myself in their eyes is by bringing you home and making you my wife. So you see, you have an obligation to me. How else am I to prove my moral character for once and for all?"

"Oh . . . oh, Peter, honestly?"

"I wouldn't lie about such an important thing."

"Are you are absolutely sure this is what you truly want?"

"Hannah!" he roared in frustration. "I love you! For God's sake, just say yes!"

"Then yes, oh, yes! I will marry you!" She proceeded to fling herself into Peter's arms and rain kisses upon his handsome face. "Oh, I love you, Peter. I cannot tell you how much. I have from the very first night. And oh, I have wanted you to k—"

Peter quickly put a finger over her lips and inclined his head toward the door, where Galsworthy no doubt still lurked. Hannah smiled, slipping her arms around his neck. "But now that we are to be married, may we forget all about being proper, Peter?"

"You may throw to the wind that decorum you've been hiding behind and unleash all the natural passion that God so generously gave you."

"You have no idea what a relief that is, for it has been a terrible strain. If you don't mind, my lord, may we begin?"

"By all means," Peter said, pulling Hannah into his arms. "Oh, by all means." He lowered his mouth to hers and began.

Epilogue

I . . . chose my wife, as she did her wedding-gown,
not for a fine glossy surface, but such qualities
as would wear well.

—Oliver Goldsmith,
The Vicar of Wakefield

Hannah closed her eyes and pushed for all she was worth, just as she had seen Mary Baker do in exactly the same situation. The fact that Peter had outright refused to leave the room surprised her not in the least, nor did she have any objection to his being there. She wouldn't have let him go to save her life.

Still, he looked unbelievably harried, and she could not help but feel sorry for him. Hannah closed her eyes and pushed one last time, and she felt the child slip from her body.

"A boy, my lady!" the midwife cried. "A fine spanking boy and an heir for you, my lord!"

"Oh. Oh, that's fine," Peter said, leaving Hannah to go and admire his son. "Yes, he's a fine specimen, I'm sure. Hannah, what do you think?" he said, carefully bringing the infant up to her after he had been warmly wrapped.

Hannah looked at him, dropped a kiss on his sweet cheek, then closed her eyes.

"Hannah?" Peter said with alarm. "You have not taken a disgust of him?"

Hannah somehow found the strength to smile. "No, my darling. He's perfectly beautiful. But I think there might be a surprise in store."

"Oh, dear God," Peter said faintly. "Twins?"

Hannah nodded and once again started to push for all she was worth. Not very much later, the midwife was exclaiming again. "Another boy! Oh, what a gift from God! Two little miracles, they are!"

Peter handed Hannah her second son, then picked up the first from the cradle and brought him over.

He looked at one and then the other. "Identical," he said. "Like two peas in a pod. I don't bloody believe it."

He and Hannah exchanged a long look. And then Hannah burst into laughter "I say we sew the ribbons directly onto their skins." She looked down at the babies, her face filled with love. "They are rather alike, aren't they?"

Peter grinned at her. "I think this news is going to throw poor Mr. Nichols into apoplexy. I am sure he thought he'd solved all of his problems by declaring you an eminently suitable wife and me an idiot and practically throwing the income at me. He's now bound to spend the rest of his days worrying that we are going to mix the boys up, and he'll be back to managing a madhouse."

"Whoever said we ceased being a madhouse? We are simply a happy madhouse, Peter, and it is just as it should be."

Mrs. Brewster, proving the point, came hurrying in some time later. Her face was wreathed in a wide smile. "Twins!" she said, beaming down at Hannah. "Aren't you the clever one, my lamb! My dear Mr. Galsworthy is beside himself—two great-grandsons, and little beauties they are, too. He'll be up in a tick with Master Wesley. They're out on the balcony listening to all of Kirby cheering outside the house. Even the messier is out there with a smile on his face. Never did see such a changed man since he came back with his tail between his legs."

"Are you quite sure they are cheering, Mrs. Brewster?" Peter asked wryly. "I would have thought they'd be crossing themselves, given what happened the last time around. Speaking of which, I don't think I can afford to have the church tower repaired again. Maybe we'll have these two christened elsewhere just to be on the safe side."

"Oh, that," Mrs. Brewster said, scoffing. "That was plain bad luck, not the devil's work at all. Really, my lord, who would have thought you'd be so superstitious?"

"Me?" Peter said with disbelief. "That's something, coming from you. Which reminds me—there is something I have always wanted to ask: Why did you go spreading stories around Kirby that the devil had come and taken my cousin's body away, when you knew perfectly well what had really happened to it? I have always been mystified."

"So you heard, did you," Mrs. Brewster said with a little wink. "I was wondering when the story would get back to you. Think, my lord. It seemed the smartest thing to do. We didn't want some disgruntled villagers coming and digging up the remains, which is surely what would have happened. Better they believed that his lordship was escorted straight to hell so that there was no doubt about the matter. A few words in the right ears, and the story was set. And don't you go worrying about the twins. I've already announced that the signs are brilliant, and indeed they are. Much happiness, they say. Now come with me, my lord, for the people want to see you and give you their approval of your fine manly doings."

Peter dropped a kiss on Hannah's forehead with a smothered laugh. "I am off to brag about my prowess," he said.

"Please, do go and tell them of your triumph, my lord," Hannah said, smiling up at him. "And then when you are finished accepting their congratulations for all your hard work, come back to me."

"Always, Hannah," he said, kissing her in earnest. "Always."

There's an epidemic with 27 million victims. And no visible symptoms.

It's an epidemic of people who can't read.

Believe it or not, 27 million Americans are functionally illiterate, about one adult in five.

The solution to this problem is you... when you join the fight against illiteracy. So call the Coalition for Literacy at toll-free **1-800-228-8813** and volunteer.

Volunteer Against Illiteracy. The only degree you need is a degree of caring.